HERE ARE MY DEMANDS

ANDREW ROFF IS A WRITER LIVING ON THE UNCEDED Country of the Kaurna people of the Adelaide Plains. His short fiction has appeared widely, and he is a former winner of the Peter Carey Short Story Award, the Griffith Review Emerging Voices Competition and the Margaret River Press Short Story Competition. His debut story collection, *The Teeth of a Slow Machine*, is published by Wakefield Press. When not writing, he is a child-wrangler and lawyer. *Here Are My Demands* is his first novel.

HERE ARE MY DEMANDS

ANDREW ROFF

A Novel

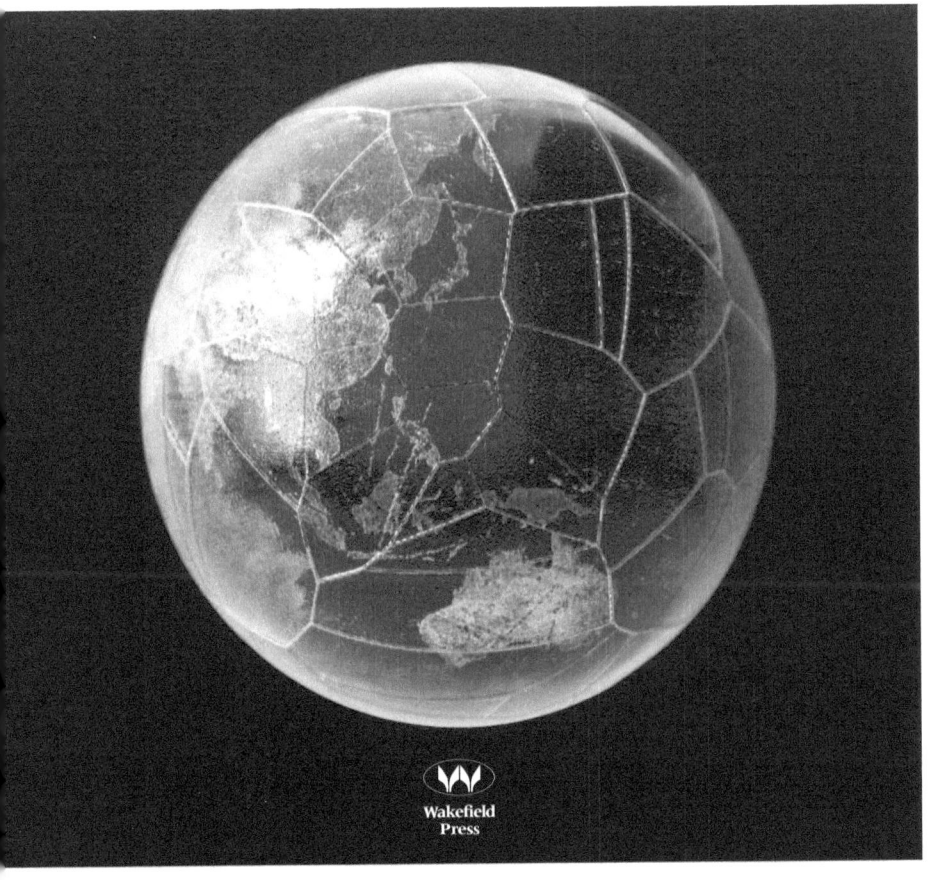

Wakefield
Press

Wakefield Press
16 Rose Street
Mile End
South Australia 5031
www.wakefieldpress.com.au

First published 2025

Edited by Maddy Sexton, Wakefield Press
Book design and typesetting by Duncan Blachford, Typography Studio

ISBN 978 1 92338 813 0

A catalogue record for this book is
available from the National Library
of Australia

Wakefield Press thanks
Coriole Vineyards for their
continued support

'BUT I AIN'T SPENDING ANY TIME ON IT—'
The Hon Robert Bellarmine Carl Katter MP,
15 November 2017

CONTENTS

↙   ↓   ↘

PROLOGUE: MAY 2058

BECAUSE SHE WAS WATCHING HER BROTHER, MAGGIE registered the noise of the blast before she saw it. The sound was so loud that in the room where her body lay, limiters tripped in her ear canals. Ringing distortion took less than a second to clear – and she turned back to the steel and glass prism housing the Department for Human Support.

She couldn't feel the explosion. And surely there would be nothing to feel, even if she'd been present in every sense. This was a not-so-special effect, another stunt aimed at virality. Around her in this endless crowd, protesters overcame their initial surprise and started to laugh, gesturing obscenely toward the huge office building as ejecta rained on the garden and the street.

The debris was a finicky detail to include. Metal shrapnel, lumps of concrete and splintered glass vomited from the site of the blast. What had been the right-hand corner of the building, a dozen floors up, was now obscured by smoke. It had been a brief, sharp bang, loud and concussive, and now it was over. The designer probably should have added a large orange fireball, flaring into the sky with a deep bass rumble, something punchy and arresting for the news wraps.

Half a minute passed before DHS employees, shaken, some bleeding, emerged from the doors. Those that could still run did so, hands clutching at eyes and ears. Others staggered as they cleared the exit, before being shunted away by colleagues. The demonstrators closest broke off their chants, heads turning this way and that, fingers touching temples to mute all overlays. Maggie's brother Tez did the same, and without thought, so did Maggie. Everything false dissolved, but the smoke, the debris, the victims – those things remained. Confusion turned to sick shock, and Maggie saw what was in front of her again, for the first time.

SUMMER

CHAPTER 1
FEBRUARY 2058

LIU: You saw it coming, Kaz—

PHILLIPS: I saw – well, we all saw it. For the conservatives, it's the nightmare the polls predicted. Their unbroken nineteen-year rule has come to an end tonight. The harvesters will take note.

'Election Night', transcript of
feed broadcast, 9 February 2058
[v:news.gov.au/election]

ON THE OTHER SIDE OF THE TURNSTILE, THE COOL and quiet of the atrium was like sanctuary. Maggie fought the urge to brush down her sleeves. A handful of other petitioners, agitated enough to make a physical journey, had claimed easy-wipe plastic chairs, and the government beige of the walls promised a lack of surprise.

An aquamarine dotted line and circle coaxed her forward. A voice, androgynous and soothing, sounded in her ear: *Welcome to Human Support. How can we help?*

It was the moment half the country had waited so long for. Unexpectedly, Maggie's boss, Brij, had delegated this meeting. *This is yours as much as it is mine*, Brij had said. *You're ready.*

'Maggie Garewal to see Tim Kinnear,' she announced, pleased by the steadiness of her voice. Not for the first time that day, she reminded herself that there was no reason to be hesitant: her team had won, and it was time to seize the machine and put it to work. With a curl of her right hand, she confirmed her appointment and found the waiting elevator. Inside, a projection of a retired football player shimmied and waved to catch her attention, and upon registering her glance, congratulated Maggie for keeping her citizen profile updated.

On level six, she followed the prompts to a cramped meeting room, featureless except for one or two finger-smudges on the walls. At the building's suggestion, her shroud replaced the far wall with an underwater scene, showcasing a reef like in the old days, with colourful fish weaving through coral, and a turtle gliding above. The movements of the fish were distracting, so Maggie blocked the image. She dragged a chair over threadbare charcoal carpet and took a seat at a table that was too large for the space. According to an alert, her counterpart was on his way.

Maggie had expected the Deputy Undersec to be old, and he was. Kinnear must have been pre-Millennial. He strode in, formal in a collared shirt. Balding, with a milk-white complexion and sun spots, he had the weathered look of someone who'd declined treatment. She couldn't help itemising the ways in which they differed, and if Kinnear chose to take Maggie's youth or olive skin as provocations, then there was nothing to be done.

Eagerly, she leaned forward across the table and they brushed fingertips, to demonstrate their mutual corporeality. There was little to fear from the contact: government workers underwent regular testing.

'Thanks for coming,' Kinnear said. 'In person. I didn't think you would.'

Not knowing what to say, Maggie offered a shrug to indicate that it was no bother. She was glad she'd decided to make the journey, even though casting in would have been more efficient, and would have avoided the scrum outside.

'It must be exciting. How old were you last time there was an OzProg government?'

She looked at him sidelong. 'The Australian Progressives have never held a majority in their current config. But the landslide in 35, before the merger … I would've been four.'

The answer seemed to satisfy Kinnear. He shuffled against his seat-back, content to wait. By reputation, the man wielded an influence that far exceeded his position in the Department's org chart. He was a connector, a facilitator, with contacts scattered through other departments, the media, and many of the harvesters that had propped up the old government. Brij had explained all this to Maggie, emphasising how important it was to get buy-in from division heads like Kinnear who would be tasked with implementation.

Conscious of his age, and assuming he would appreciate the old courtesies, Maggie smiled. 'I'd like to brief you. You and I will be working together.'

When Kinnear answered, it was as if he was trying to overlook some impropriety. 'You're new at this, I know. And I don't want to be a pedant – but we'll never work *together*. You're a lobbyist.' The downward turn of his mouth conveyed his distaste. 'I consult with all sorts of stakeholders. But I am government.'

'You know who my boss is.'

'Yes.'

'You know that their proxies made the difference.'

'So the commentators say.'

Maggie pressed. 'And I'm sure you know that our support was contingent on certain assurances.'

'In a general sense, I know what Bridget Sutton stands for. Plate reform. Foreign policy reset. Tackling inequality.'

'It's that last one I'm here about.' Maggie held Kinnear's gaze, willing the old man to heed her. He kept silent, motioning for Maggie to continue. 'We'll be establishing an Income, and we need your team to start modelling.'

Kinnear sucked air through his teeth. 'Can't be done. Modelling work, I mean. Not until we get a formal request from the Minister's office. There are protocols—'

'Protocols change,' Maggie cut in. 'The Department will need to change.' She shouldn't need to remind Kinnear in so many words that the new government could clean house. He was clever enough to work that out for himself.

Kinnear inclined his head as if to concede the point, but he held her gaze a second too long. 'What was it like out there?' he asked, and Maggie knew he didn't mean the weather. He murmured, 'Front courtyard, augmented.' Between them and off to the side against the wall, a high-angle live feed of the protest formed up.

For the most part the participants were static, content simply to fill the space. It wasn't like they had anything better to do. Maggie had thought that after the OzProg victory they might have dispersed, but in the vox pops, people said they were sticking around to make sure the new mob kept their promises.

The occupation had started small and metastasised. Now there were too many for the grounds of the DHS building, and the crowd spilled over footpaths and down Soward Way, to the edge of Lake Tuggeranong. Ignoring the baked bark of the gums, demonstrators milled around virtual bonfires distributed haphazardly up and down the street and in the yards. For the most part, the cosplay was in keeping with the theme, with convicts and gentry in abundance, redcoats and squatters and miners.

That morning, when she'd arrived at the drop-off point, Maggie had made directly for the front entrance. There'd been no need to dodge. Unlike the protesters, she was here in the flesh, and that made it her reality. She'd moved through their projections unflinchingly.

Vision on her feed, called up on the ride over, had let her know what to expect. But here with them, there was a different energy. They'd been camped for days, off and on, tens of thousands. Individuals spawning and dissolving on a whim, or logging off for an hour to answer the demands of their bodies, wherever their bodies called home. They stood at odd angles, talking to each other, smiling and gesturing languidly, but somehow not entirely at ease.

The focal point of the protest was a simulated wooden barricade, projected on top of the sand garden in the DHS courtyard, thick timber boards nailed into posts. Massive banners, rippling in a counterfeit breeze, draped from crude platforms on either side of the main structure, proclaiming, *WORK IS OUR HUMAN RIGHT*. Raised crosswalks bristled with activists, but the unauthorised structure was dwarfed by the sprawling,

7

twelve-storey government building behind. *New Reeker Stockade*, one tabloid had dubbed the protest, an unfortunate handle that had stuck. A gift to political satirists, and a curse for the movement's PR officers, who'd hoped to engage on the merits of their ideas. From where Maggie had stood, the occupiers looked unequal to their mission.

So that she could see where to place her feet, and hear herself think, she'd turned down the opacity and volume of everything augmented. Now that the demonstrators were half-mute and transparent, and costumed as they were, Maggie felt as though she walked among ghosts.

A fat man in pirate garb – surely this was stretching the dress code – had lumbered toward her. Maggie's no-nonsense blouse and dark red pencil skirt marked her out, and he called, 'You government?' Not waiting for an answer, the man shouted to his faded comrades, waving them over. 'Oi! It's government!' Others closed in.

'I'm not government,' replied Maggie. And that was true, but the pirate didn't seem to hear, or care.

'Priv,' someone spat as she pressed forward.

'What you got? Thirty hours? Thirty-five?'

'Share it!' another voice added, to cries of affirmation.

Maggie didn't check her stride as she passed through the space the pirate occupied, passed through the sham stockade. 'You've got it wrong,' she said, but her words were lost.

Maggie was no stranger to precarity: if she didn't perform for Brij, it would be back to freelancing, and an overcrowded dorm. But this was her chance, her first real test. After years of quiet striving, she had earned the right to get closer. As usual, any pride she felt at that thought – any reflexive impression of having *earned* something – came with a chaser of guilt, and fear that she would be exposed as a pretender. She tried to shrug it off. Important things didn't happen streetside; they happened in stale-aired offices.

Across the meeting room table, Maggie indicated toward the image Kinnear had called up. 'Those people have cause,' she said.

'They think the system is rigged. As a representative of the Department, I'm constrained from expressing any kind of opinion. But no one here is blind.'

Maggie nodded, gratified that he could at least tacitly acknowledge the problem. She tried to lay out a trail for him, saying, 'But they're wrong about the solution. Rationing, stopping anyone from working more than twenty hours a week: it's crude. And it lets the rentiers off the hook.'

Kinnear pressed the top of the table with his palm, like he was trying to massage a bump he'd found in the surface. 'They advocate sharing. You want a universal income. And there are other proposals. We can't be taking instructions from every harvester rep that turns up, or we'd be chasing our tails.'

'In the last fortnight of the campaign, OzProg adopted our position paper.'

Kinnear arched his brow. 'Candidates make all sorts of promises,' he said wearily. 'As of this week, I serve a party that has sat in opposition for nearly two decades. And once the Department has briefed the new minister, and explained some home truths, and the difficulties inherent in actioning certain complex initiatives – noble as they are in principle – well, once we've been through all that, if we're instructed to pursue an Income, that's what we'll do.'

He settled in his chair, content to let the silence become an unbreachable gulf. It dawned on Maggie that he thought the meeting was over, and anger made her face run hot. She was here to speak for the hundreds of thousands who Brij represented. Others had worked just as hard; so many who, through bad luck or some superficial failing, had been condemned to a life of hustle. A generation—

Struggling to keep her voice level, she asked, 'Is there any point discussing specifics with you?'

'I'd welcome that,' Kinnear replied, as he shook his head in the negative. 'But it's only been nine days since the election.'

Beneath the table, Maggie raked her fingers over her skirt. 'I need to take something back. A next step ...'

For an instant, something softened in Kinnear. But then he looked away, turned again to face the image of the protest. 'We have tenure here at the Department. Good conditions.' His voice was low, as if he didn't want to be overheard. 'Do you know how we kept those things, even as others surrendered them?'

'Corruption?'

Kinnear allowed himself a fleeting, dry laugh. 'No. It's because public servants are a different breed. Those people out there, they've been atomised. That's why all the dissent has come to nothing. They're co-located, for the time being, but they're not *together*. Their demands are easy to ignore.'

'They're coordinated. Movements don't need a single leader.'

Kinnear nodded, acknowledging the point, but quibbled, 'They could lead themselves, if they knew who they were. As it is ... look at them! Fake troopers, imitation prospectors – they've got both sides of a rebellion singing songs and holding hands.'

Maggie shifted in her seat. 'Maybe so,' she said. 'But I'm here. We're both here, now.'

'Perhaps an Income would work. Perhaps not.' The look on Kinnear's face conveyed his own view plainly enough. 'I shouldn't give political advice. But.' He pressed the palms of his hands together, as if praying for understanding. 'What you're attempting is dangerous. Once it's started, you could easily lose control of the process. So wait a year; let everyone settle into their roles. Let the people outside get bored and go home. Most importantly, give yourself time to learn.'

He wore the suffocating, unperturbed half-smile of every comfortable man. Coldly furious, Maggie raised her voice. 'Things have been low-key fucked for a long time. Me, the people out there – we just won an election by calling that out. We might not agree on everything, but on that much, we stand together.' In that moment, she believed it was true. 'You won't dismiss us, and you won't gaslight us. If you try, you'll deserve what comes your way.'

This was supposed to be a victory lap, the repurposing of old tools to new ends. Instead, Maggie realised that she had lost control, was venting her frustration like one of the placard-bearers outside. There was an ache growing behind her brow, and she knew she needed to get out, in case her eyes betrayed her and her credibility was shot forever. 'We'll be in contact.' Aware of how passive that sounded, she rasped, 'With you, if you're still here next time we call. Stay clean.'

Kinnear stood, and his hand swept toward the door. 'Stay clean.'

On her way to the elevator she traversed a long, windowless corridor flanked by portraits of former departmental secretaries. She couldn't remember having come this way on arrival. The paintings were real, framed in thick, stained wood, and featured unsmiling women and men. If she'd done an image search on any of the subjects at random, Maggie could surely have pulled up a list of achievements, but that was beside the point. Their contributions had been noted and were to be taken as read. She felt eyes all around her has she moved, and the silence gave her no comfort at all.

CHAPTER 2

Proxies (Australian_democracy)

… A response to the plebiscites of the early 2040s. With the senate deadlocked, the Roy Government used non-binding online surveys to pressure independents into supporting legislation. But it wasn't long until voters became resentful about being polled so frequently … The High Court's *Harvester (II)* judgment established that a right to vote in a plebiscite implies a related right to delegate that vote to another. Shortly after the decision was handed down, a class of professional 'proxy harvesters' emerged, offering the public a way to make their views known without the burden of following a busy legislative agenda.

Further reforms followed, allocating public funding to successful harvesters as an anti-corruption measure. Subsequent court decisions barred the direct purchasing of proxies, though some corps still offer incentives for grants to their preferred nominee …

– [AlltFeed Knowledge, accessed 16:54:03, 18-FEB-2058]

NGUNNAWAL-NGAMBRI CANBERRA WAS COMFORTably set in its ways: each suburb an enclave, too isolated to walk from one to the next. Too dusty dry, in the summer, to be outside for long, so everyone was whisked. For Maggie, the ride from Greenway to Barton was like coming home. Toward the centre, the structures were less like prefabricated bunkers – blockish, pockmarked with vents for aircon, filtration and de/ re-humidifiers – and more their own entities. Curved, insulated glass. Reclaimed water systems nursing hardy plants. Back here, the structures were individualised in subtle ways, displaying the hallmarks of intelligent design.

At the office, Maggie was intercepted as she stepped off the elevator.

'How'd it go?'

'Not great,' replied Maggie. She stepped to pass by, but Cass held her shoulder.

'Hang on. She's on a call, anyway.'

Maggie let out a breath she'd been holding for suburbs. 'Of course.'

'Drink tonight?' The too-casual way Cass asked made it a challenge. Her auburn hair was cropped to a messy shingle, accentuating her already expressive features. A tiny silver skull-and-crossbones adorned the flesh below her left cheekbone, and a black teardrop hung suspended on her right, each ornament clipped into a stud fused to her skin. The studs, with their constantly changing jewellery, made her face a constellation, and Maggie felt her gaze shifting from Cass's eyes to her mouth, to a stud, and back again.

Maggie turned to see if they were disturbing any of their workmates, but the office was quiet. Brij had fourteen staff, but they were almost never in the same space at the same time. And those who'd cast in could easily mute Cass if she bothered them.

'I can't tonight. Family dinner.'

Cass took a half-step backward, audibly drawing air through her nostrils like she was trying to summon a reserve of patience, but by now Maggie knew this to be an expression of no more than mild annoyance. The pair had started as volunteers in the same intake, almost four years ago, and Maggie had fully expected that they'd be shown the door at the end of their trial. When Brij announced that her base had grown, and she had room in the budget for both of them, it felt like dumb luck. Though they drew from the same pool of resources, Maggie couldn't bring herself to resent Cass, whose lack of diplomacy cut through the priggish vibe that Brij's team was sometimes prone to.

The bullpen was large enough to accommodate eight work-spaces, most adjacent to a window overlooking the leafy street. There was a separate conference room, and a dark space for casting. Brij had an office to herself at the far end, and everyone else shared. The decor was minimalist, muted greys and blues, but each year Brij engaged a designer to create a couple of new shroud themes. Maggie stuck to the current default, all blond wood panelling and ferns, believing that an office should look like an office.

Cass grimaced. 'You're in robot stress mode. Enjoy that. I'm gonna crash the Barbecue.'

'Happy hunting,' Maggie replied, but Cass had already turned and started toward the darkroom.

Self-conscious now she was alone, Maggie approached her boss's closed door. Knocking, she poked her head through and raised her eyebrows in a question.

Brij was speaking rapidly to someone: '... won't get up unless we can get Reeve on board, and there's little chance of that if the Truvies come out hard against ...' She held up a hand to Maggie, fingers splayed.

Five minutes could mean anything. Maggie took a seat at the nearest desk. It was unadorned, nothing more than a place to sit and stare, and to rest wrists. Idly, she scrolled through her messages.

She'd worked with Brij for years now, but Maggie couldn't relax in the older woman's presence. What if she said something intemperate, and that nudged things? Brij was one of the most powerful people in the country. Maggie was a policy advisor; it was her job to advise, but still, venturing an opinion in Brij's presence felt like letting something hard and heavy slip from her fingers.

Soon enough, she got a ping. She stood quickly and returned to Brij's office, taking a chair on the other side of the harvester's vast desk. Jarrah, she'd heard Brij say once. It was the sole extravagance in this space. Brij herself was compact with a round-faced, sated look, as if she'd internalised every proxy she'd been loaned, holding them within to ride out a coming period of hibernation. Her dark hair was raked back, emphasising her forehead, and Maggie had always supposed that this was deliberate. A claim, or a repudiation.

On the ride back to the office, Maggie had rehearsed explanations, but everything sounded like an excuse. Now she made to speak, but Brij was faster. 'There's another interview starting in ten. I need you to pull together our next grantor burst. Watch the tone: we're not smug. We're focused on what happens next.'

Maggie nodded, starting a transcription. A dim amber light on her brow let Brij know that audio was being taken.

'We need to lay out our agenda,' Brij continued. 'What we expect to see, what we'll be pushing for in these first few months. Of course, you'll write the Income section. You can do something on crypto-baskets, too – why the default needs updating. Get a blurb on plate reform from Cass, and ask the others for project summaries. Nothing too long.'

'Okay.'

'Ah. And there's a new intern starting next week. I want you to supervise.'

Maggie paused the recording. 'I'm not sure—'

'The timing isn't great, but it's Chase's sibling's kid. I know! They'll probably be hopeless.' Maggie found it hard to get a word in once Brij got going. 'But if we can get Chase onside, it would help. God knows why they picked us. Anyway, that's how it is.'

'About Kinnear …'

'That bundle. How'd you get on?'

There could be no hedging; Brij was always pushing forward. 'They blocked me. I tried, but they won't start work until the new minister issues an instruction. Brij, I'm sorry, I—'

'Don't worry.'

'I know we need momentum.'

At this, Brij laughed, her face settling into a wry smile. 'And you thought the Department would make it easy? After all these years, the place is a dumping ground. They were never going to listen to you.'

Maggie pressed her fingernails into the flesh of her palm. She'd thought Brij might be angry, or disappointed, but this blitheness was worse. It spoke of low expectations. Unsure if she wanted an answer, Maggie asked, 'So what was the point?'

'Because now I can message an old friend. And I'll tell him, so sorry to bother you, but we tried the proper channels ...'

Realisation came as a bilious feeling. Holger Tan, the new Minister for Human Support, had history with Brij. Now it made sense, why Maggie had been allowed to take the lead with Kinnear.

Something must have shown on her face, because Brij said, 'It was good experience. If we're going to get this over the line, we'll need to sell it, and I'll be stretched too thin. It will have to be you, Maggie.'

'You could have told me.'

'For all I knew, Kinnear might have seen the way things were going. That dult is smart.'

Trying and failing to move Kinnear had felt like fighting for breath, but Maggie put her frustration aside. Brij had her reasons, and, besides, Maggie owed her everything: her loyalty and her trust. She'd plucked Maggie from the big drift, creating a debt that could never be made good.

'The more you tell me, the more I can help.'

Brij was inscrutable. 'I know,' she said, her mouth a line.

From experience, Maggie knew that this was as much as she'd get. Swallowing her first response, she hesitated, tried again. 'What's next?'

'Budget meeting next week. All that new money, and I'm sure you'll come ready for the fight. In the meantime, I'll set something up with Tan. Do you want in?'

'... yes.'

'Good. Oh! Shit. It's starting.' Brij's eyes flicked to something only she could see, and her face eased into a practiced expressionlessness. She smiled. 'Thank you, it's nice to be here.'

Over the past week, Maggie had watched her boss conduct dozens of these brief victory-lap interviews for news aggregators, audiocasts and fan sites. Dull, but important for consolidating the base, to make them feel like their long-standing faith was about to be rewarded. Maggie let herself out.

CHAPTER 3

Congratulations! Your parents have decided that you are ready for a shroud. Getting a shroud installed is part of growing up and becoming a dult.

Q. ? Whats a shroud?

A. A shroud lets you use augmented reality. These days, shrouds are implanted around your eyes (three tiny projectors around each eye, and a camera and a microphone on the bridge of your nose) and your ears (two buds). As you grow, your shroud technician will make adjustments and upgrades to make sure that your shroud stays clean and grows with you.

Q. ? What can I do with a shroud?

A. With your shroud, you will be able to see and hear projections. Projections are people and things that have been placed in the world around you. They are not really there – you cant touch, taste or smell them ...

... Depending on the settings your parents choose, you might be able to cast yourself into other places. To do this, sit in a dark, quiet room. Then choose where you want to go. You will be able to see and hear whats happening at the place you cast into (or, if no one else is there and theres no cam, you will see the place as it looked the last time someone else with a shroud visited IRL). And other people wearing shrouds in the same place will be able to see you, or at least, they will see the avatar you project.

You can read messages and your feed, make calls, and listen to casts. A shroud will help you find your way around, and highlight interesting things nearby. With a shroud, you dont need your kidScreen anymore!

…

!Safety First!

The hardest thing about learning to use your shroud is working out whats real. Projections cant hurt your body, but real things can.

To help you start, projections will have a max opacity of 75%. That means they look faded, and you will be able to see through them a bit …

… Even once you can tell whats real and whats not, projections can be dangerous if they distract you. Thats why your shroud will automatically hide projections when you run, or if you are up high, or near something that looks like it could hurt you.

!Things to remember!

You can turn off all projections – and return to your body, if you are casting – by saying 'Sever!' You should practice doing this so you can remember for later.

Sometimes, projections might appear and then disappear suddenly, or you might not be able to access a projection you were expecting to see. Your shroud will block some rude things.

Some kids need a bit of extra help adjusting to their shroud. If it makes you scared or sad, or you are having trouble sleeping, thats ok. Just tell a parent or your shroud tech.

– Extract from 'My First Shroud –
a FAQ for kids', GazeUp Australia, 2054
[Grammar setting: English Junior]

ALWAYS, THE SMELL OF HER PARENTS' KITCHEN
registered first. It was the warm, earthy undertone of garam
masala, worked in to the benches, masked but never entirely
displaced by whatever else was on offer. Maggie let herself in
through the back door, and Liv and Raman greeted her from
the other side of the breakfast bar.

'Gnocchi!' Liv said, proudly. Red sauce bubbled in a pan
next to a pot of boiling water.

Maggie's dad smiled apologetically. 'Peasant food.' To the
continuing embarrassment of his wife and children, Raman
liked to eat meat every day.

The lights were dim, and steam from the pot made the air
feel soft – a relief from the outdoors. The house was a jumble
of things: photo frames, vases, souvenirs from family holidays
decades ago. Paintings on the walls. All of it could have been
digitised, converted into a shroud theme, but like many older
people, Maggie's parents must have enjoyed being surrounded
by objects. In her idle moments, Liv would run her fingers
around the rims of a set of lacquerware bowls stacked, inexplica-
bly, on the wide windowsill facing the back garden. That seemed
to be the bowls' only function: Maggie couldn't remember them
ever having been used for food.

'Where's Tez?' Maggie asked. Liv responded with a vexed
look and a shake of her head.

'We're a few minutes away,' said Raman. Not quite sixty, he

had retired two years ago. He said he wanted to free up his job for some young person, but Maggie suspected that he'd been waiting to quit for a long time. The fact that he'd never made partner at his former accounting firm didn't bother him: Raman just put it down to a lack of vision on the part of his colleagues. He was much happier now, cooking and tinkering in his shed when the evenings where mild. Liv continued to work two days a week as a hospital administrator. Her pay and their savings afforded them a comfortable existence.

Maggie walked to the fridge and searched through a collection of wax paper wraps for the block of parmesan she knew she'd find. 'Where's the grater?' Without taking his eyes off the sauce, Raman pulled open a drawer.

When the gnocchi had been drained and served, Liv picked up a bowl and walked down the corridor that led to the front of the house. 'Tez! Dinner!' Her words bounced off the polished concrete, back to Maggie and Raman, who took their places at the table. Catching Maggie's look, Raman returned a sheepish expression.

When Liv walked back in, her hands were empty. She joined the others and said, 'He'll cast in.' Raman nodded and fumbled for the glasses he'd need to see his son. He'd never gotten around to having implants installed for a shroud, and now he said he was too old to bother.

Maggie's older brother materialised at the foot of the table. In appearance, Maggie took after Raman, but Tez was fairer, more like Liv, with short brown hair and delicate features. He had the courtesy to at least fade in slowly, but Maggie could tell straight away that this was a placeholder, not really showing

Tez as he was. 'Hey, Mags.' The mouth moved, but his avatar's expression remained vacant.

Maggie didn't try to hide her annoyance. 'You won't be joining us?'

'I'm on a deadline.'

'It's a big competition,' Liv added, her eyes apologising. 'If he wins, it's twelve months, committed.'

Maggie imagined her older brother in his room, half-reclined on his bed, wolfing down his plate of gnocchi. The air would be close, reeking of unwashed sheets. 'What is it this time?'

'A new hotel in the desert. Underground, so there's no exterior to worry about. All the focus is on flow. And cost. I've got a good shot at this one.'

Tez had graduated almost a decade ago. Since then, he'd spent his time submitting to design competitions run by the larger architecture firms. For those without a personal connection, it was the only way into a career.

When he'd started, Tez had seemed inspired by the briefs. And some of his concepts were breathtaking, even to Maggie's untrained eye. Back then she was still in high school, and he'd visit her room and explain what he'd drawn. But for each opportunity, there were thousands of applicants. After years of failure, Tez's efforts had come to resemble an obsession.

Maggie had tried to talk to him about it a few times. Recently, she'd heard of a job going at an indoor plant hire business – there might be some aspects of interior design? But Liv and Raman had ruined him. They'd say things like, *Follow your heart.* Perhaps that used to be good advice.

'Dada ji's party is coming up,' said Raman, his mouth full of half-chewed gnocchi.

'Yeah,' said Maggie. 'I'll be there.' Raman's father – Maggie's paternal grandfather – had always doted on Maggie. Growing up, her cousins had teased her about being the favourite.

'Are you stressed?' Liv asked. 'Now that the election's over, you should take a holiday.'

'Ha!' Tez laughed. The laugh was genuine, but without the expression to match, his avatar looked uncanny. 'Mum, have you met your daughter?'

'Like you can talk,' Maggie shot back. With an effort, she swallowed her annoyance. 'You should come along next time Cass and I catch up. Maybe you can charm her.'

'I don't need your charity,' replied Tez. 'I do alright.'

'Yeah, wanking off to projections.'

Raman grunted, trying to hide his amusement and almost succeeding. 'Hey! No fighting at the table. Take a breath. Taste this meal I made. Basil, oregano – what else?'

'You think you're any better?' There was hurt in Tez's voice. '*You're* the indentured fucking servant.' Before Maggie could respond, Tez's avatar darkened and froze.

Raman studied the water jug.

Liv said, 'For a couple of days? You could go to Tasmania, see some tall trees.'

Maggie shook her head. 'There's too much on.'

'You've done very well,' said Raman. 'Doesn't it bring you pleasure?'

That was so typical. It showed that he didn't get it. It was fine for him and Liv: they swanned around. They could have done something, but instead they'd been happily diverted. Inspo, and lifeporn. Learning how to hand-roll gnocchi.

Rather than rekindling the old fight, Maggie glanced at the inert form of her brother. 'Tez needs some sun.'

'He's following his own path,' Liv said gently.

'It's not kind,' said Maggie. 'This pretending. If he was going to succeed, it would have happened. He should be out there attending conferences, networking. Looking for his chance.'

Raman ran his spoon around the inside of his bowl. 'We'll see.' He slurped lukewarm sauce like it was soup.

'I've got an early shift tomorrow at the co-op. Can I help tidy?'

'Don't worry,' her mum said.

'Remember about Dada ji. He'll want to see you.'

'I will.'

IT WASN'T LATE BY THE TIME MAGGIE GOT HOME. The long dusk had ended and it was properly dark, but it was only nine.

Inside her apartment, the only sound was the muzzled puff of the aircon. With her job, Maggie had been able to rent one of the new-style apartments in Bruce. Small, with no windows except those the shroud added. A tiled entryway for taking off shoes, and a kitchenette, and for the rest of the main room, Maggie had laid faux-tatami. A separate bedroom doubled as a space for casting. She had her own ensuite, so she didn't have to share with anyone, except for laundry.

There was nothing to tidy or prepare, so she lay on the sofa and called up her feed. Top suggestion was a panel argument about the Leadbeater's Possum. A group in Victoria had spent the last few years cultivating a habitat in what remained of the Central Highlands after the fires. They'd found substitutes for the old ash and gum trees the animals had made their homes in; printed fake twigs and ribbons of bark that could be used to build nests. 'We've got everything ready,' said a conservationist involved with the project. 'Now all we need are the animals.'

The plan was to implant fertilised embryos, grown from materials preserved before the last specimens died back in the thirties, into common brushtail possum surrogates. The first animals would show that a viable community was possible. Support a crowdfunding effort.

'Things happen for a reason,' said one of the other guests. 'This possum isn't a survivor. We should spend that money on endangered livestock.'

The same words as always, tumbled like spray. But now it would be different. She turned over to the pleb channel, checked which bills were coming up in the next fortnight. Mostly procedural stuff, repeals, following through on campaign promises. Starting with the restoration of Medicare benefits to over-70s, there was a backlog of measures with public support that the old government had refused to bring to a vote. All these things would compete for attention in the coming months.

Once she'd scanned the list, there was nothing else for her. Maggie switched off, padded through to the bathroom to have her teeth brushed. She changed for bed, found a channel streaming slee-slo. With the closing of her palm, she stopped the lights. Settled on her mattress. An hour later, she was still awake.

CHAPTER 4

Abstract:

The Australian hybrid system is unique. Falling somewhere between Europe (in which parties propose, and citizens dispose), and the old-style representative arrangements of the United States and South England, Australia's form of government has variously been described as 'half-baked', a 'mongrel', and 'unfinished'. One commentator went so far as to describe it as 'the worst of all possible worlds', but that is hyperbole, given Aotearoa's democratic regression in the early forties ...

There is, of course, no constitutional requirement that bills be referred to a plebiscite. The concept of the people as a third chamber of parliament, and the 'two out of three' rule are nothing more than conventions. In practice, it would be unthinkable for a bill passed by a chamber of parliament, and successful in a plebiscite, to be blocked by the third chamber. This paper considers a related question: could a bill that does not have popular support (either because it is never put to a plebiscite, or is put and defeated) be made into law by House and Senate alone? Formally, there is nothing to prevent this ...

The author will argue that such a possibility, even if never realised, functions as a final safeguard against tyrannies of the majority.

– Unthinkable, but Indispensable: Unpopular Legislation as a Last Resort
Ramsay, D., *Journal of Good Government*, (2055) Vol. 23(2)

MAGGIE SPENT THURSDAY MORNINGS AT HER LOCAL childcare co-op, banking credits. She wasn't sure if she would ever want children, and at twenty-six, the question didn't yet feel urgent. But in case the day ever came, she was building a buffer.

In truth, Maggie enjoyed the way the shifts broke up her week. A four-hour stint was manageable, though the morning shifts were easier than the afternoons, when the younger ones grew tetchy. Afterwards, she took pleasure in the quiet and order of her usual routine.

Today she was on toddler patrol. It was more difficult to look after pre-shroud kids, because you needed real stuff to keep them occupied. Maggie and another volunteer, Ram, had cordoned off a small territory at the back of the centre, bringing over armfuls of toys to spread out on the carpeted floor. The main hall was the size of two large classrooms. It was able to be partitioned, but rarely was, so noise and activity always carried from somewhere on the periphery. Down the other end, Kei, the centre's director and its only paid employee, was helping some older kids with their homework. In an adjoining kitchen, more volunteers would be cutting up fruit for breakfast.

Maggie crouched on the floor next to a gaggle of children, showing them how things could be made to stand for other things, or assembled to form a gestalt. She mediated the inevitable fights. Unlike projections, you couldn't clone a coveted toy. And scarcity made people strange: Maggie watched as a little girl abandoned a trove of objects, her attention caught by a horse figurine being dragged along the ground by another.

Because the centre was continuously staffed, children could be deposited and collected at any time, so the population was always changing. But there was often a high turnover before lunch, just as Maggie's shift was ending. By now she recognised many of the parents, and she smiled as one of the dads, Jaxon, approached to collect his child.

'Has she been a pain?' he asked. He was unshaven, and reached down hurriedly to swoop up his daughter, not meeting Maggie's eye.

'Not at all. They've been playing with Micah.'

'Okay.' He didn't sound pleased. 'I guess we'd better use this place while we can.'

This was bait, unmistakably, but Maggie's curiosity won out. 'Why's that?'

Jaxon scowled. 'Well, OzProg'll probably try and shut it down.'

'I don't think so. If you look at their statement on—'

'Well, maybe not shut it down,' he cut in. 'But they'll ruin these centres, somehow. Too much regulation. A government takeover.'

'If they tried, they'd have to get it past a 'scite. I wouldn't vote for something like that. Would you?'

'They'll sneak it through. Bribe some harvesters,' he said pointedly.

'That's an idea,' Maggie replied. Brushing past him, she spotted some old-style picture books on the other side of the play space that needed putting away.

LATER, AFTER SHE'D FINISHED HANDING OVER TO the afternoon crew, Kei arrived to check in. 'I saw Jax bail you up. I'd tell you not to feed the trolls, but ...'

'How did you know?'

Only a little taller than Maggie, Kei Arakachi presented like the sort of man you could entrust your children to. Slim, with a kind, open face and long dark hair, his accent retained the barest trace of his Japanese ancestry. His parents had emigrated to Australia from Okinawa, at the tail end of a Ryukyuan diaspora that had lasted for centuries. She envied the relative closeness of Kei's connection to that culture. When people asked about her background, it was usually but not always with friendly curiosity. Maggie would reply that her mum was from Wollongong, and her father's father was Jat, born in Gujarat. The follow-up questions, when they came, were never about Wollongong.

Maggie had never been to India – had never left Australia. Physical travel was dangerous, expensive and, at least since the last cold war, administratively difficult. Some millennials and their predecessors still managed it, hopping on one of the year-long sea cruises that never stopped at any port, but that idea had never appealed to Maggie.

She had never learned Gujarati, or Hindi, or any other language. When she thought about her Indian heritage, which was mostly when she caught up with extended family on her dad's side, she felt acutely embarrassed at her ignorance.

Kei asked, 'Do you know what Jaxon does for actual?'

Maggie shook her head.

'Vehicle manager. Looks after half the cars in town.'

'That explains it,' Maggie replied. Jaxon's overlords in the capital class had not been pleased by the election result. 'Hmm. I've got to run. I've got a lunch over at Manuka.'

'Fancy.' Kei's mouth gaped in a sarcastic approximation of awe, and then his expression cleared. 'Any chance I'll see you tomorrow night?'

She smiled. 'I'd say you're in with a shot.'

TAN AND BRIJ HAD DISPOSED OF HALF A BOTTLE OF wine by the time Maggie arrived. The place was crawling with government workers, and she was conscious of sideways glances as she brushed digits with the new Minister for Human Support and took her seat. It was odd to meet this person in the flesh, after years of watching them on her feed, and she registered all over again how physically small they were – short-statured, and so skinny as to suggest frailty. Tan had updated their look for the election campaign, losing the mess of unfashionable bleached white hair they'd sported for years, shaving their head. Perhaps an advisor had suggested it, to make them look less professorial, or like they had nothing to hide.

'Brij's told me about you,' said Tan. 'Says you're a good analyst.'

'That's true, I think.' Maggie felt her cheeks grow warm. Beside her, Brij nodded confirmation.

Tan continued a story that Maggie must have interrupted. Something about a disgraced lecturer from their student days, who was trying to rehabilitate his reputation by conducting what he'd dubbed a 'national atonement tour'. Brij thought the academic's remorse might be sincere, if bombastic; but Tan insisted that this was more likely a set-up for some new, pre-meditated outrage that would keep the lecturer in mentions and paid appearances for a while yet.

Maggie glanced at a menu, picked out a phở made with real beef. This was an old-school place, with white linen and metal cutlery, and people to bring over their meals. She would never have come here if she'd been paying, but this was on Brij's account. It was something Maggie's boss would need to report in a lobbyist disclosure, which made this a business meeting, no matter how pleasant the surrounds. Other diners were watching their table, and one or two red lights on the brows of those nearby meant that vision was being recorded. Obnoxious, but there were always a few.

'Thanks for doing this,' Brij said. 'Meeting here, I mean. You won't believe what this will do for our numbers, once this hits the boards. Everyone likes to feel close to power, and that's you, now.'

'How am I meant to behave?' Tan asked quietly, rubbing the back of their neck. 'I mean, is this okay, to go out for lunch? Until now I've laboured in obscurity.'

'It's been a long time since the teams changed,' said Brij. 'You can make your own rules.'

'It's alright for you,' Tan replied. 'You're used to the attention.'

Brij aimed a weary look in his direction. Perhaps this talk of scrutiny reminded her why they'd gathered, because she said,

'We're very pleased that OzProg supports our Income proposal.'

'It's good. Comprehensive. You worked on this, Maggie?'

'Wrote most of it,' replied Brij, before Maggie could respond.

Tan nodded. 'And say I want to pitch it. To cabinet, or to plebs.'

Maggie had wondered why she'd been asked to lunch. 'Cabinet's easier,' she said, trying to sound confident. 'You tell them that if OzProg doesn't deliver, there are going to be riots, and not just in shroudspace.'

Tan winced. 'That's stretching things, don't you think?'

'Why do you think you got in, after all this time? People are angry. And they have a lot of time on their hands.'

'These angry, idle people: how do we bring them along?'

A soft question, with a straightforward answer. 'They're already supportive. They've been crying out for something like this for a decade. We just need to convince them that an Income – a universal basic income – is the right way to solve the employment problem.'

The edges of Tan's mouth turned upwards, as if the politician was enjoying a private joke. 'The employment problem, yes. What actually *is* the problem? How would you describe it, if you were the one doing interviews?'

Tan was no moron. They knew the statistics just as well as Maggie, so her sense of being tested grew stronger. 'Almost half the country lives below the poverty line. They'd work if they could, just to earn more money. But there aren't enough human jobs to go around, so they're stuck.' Even as she spoke, this explanation felt trite to her. 'And then there are people out there, with good jobs, who would prefer to work less, if they weren't terrified of losing what they have.'

'So it's an imbalance?'

'In part. But you can't fix it just by rationing. Some people want to work a lot, and they have specialist skills. We need them. But others would rather not work at all in paid employment. And with the gains from automation, we can say: that's valid. Contribute in other ways. Volunteer. Make art. Look after others.'

'An Income would let people make that choice,' added Brij. 'It would give them dignity. It's a mindset as much as anything.'

'And how do we pay for this?'

'Easy. We tax the robots.' Thinking of her run-in with Jaxon, Maggie said, 'Or, more precisely, we tax the owners of the machines that have replaced human labour.'

'Those owners – they won't be thrilled.'

There was no arguing with that. Harvesters in the pocket of big business had kept tax reform off the agenda for years. 'They'll run a scare campaign,' Maggie conceded. 'And you'll explain that the point of automation should be to free humans from drudgery. To give them a chance to find their own meaning. All we'd be doing is allowing some of the benefits of automation to flow to the people, instead of the capital class.'

'What will the Chinese think about this? The Americans?'

'What's that got to do with getting it past a pleb?'

Tan's glass was halfway to their mouth, and they stopped, eyes searching for Brij, who shook her head as if she were embarrassed by Maggie's question. Sensing that she'd mis-stepped, Maggie added, 'I suppose the Americans will hate it.'

'And the Chinese?'

Maggie hesitated. 'They might like it just because it annoys the Americans. But they won't understand it. In some ways, it'll be too socialist for them. If they were doing something like this, they'd tie it to existing credit. Make graduated payments, conditional on a citizen score. But then it wouldn't be universal.'

Tan looked unconvinced, so Maggie hurried on. 'There's precedent for this, as you know. Decades worth of positive data out of Europe. We have a pretty good idea of what works.'

Their meals arrived. A server placed a large bowl in front of Maggie and the aniseed smell of the soup made her mouth water. At the same time, she regretted ordering something liable to spatter. Tan and Brij had both opted for dry noodle dishes. Gingerly, she raised her spoon to her lips and slurped broth.

The conversation turned to gossip, the kind concerned with staffers and election-night parties, and the perennial flow of traffic between the commentariat, the harvesters and government offices. Brij and the Minister filled all the spaces with their words, but now Maggie could sense that something was pending; unresolved between the two. Brij motioned to order another bottle of wine, but Tan stopped her, his eyes flicking from table to table around the room.

'Have you asked them?' Tan said, speaking to Brij but looking at Maggie. Maggie searched her boss's face for some clue.

'Not yet,' Brij replied. 'I wanted you to meet her first.' She looked at him and Tan nodded, as if giving permission. 'Mags, we need a liaison.'

Tan jumped in. 'I support the push for an Income, Maggie. It's an idea Brij and I have kicked around since university.

But the hard work on this is going to be done at Treasury, up in Sydney. They've already begun drafting a White Paper.'

Maggie straightened. This was happening.

'I'm worried that we'll lose control,' Tan continued. 'There are too many interests, within OzProg and without. Once the gnomes get their hands on this—'

'That's why we need someone,' Brij said. They were trading verses; they'd worked it all out beforehand. 'To keep an eye out.'

Maggie understood that she had just been nominated. She didn't disagree with anything Brij or Tan had said, but she was conscious of all the things she didn't know. This would be a major reform, maybe the largest in a generation, and Maggie had never been part of turning a proposal into government policy, policy into legislation. Being chosen for this task showed that Brij, even Tan as the new Minister, were making this up as they went along.

It wasn't as if the election result had come as a shock. The new PM, Jack Alpen, exuded likability, and during the campaign he'd maintained his party's comfortable lead in the polls, even after the 'LawnGate' beat-up, and the leaked pictures of his prepper bolt-hole on Bruny Island. But the progressive side of politics had been marginalised for so long, had settled into careers of resistance and opposition, cut off from donors, alienated from most of the ordinary people they claimed to represent. Bridget Sutton and Holger Tan were trying to implement the kind of change they'd advocated for decades, and still, it felt ad-hoc.

'Why me?' Maggie asked. 'Why not someone from inside Human Support?'

Tan laughed. 'You've met Kinnear. Should I send him?'

'I take your point.'

'And Brij represents the everyday voters of Australia. Or two and a half million of them, anyway. She should have eyes on how the plan is shaping up, and a chance to apply pressure if things slide.'

Brij turned toward Maggie, held her gaze. 'And you want this. Don't you.' It wasn't a question.

'Yes,' Maggie said. And it was extremely true.

CHAPTER 5

After all that hype, the marketing campaigns, the billions of
research dollars! The labs and the processing centres ... Why
does it feel like I'm eating defrosted earthworms?

> – [User comment, AlltFeed/Synthmeat,
> accessed 16:04:48 21-FEB-2058]

MAGGIE AND BRIJ SHARED A CAR BACK TO THE OFFICE.
A two-seater, configurable so that they could have faced each
other. But when they entered and settled, both looking out
the windscreen, neither of them made an adjustment. Being in
close quarters like this no longer made Maggie nervous, and like
everyone, she was used to being ignored in small bursts. Judging
by Brij's vacant look, something in her feed had captured the
older woman's attention.

'What we talked about at lunch,' Brij finally said as their
vehicle slowed and veered to navigate an intersection. 'Don't
mention it to anyone else. It'll take me some time to get you
embedded. It might not even happen.'

Maggie nodded, and then, because Brij was still watching
her feed, said, 'Okay.' She could ask for an explanation, but all
the beginnings sounded petulant, so she looked out the window.

Half a minute later, she realised that she was idle, that this time could be utilised for work. With an effort, she focused up, selected a saved tab in her feed, and resumed a UN keynote about the situation in the Arctic.

Almost everyone on Earth had become an expert on what used to be called permafrost, but was now mostly referred to as the Polar Bomb, or just the Bomb. Over the course of Maggie's childhood, a list of likely culprits for the apocalypse had been studied and treated, with varying degrees of success. Ocean acidification: bad, but adaptable, if you were not a maritime creature. Sea level rises, ditto, as long as you didn't live near the coast (it was not going so well for billions who did). But as Maggie's teenage years sped by, the emerging scientific consensus was that as hard as things were, it would be the tundra that would doom humans, if its ice cover vanished and all the methane trapped beneath was released into the air.

The UN's yearly report had dropped a couple of days earlier, so Maggie already knew the headlines: despite all geoengineering efforts, the likelihood of a significant methane release event within the next 20 years had been upgraded from 42 per cent to 48 per cent, largely due to warming that had occurred decades earlier. But the keynote itself was important for Maggie's work, because the messaging would influence OzProg's climate policies over the next few years. She tried hard to pay attention.

WHEN THEY ARRIVED BACK AT THE OFFICE, SOMEONE new was sitting at one of the bullpen desks. Knees together, hands in lap, he appeared to have no choice but to listen as Cass held forth, gesturing extravagantly and standing over him.

'We should intervene,' Brij said under her breath, to Maggie or to herself.

They approached in time to catch the end of Cass's diatribe. '—just there to sell subscriptions. reFolk is pure marketing. It's the exact opposite of what real musicians are trying to do.'

The youth – he couldn't have been more than twenty – nodded politely while his eyes roamed. Alighting on Maggie and Brij, he smiled an appeal.

'What is it this time, Cass?'

At the sound of Brij's voice, Cass turned. She was unabashed, and she didn't try and hide the fun she was having, but as her eyes found Brij's, a look passed between the two. Something intense, and out of place. Cass's face framed a question, and almost imperceptibly, Brij nodded in response.

Oblivious, the young man answered Brij. 'I asked Cass what music they listen to.'

'Maggie, this is Felix Reeve. They'll be doing work experience here for a few months.' Perhaps unconsciously, Brij had emphasised his last name.

'He/him,' Felix said, as he reached out to brush fingers. His warmth and confidence caught Maggie off guard. Sitting, he appeared small, although when he stood, he'd probably be taller than Maggie. He had a mop of dirty blond hair that should have made him look unkempt, but Maggie could tell that his clothes were expensive. He was overdressed for this place, in a charcoal suit and ivory button-up shirt, like a teenager forced to scrub up for a formal event.

'She/her.' She grazed her fingers against his.

While Felix looked on, Maggie and Cass fetched chairs, and Brij disappeared into the kitchen and returned with jars of cold tea, which she handed around, and all four of them sat in an impromptu huddle. 'Cheers,' Felix drawled, and sipped.

Maggie set her face in a smile, and lowered her expectations. He'd allowed Brij to get the tea. Didn't he know – he should have known – that everything was a test? With an effort, she fought back annoyance. Asked him, 'What brings you here?'

'You probably know my uncle.'

She did. Chase Reeve spoke for nearly four million votes, making him the third most prominent harvester in the country, carrying greater sway than Brij when judged by raw numbers. But more than that, he occupied the dead centre of the political spectrum, making him a swing vote on key plebs. He sold himself as a dult driven by common sense, wary of ideology. But to Maggie, this was a reframing of what really amounted to a lack of principle. It was striking how frequently common sense led Chase to support the interests of his corporate donors.

'I'm interested in the family business,' Felix continued. 'And Chase said I should get experience, from all sides. Even with bleeding-heart lefties like you.' He chuckled as if he'd amused himself.

'Admirable,' said Brij, giving nothing away. Next to Felix, Cass looked like she was about to choke on her tea. 'We're very pleased to have you here. You've already met Cass, and perhaps she's told you what she's working on. Now, Maggie – her focus is Income.'

'As in, just give everyone money?' When he saw that no one was smiling, he moderated his tone. 'That … ah, that's interesting.'

'It's a challenge,' Maggie allowed. She didn't feel like justifying herself. 'It's the most effective way to reduce inequality.'

'And you'll be helping her,' said Brij, in a tone that didn't invite argument. 'There'll be lots to do. Research, and working out how to explain our plan. How does that sound?'

This must have been meant rhetorically, but Felix pursed his lips, made a show of thinking it over. 'It'll expand my horizons,' he replied, magnanimously.

'Good-o,' said Cass.

They spoke for a while longer, probing him. Felix was studying political science, with a minor in metadata analysis. He played pickleball at the indoor complex in old Legacy Park. After a while, Brij excused herself. Maggie followed, mouthing an apology to Cass and Felix.

She stalked her boss back into her office. 'This isn't going to work.'

Brij's eyes were sympathetic, but her mouth was set firm. 'You know what your job is. And you're smart enough to understand why Felix is part of that. I shouldn't have to remind you.'

LATER, MAGGIE AND CASS COMPARED NOTES. THEY'D met for sunset drinks at the Gungahlin Yacht Club, a bar at Ngunnawal city's meniscus, with medium-rise shops and apartments on one side, and paddocks, returning to scrub, on the other. A decade ago, some entrepreneur had levelled out one of the gently rising hills to create a vast AstroTurf 'lake' for sail-powered buggies, and for a summer or two, it was the hottest ticket in town. Now locals had reclaimed the place from the hipsters, and the only working infrastructure that remained was the vestigial bar that abutted the old dock. Cass lived nearby, and she blended like a skink into the vibe of gentle decay.

'He's a smug little prick, that's for sure,' Cass opined when they'd found a table up the back, away from the windows overlooking the patchy field. She gulped beer.

Maggie laughed and took a sip of her vodka and lime, easy on the vodka. She didn't particularly enjoy the taste of alcohol, but wanted to spare herself the eyeroll she'd receive from Cass if she ordered a mocktail. 'You're not the one that has to babysit.'

Just as she was about to complain about the injustice of being stapled to Felix Reeve, she noticed that Cass's attention had shifted. Strange: whatever Cass's other qualities, her presence could usually be relied on. But now she stared absently at a couple of barflies as they tried to get the pool table to take their payment chip. To bring her back, Maggie clinked her glass against Cass's where it rested on the table. With her palm, she pushed against her friend's shoulder, and waited.

'Weird day,' Cass said after she'd tuned back in.

'More flamin' mongrels?'

'Mmm.'

Cass had been spending her time at a shroudspace locale called The Big Barbecue, a hangout for pro-meat activists. Maggie had seen the vids. Leaning into their reputation as savages, and relishing the incorrectness, the ringleaders had adopted a tribal village aesthetic, featuring a circle of crude huts surrounded by jungle. The central clearing was dominated by a huge bonfire, over which they'd suspended a pig the size of a baby elephant, rotating slowly on a spit. The only thing they couldn't replicate in shroudspace was the smell.

Brij stood for greater equity in the distribution of natural proteins, and Cass had been lurking there off and on as a form of opposition research. It was a public locale, so no one could stop her.

Since production had been reduced to a level consistent with emissions targets, meat prices had soared. Brij's idea was to give every dult and child vouchers, enough to allow them to eat meat three times a week. Those who didn't want to use their vouchers could sell them, creating an incentive to transition away from carnivorism.

'They say rationing like it's a bad thing. Ignorant fucks.' Cass never minced words, but the bitterness in her tone was unusual.

'What happened?' Maggie asked.

'I mean, most of those bogans can't afford it now anyway. But they think we're taking something away from them.'

'Cass, what happened?'

Cass stared at the pockmarked surface of the bar, running her fingernail along the scar of a name that had been gouged into the worn plastic. 'They took the pig down from the spit. Shrank it to the size of a golden retriever. And re-animated it. It ran around screeching, smoke still coming off it, and they all stomped around trying to catch it.'

So far, so familiar. Maggie had seen comment pieces denouncing this kind of behaviour, which of course was the reaction the meat-eaters were counting on.

'Next thing, Brij's face was superimposed on the pig's head. They'd done a good job with the modelling, it was clear who it was meant to be.' Cass took another sip. She considered her drink for a while, watching the foam slide back down the glass. 'Anyway, a couple of guys tackled it, held it down, bum in the air. And they got a carrot, and—' Thrusting her arm forward, she mimed the action. 'So this pig with Brij's face is screeching, the sound is horrendous, and then LuLu shows up,' – Louie Lewis, their spokesman – 'and he squats down, so his face is in front of Brij's. Nose to nose. And he says, *Don't fuck our industry.*'

'Jesus.'

'They took a recording. It'll be on the wraps tonight.'

Despite herself, the tactical part of Maggie's brain spun up, already considering the angles. What the carnivores had done wasn't illegal. It had been a virtual pig. Maggie had no doubt that they would have flagged it in advance for the content filters. In theory, Brij could claim it amounted to a threat of violence against her, and try and press charges, but that would be self-defeating. Still. 'How can they possibly think this'll help them?'

'It's one way to get air. And it might scare off other harvesters. Maybe even make OzProg think twice about the fights it's picking.'

'Sorry, Cass.' But it was Brij that Maggie was thinking about. Her boss's distance and abruptness on the way back to the office, as she watched something on her feed ... that made sense.

'Brij's tough,' Cass said, as if she could follow Maggie's line of thought. 'But she's got a lot going on right now.'

They sat for a while with the news, with each other. And then, recognising how dour they must both have looked, cracked sardonic smiles. Maggie said, 'You'll talk them round,' meaning it flippantly, but Cass seized on the comment.

'Fuck me dead, Mags, you actually believe that, don't you? I mean, maybe not the meatheads, but you actually think we can change things.'

'Well … yeah.' Maggie wished she could offer more, but it seemed so obvious. Why else would anyone work for a proxy harvester?

Cass huffed, and Maggie knew this as a sign that she was in for a lecture.

'Even the weakest of the *keiretsu*, the conglomerates, hold more power than any government. They're building literal pyramids in space, Mags, and people are begging to be used as slave labour. Meanwhile, the government, of which we are a weird appendix, fusses with admin, fiddling the knobs, adjusting the humidity up and down.'

'Weird analogy, but sure,' Maggie said, unperturbed. 'If that's true, then why do you bother? With work, or with … anything?'

'Because the fight is worth having, even if we lose. The fight is beautiful. You're too results-focused.'

While they bickered, one of the pool players approached them, sidling up to Cass. He flashed a smile, eyes trained on hers. 'Hey,' he said with a nonchalance that came off as affected. 'Do you, uh. Do you want to rub units? We could go back to mine.'

Maggie watched Cass size him up. She took her time, making no effort to hide the fact that she was appraising his body, his clothes. He didn't look too bright. He had a scruffy, sand-coloured beard which made his head look too large for his body, but his tight shirt advertised the definition in his arms and chest. 'Fine,' Cass eventually replied. 'But I'm here with my mate, freeing her of some childish ideas. So you'll have to wait until I'm finished.' He nodded and wandered back toward the pool table.

Maggie and Cass had hooked up once, years ago, back when they were still interns. As a one-off it had been enjoyable, but it was clear enough to both of them that they weren't suited romantically. They didn't speak about it much afterwards, but neither was it awkward, even at the time, and certainly not now that other partners had come and gone. It was a small part of their shared history, and it did nothing to diminish the amuse-ment Maggie felt now, watching this random trying to score with Cass. 'Do you know that guy?'

'No … but I've got a good feeling about him.'

Something else nagged at Maggie. Cass had said, of Brij, *She's got a lot going on right now* … The words struck Maggie as intimate. As if, through this shared experience, Cass had formed a bond with Brij that Maggie couldn't hope to replicate. A jealous feeling flared up, and then a wash of shame. The idea that Maggie might want trauma, to give her an opportunity to prove her resolve … it wasn't the first time she'd had a thought like that. The rational part of her understood that only the safe could afford to indulge in those kinds of fantasies. Maggie sus-pected that Cass knew better.

'If you need help, ask me, okay? I want to help if I can.' she almost winced at her own mawkish words, but Cass appeared to take them at face value, smiling and giving a quick shake of her head.

'Thanks. Anyway, how was your lunch?'

If Cass didn't want to talk about the Barbecue, Maggie wasn't going to insist. 'Okay, I guess,' she replied. 'Kind of awkward, but it looks like we've got some buy-in.'

'So what's next?'

'Ah. I'm … not supposed to talk about it.'

'Come *on*! Spill your guts, Garry!' Maggie hated that nickname, as Cass knew all too well. Maggie looked skyward, and she could tell they were alright.

Almost in parallel, some part of Maggie worried over Kinnear. She hated where she'd left things at Human Support. She had let herself down, and worse, had failed to make progress on the Income. With the fight over meat rationing, Brij wouldn't have time to hold her hand. Maggie thought about what Cass might do if it was her problem, and realised she would have to push things. Take a risk, try and offer the man something he'd want enough to make a deal.

Cass said, 'How are you going to ditch your new mate? Young master Reeve?'

Shuddering, Maggie let out a long sigh, knowing that Cass would appreciate the melodrama. 'My problem is I'm too polite. I need coaching from a rude bump like you.'

They ordered another round, enjoying the spectacle of the man throwing thirsty, frustrated glances at Cass from the other side of the room.

ALT+TAB

TEZ GAREWAL SPRINTS UNTIRINGLY THROUGH THE twilight bush, setting possums to scatter. His footfalls thud in metronomic time. Tree roots, rocks and scraggly branches present no obstacle. Tez is the seventeenth-ranked B-Fly hunter in the whole of Australasia, and he has nothing to fear.

In the lower-left corner of his visual field, a live map shows the location of his squadmates, who've fanned out to cover more ground. On this map, three beefs per square kilometre is an algorithmic certainty. It's just a matter of finding the little b-b-bastards. Tez has named himself catcher, which is his right as the highest-ranked player in the party. The rest of his crew are assigned to control. They'll be happy just to have matched with someone like Tez. Everyone's a stranger, but at 10:30 Ngunnawal/Eastern time on a Tuesday morning, the servers are quiet, and beggars can't be choosers.

This map has a highland forest aesthetic, and the sun slants through ferns, stringybarks and waratahs, turning random patches of dirt and leaves to gold. A steady breeze roils the landscape, adding to the difficulty of their task.

'Flapper, twenty metres. I think … yeah, for sure.' Some gruff-voiced teammate, whose avatar looks like an homage to Rosie the Riveter, has spotted their prey.

Tez sets a waypoint and sapphire-coloured arrows guide him through the forest. 'Thirty-five seconds.' The rest of the team converge, reporting their ETAs.

'Tez, there's juice for you in the hallway. Please don't forget about it; you know how hard it is to come by oranges this time of year.'

This comment is not part of the game. It's Liv – his mother, but he thinks of her as Liv – intruding. He grinds his teeth. In calmer moments, he can admit that without her, Tez wouldn't be able to spend so much time hooked in. Besides, he's told his mum he's working on an entry. He *should* be working on an entry.

'Give me a sec,' he says in-game, and then dials down the opacity of his shroud to thirty-five percent. Tez leaves audio on so he can still hear the other players as he registers the room around him. He shuffles out of the casting chair jammed against the foot of his single bed, realises that he's cold, and hunts for a jumper among the tangle of clothes at the base of his closet. Unbidden, Tez's shroud offers him a thumbnail, high-angle view of his room, and his slender, unkempt form slouching in the middle. Idly, he takes in all this stimulus – the faint overlay of the game, the third-person perspective, and the data from his real eyes – as he shrugs the jumper over his top half, leaving hairy legs and boxers exposed. He stumbles to the door, wincing at the assault of sunlight as he opens it and retrieves the orange juice from its place on the floor nearby. He takes a gulp and stows the glass on his bedside table, well out of gesticulating range. When it's fully engaged, his shroud blocks out everything he doesn't want to see and hear. But meatspace still cradles his body, so he's got to be careful where he waves his arms.

When he dives back in, the rest of his party are assembled, ringing the target at a respectful distance. Their avatars are a riot of contrasting aesthetics, but each carries a large backpack, connected by thick tube to a flamethrower. Tez is unburdened by weaponry. He holds a butterfly net.

'Soz,' Tez mumbles. 'Ready to go.'

He edges toward the centre of the perimeter established by the others. Sure enough, a dappled navy-and-white butterfly flits, oblivious, between the branches of a pink-flowered sassafras tree. Everyone confirms that they are in place and waiting. Back in meatspace, Tez stacks his fists one atop the other and swings experimentally, confirming that in-game, the hands that grasp the pole of the net follow his movements.

He edges toward his quarry, right leg leading, side-on so that he is poised to turn and run if need be. On the other side of the circle, he catches sight of one of his squadmates, red-robed, face hidden behind a fox-shaped kitsune mask, who nods at him. Tez nods back, and brings the net down.

The beef dissolves, and a shower of coins rains down from the trees above them, disappearing as they hit the dirt. While everyone stands down, Tez checks his in-game balance, and confirms that they've been paid. As catcher, he's received the largest share of the prize, which is only fair, since he's taken most of the risk.

'Yum yum,' someone says from behind Tez.

'Is everyone cool for one or two more? We could try out east.'

'Not like I got anything else to do. Descartes, You good?'

This is directed to Tez, via the username he's chosen for this game.

'Always hungry for more,' he replies.

As they dash toward their next hunting ground, the party chatters about inconsequential things: celebrity hookups, football, procedurally-generated sitcoms. Tez doesn't say much. He's been playing Flûttr for long enough now that the search phase, which comprises the bulk of the game, has started to feel like a chore. In auto-matched squads like this, he gets the sense that he's older than most of his teammates. He'll be 30 before long, as his sister never tires of reminding him.

The player in the kitsune mask – username Hanabi – DMs him.

[Hey man ur really smooth]

[thx]

[U pro?]

[Nah.] The coins collected in-game are convertible, but even though Tez is elite, if he cashed out all of his winnings from the last couple of years of play, it would represent a pittance; barely enough to cover a week's rent at one of the new places over in Belconnen.

[What u do outside?]

Tez's avatar momentarily judders to a stop. It's an impolite question, in a community whose members value their anonymity. He starts to tap out a response, telling this kid where to go, but then he pulls in a breath, lets go of the indignation.

[I trained as an architect]

[Oh man thats rough. I thought it was just dumbfucks like me on fluttr]

They are skirting the edge of a lake, the twilight swallowed by cloudy, greenish water. They've been playing for almost two hours, and the stubborn lodgement of the sun just above the horizon is a reminder that what they're experiencing is not original-flavour reality.

Tez sets his avatar to auto-follow the group, and back in his room, stretches out an ache in his shoulder. Though he'd prefer not to, he remembers the buzz he'd felt as a graduate, at the start of what might have been a new career. He'd been inspired by the design competition briefs, and proud of the concepts he'd come up with. The occasional long-listing or word of encouragement was enough to keep him going. But after years of obsession and failure, Tez has started to explore other diversions offered by the shroud. Of these, Flûttr has been the most long-lived. He imagines most of the players on this server have a similar story.

In primary school, Tez had been taught about how automation wiped out most of the old, low-skilled jobs – not that his teachers had put it exactly in those terms. While he was growing up, it came for accountants, too, and winemakers and auctioneers and middle managers. Turns out, architects are just as replaceable. Aside from high-EQ roles and certain specialties, the human work that remains is manual: too grubby or fiddly for machines to do efficiently, meaning it's still cheaper to pay a pair of hands.

It takes them another twenty-five minutes to locate the next beef. It loiters in a thicket of slender-trunked wattles, which means that the usual tactic of enclosure will be harder to pull off. Tez calls a huddle, thinking about the data they are generating. Flûttr is free-to-play because really, it's an org-psych study about cohesion. The designers watch how tactics evolve in the gameworld. What is the optimum squad size? Why do teams succeed or fail? Bitterly, Tez wonders if this discussion will yield any insights for the faceless corps that sponsor the game.

At Tez's suggestion, it's decided that control will split into two equal-sized mobs, fifteen metres apart from each other, and twenty back from the target. If things escalate, Tez will run between the two squads, so that they can pince. The plan will leave Tez exposed while he retreats, and dependent on his teammates to eliminate any threat before he gets got. But Tez never believes in the monster, until the exact moment the monster appears.

He picks his way through the undergrowth, until he's close enough to the beef that he could reach forward and crush it in his fist. This one is black and orange, with an abdomen about the length of his thumb. Cash or carnage: there's no way to tell. He hoists his net and brings it down.

The feedback sensors on his fingertips buzz. It's what Tez is primed for, and he jumps back even as the beef swells and sprouts limbs. Every monster is different, lethal in its own way. Tez has no time to inspect; he gets a fleeting impression of slavering jaws and spiked forelegs as he turns and bolts back the way he's come, checking to see that his party are moving like they'd planned. The group to his left are slower off the mark; it means that the others will arrive a split-second too soon. To correct, Tez jinks leftward, listening for the rustle that marks his pursuer. The monsters are designed to be faster than players can run. It's all about timing, about waiting until the instant before the killer blow will land.

Now: Tez plants his leg and dives sideways, pressing flat against the ground. 'Do it,' he shouts. Above him, the air turns to flame.

The beast lets out a rasp of pain and anger, flailing. Then it pitches, running straight at the mob that had been too slow, limbs scything the air. Another burst of flame blocks Tez's view, but he clocks dark spatter on the bushes nearby. By the time he regains his feet, it is done.

Once again, coins rain from the sky. The glint, and the dopamine hit, mean that Tez is slow to do a count. They are down three people.

'Messy,' says Hanabi, who'd been leading the mob that had reacted faster. 'Those eyeballs deserved to wipe.' With their reduced number, the bonus for killing the monster will be split nine ways instead of twelve. Some of those that have survived execute pre-configured victory dances. One player, whose avatar's skin is scaled like a snake, recounts how he dodged one of the creature's spines.

Someone else interjects. 'Hey all I need to drop. Fuck if I got anything else to do, but I'm at the library and they're telling me I gotta move. Game.' Their avatar blinks out.

Hanabi makes a show of looking over the remaining players. 'More grind?'

'Seven's pretty thin for control,' Tez replies.

'Yeah but we prolly won't get another monster for a while,' a player standing behind Hanabi pipes up. And they're right: the chances of any beef morphing into a monster are fixed at one-in-seven.

'Does happen, though,' counters Tez. 'I had three in a row, once.'

'Rough.'

'Come on,' says Hanabi. 'Don't be soft. Who's got something

better to do this morning?' Their voice is androgynous, and modulated for anonymity, but all the same it drips with sarcasm.

Among the group, Hanabi's query provokes a bout of wry self-examination.

'Not me.'

'Wouldn't be here if I was, would I?'

'Fucking privs can keep their jobs, if you ask me.'

'I don't know, mate, I wouldn't mind some real cash once in a while, ay?'

Tez is aware that Hanabi's watching him. The face of Descartes, Tez's avatar, isn't masked, which means it mirrors the expression he wears in meatspace.

'It's fucked, for sure,' Hanabi agrees, still looking straight at Tez. 'But privs gonna priv. They won't share jobs by choice, it's gotta be a mandate. No one should get more than twenty hours, not while some can't get anything.'

'Maybe OzProg'll sort it,' Tez ventures.

One of the others, a clunky anthropomorphised hedgehog who hasn't spoken before, laughs sardonically. 'Nothing's gonna change unless we *make* 'em change. You guys been at the protests?' Three, including Hanabi, confirm that they have; the rest shake their heads.

Tez is bewildered by this politics talk, coming from a bunch of dropkick strangers. 'Can we just play?'

But Hanabi pushes back. 'You gotta take care of your shit. You've got it together in here, right? You're elite. But we all live in meatspace, too. Be a boss, everywhere.'

Back in his room, Tez feels rather than hears movement. Dimming the game, he catches Liv fossicking, a washing basket balanced on her hip. 'Don't mind me,' she says. 'Keep going with your ... work. Lunch in half an hour, if you're ready.'

''Kay'.

Everything's fucked, but everything's fine. He lives, surrounded by family, in a house. There's no cause to complain.

IN-GAME, THEY SPREAD OUT AGAIN, ON THE LOOK-out. Tez is trying to focus, trying to pick out any flash of exotic colour from the camouflage, but it's hard to get in the groove. There's pleasure in losing himself in a task, even one as mundane as this, so he's irritated when Hanabi DMs him again.

[Why don't you do game design?]

[??]

[I mean, with your training, and your beef skillz, I bet you could get a job making maps.]

In the real, Tez snorts, and his avatar does the same.

[I know materials. The tensile strength of steel, bamboo. I know physics. How to cantilever, how to build bridges that can stand against gravity and waves. Shit that took me years to learn. But none of it matters here. Flûttr is kids' stuff.]

Although he'd never admit it round these parts, Tez enjoys how in meatspace, matter is immutable. Here, the devs never stop tinkering, adding code, summoning and altering and dispatching. And rules are bendy. Tez knows hacks that would let him grow his avatar to the size of a building, or teleport to the other side of the map. He's built something here. He's fucking *Descartes*! But it feels provisional.

[Yeah ...] Hanabi DMs. *[I feel that. U deserve better, ay?]*

Minutes later, snakeskin spots another beef.

'I better drop after this one,' Tez tells the group. He should do some real work before lunch. The thought of the competition brief, a design for an underground hotel, is a snarled knot in his stomach, and he tries to focus on what's in front of him. Like he told the others, this beef could be a monster, too.

Once more the group fans out around their quarry, Tez in the middle. There are fewer of them now, and Tez notices how wide the gaps are in the defensive ring. He decides that if a monster spawns, he will bolt toward Hanabi, make it their problem to deal with.

He lines up and swings the net. But this time, it's just cash. Although he's made a good profit this session, and his ranking points will reflect that, Tez is disappointed, and puzzled at his disappointment.

'Game, everyone,' he says. 'Catch you around.'

The other players maintain position, surrounding him in a loose ring. 'Hold up,' says Hanabi. 'Something we need you to hear.'

We? Tez had assumed these players were all strangers to one another, as well as to him.

'Big meatspace update gonna drop on May eighteen,' Hanabi continues. 'May eighteenth, you listening? Special protest, at Human Support HQ. Hundreds of thousands. We're gonna make OzProg ration work.'

'Yeah, not interested, sorry.' This is not the first time someone's tried to spam Tez in-game, but it's usually shitcoins being pushed, not politics.

Hanabi shakes their head. 'You don't get it. We need *you*

59

there, Tez Raman Garewal. You're elite. If you go, other beef hunters will, too.'

At the sound of his birth name, Tez swallows. They've doxxed him. How? What else do they know? If they have his name, they could have his location. His contacts? The password to his wallet? He is taking shallow breaths. He has been careful, this has never happened to him before. It feels like violence.

[do it tez]

[yeh do it fucker]

[yr names on the forums, we told everyone you gonna be there]

Is it true? some part of him wonders. *Would it matter if I went?* No, he decides. These punks probably pull this trick all the time, to recruit for their stupid demonstration. Tez is not special.

'I'm DMing you the details,' says Hanabi. 'If you're there, we'll remember it. And if you're not, we'll remember that, too.'

Tez feels heat and sweat collecting under his armpits, on his palms. He can't bear to stay here, in this circle of jerks. But then he remembers what's outside, and suddenly he can't take the thought of that, either: another design project that won't amount to anything. Liv, with her inexhaustible reserves of patience, watching as he eats the sandwich she's made.

No vessel can hold him. He will bust, or burst. His thumb twitches and his avatar runs, past the punks, between limbs and leaves, indefatigable, straight at the horizon. He knows an exploit. Using it will get him booted, he'll forfeit all the coin he's accumulated this session, but he can't care. Through the sheer side of a mountain that signifies a formal limit, he bursts into grey space, unregulated and uncreated, and still he runs, quickening, impossibly so, until he's faster than sound, faster than consequences, until the universe is a dot receding over his shoulder.

CHAPTER 6

You gave Triple-Bobble a red-hot go, until it got too freaky. You pretended to enjoy ASMRapture, but your partners caught you microsleeping. You need something new, something spicy. Don't worry! We've got your back.

After months trawling the darkest and most depraved corners of AugSex, we present, for your edification, 11 entirely new techniques to try at home. (Must have latest shroud firmware, easy-clean wet area, grab bars, robust sense of humour.)

– [AlltFeed/sex_rel, accessed 09:33:22 23-FEB-2058]

WHEN MAGGIE STIRRED, AND FELT KEI'S WARMTH and weight next to her in the bed, anxious half-thoughts surfaced. In that split second, she perceived him as a threat, as if he were an error that threatened to expose her.

But then she remembered him better. Remembered that she had chosen him, at least as much as he had chosen her. For his forbearance. They had been seeing each other outside the co-op for three months now, at a cadence dictated largely by Maggie's work and her preferences.

She rolled over to face him, and the movement brought him out of sleep. He tested the light with his eyes, and when he found Maggie, he smiled. 'Morning.'

'Good morning.' Her room began to let in the day, and as Kei yawned, Maggie was close enough to make out the black threads of his hair, and the pores on either side of his broad nose. Even more now than the night before, she felt him laid open to her, and she enjoyed regarding him, thinking her own thoughts.

'Let's sleep in,' he said, but he must have known that she wouldn't go for that. She was already peeling away the bedspread, primed for an exit. She paused, turned to him, and they kissed.

His hand slid down her shoulder to her elbow, and she pulled away. 'I have to pee.'

As she found her feet, walked unclothed to the bedroom door, she imagined how she must look to him. Her wide hips and not-insignificant thighs were facts, unchangeable features of her body, and for the most part she accepted them as such. There was nothing to stop him taking a picture or video, even while they were having sex. A light on your brow was supposed to glow red when recordings were being made, and it was a crime to tamper with that, but it was easy enough to download a patch. Kei didn't seem like the type, but what was impossible to know was whether it was always *her* he was seeing when they fucked. She supposed she should just come right out and ask him.

When she came back from the bathroom, he was dressing. He stopped, half finished, his head tilted, waiting for her to tell him what next.

'Food?' Maggie asked, motioning toward the door. He tugged on his shirt and followed her.

Breakfast was muesli and fruit. Growing up, Maggie's parents had spoiled her, and she still allowed herself yoghurt, and cow's milk in her coffee. Kei had no compunctions, and when she'd served him up a bowl, he set to with his spoon. 'Good,' he said between mouthfuls.

It was her day off, and one of his. She hadn't invited him to spend it together, but she wondered whether he assumed. She asked, 'What have you got on?'

'Nothing much. There's a rugby game tonight.'

'I've got a few things to do …'

'No worries.'

She frowned, not sure if he was picking up what she was putting down. 'Maybe we can share a car back to yours? And then I'll keep going into town.'

He shifted to get a better look at her. 'Sounds good. You're not going in to work, are you?'

'Not for very long.' She stacked up their dirty plates on a tray and walked them to the alcove outside her front door. In a cupboard below were clean replacements. She hardly ever saw the machine that did the rounds early in the morning, but sometimes she heard the rattle as it slid the tray into a slot in its chest and trundled away on rubber tracks.

When she returned, she said, 'Have a shower, if you want. I've just got to vote.'

He snorted. 'Doesn't Brij get annoyed that you don't give her your proxy?'

'If I didn't have thoughts of my own, what use would I be?'

He wore a vague look of distaste. 'Some of the things she says are nuts. Does she listen to you?'

'Sometimes.' She wasn't sure she appreciated Kei's take. 'I like what I'm doing. It's hard, in a good way.'

'Me too,' he said. 'I'm happy doing what I'm doing, too.' It sounded like he was confirming something he'd long taken to be self-evident, the words like smooth grey pebbles, the kind you could buy in bucketfuls at a hardware store to cover a patch of dirt. He flopped down on the couch and started playing with something in shroudspace.

Instead of joining him, Maggie took one of the high stools at the breakfast bar. Voting felt to her like something that should be done in private. Irrational, this need for distance, because even if she'd been sitting right next to Kei, he wouldn't have been able to see what her shroud displayed. Her shroud was hers, as personal as the data transmitted from her own biological eyes.

Twenty-eight motions were marked for her attention. Mostly these were minor amendments to existing legislation; procedural changes that OzProg had long promised to roll out if they formed government. A few regulation changes that the opposition sought to disallow. For each measure, a graphic summarised how the parties had voted in the originating chamber, and Maggie took this as her cue, voting along party lines to support the new government.

Three of the measures had exclamation marks next to them, to flag something substantive or controversial. The first was the restoration of Medicare benefits to over-70s. During the campaign, this had formed part of the OzProg policy platform, although Maggie knew there was plenty of dissent within the party, and many of the centrist harvesters had withheld support. The Libs opposed, of course, claiming that now human life could be reliably prolonged past one hundred, government-funded care was fiscally irresponsible, and no one was entitled to extreme old age underwritten by the taxpayer. But the Truvies supported the measure, standing firm on the right to life. It was one of the rare points of intersection between the True Values party and OzProg. Maggie cast her vote in support. The plebiscite would close in another three days, and then the result would be announced.

When she was done with the full list, she blinked herself back into the room. She walked over and sat down next to Kei, letting her side graze his. After a few moments he turned to face her. 'Done already?'

'I don't muck around.'

He laughed and pulled her to her feet, drawing her into a bear hug. He held her tight, and when he released her, he said, '*Ikimashou?* Let's go.'

Maggie heard something like exasperation in his tone. She said, 'It must be boring, sometimes. Being with me.'

He shook his head. 'Not boring.'

He held her eyes, but it wasn't enough. 'Kei, what do you want for us?'

Now he backed away, dropping his arms. He could see that she was serious. 'It's a bit soon for the talk, isn't it?'

Maggie grimaced. 'I meant to say something. I might need to spend a while in Sydney, for work. Could be a few months.'

'Sydney?' He sounded relieved. 'That's okay. We can visit each other. Cast together.'

'Yeah.'

'And.' He hesitated, mouth half open. His eyes slid past her.

'If you get lonely … I don't mind if you hit shuffle.'

This. *This* was what she'd been waiting for, and hoping to avoid. She'd felt it there, below the surface of their interactions. 'I guess we've never talked about that.'

They'd had the usual conversation when they'd started. Had both agreed not to take other partners without discussing it first. For something casual, that was all that was needed. But they were three months in, now, and she was leaving town.

Kei frowned, choosing his words carefully. 'I mean, I guess I assumed, what with your job and the people you work with, you're not against that kind of thing.' He sounded defensive, but he hadn't done anything wrong.

'I'm not against it. I'm just not sure it's for me.'

'You've never tried? Multiples or anything?'

She shook her head.

'Ha.' He studied his fingers, running the pad of his thumb against his nails. 'I guess that means you'd rather I didn't, either.'

'Yes. Sorry, but I know what I'd prefer.'

'Okay.' There was a studied neutrality in his tone.

'This is what I mean, about being boring. I *am* boring.'

'No, it's fine. And you know me. I love simple. Simple and easy.'

If he thought this was the right thing to say, he had misread her. She wasn't simple, was not interested in providing simplicity as a romantic service. 'You love getting laid on a regular basis.'

He nodded. 'True. But this won't be forever.'

Maggie traversed the room, hunting for shoes and a canvas bag. Leaving was no problem: she carried credit, phone and keys in her skin.

'We're fine,' he said. And though she studied his face for signs of ambivalence, of insincerity, she could find no fault.

'Still want to let me drop you home?' she asked.

'Definitely.'

MAGGIE SWITCHED INTO THIRD-PERSON, TAKING IN her surroundings, her vantage point floating behind and above the spot where her avatar had materialised. She'd cast into what looked like a rehearsal space. Plywood floor, painted black, with rows of banked seats skirting two sides of the room. The lights were diffuse, dim, and the walls were covered in halved egg-cartons, visual cues that suggested privacy. It looked custom; Kinnear must have architected the space himself.

'Thanks for answering,' she said.

The old man came across less rigidly here than he had at the DHS Building. His linen shirt and dark leggings were functional, unpatterned, eschewing the current tendency toward flamboyance. Even beneath his loose-fitting shirt, Maggie noticed the slight hunch in his avatar's back and shoulders, mirroring his meat form.

The seats in this auditorium were exact clones of each other, and they were pristine, as if none of them had ever been sat in. But the surface of the stage was mapped with scuff marks, fragments of old tape, divots exposing the wood under the paint, and lighter-coloured swirls that looked like someone had tried to rub away chalk. Far from being a generic texture, every one of these imperfections had been deliberately applied. This stage was Kinnear's. He knew it intimately, had spent time here.

They were casting, and Maggie knew in her forebrain that she could exit at any time. But her body took in the data from her eyes and ears and replied with warnings, unsubtle clouds of epinephrine and cortisol. She was alone with this person, her limbic system told her. In a dark room, with no way out and no one else around.

He said, 'I didn't think I'd be hearing from you so soon. Especially after your lunch yesterday with our respective bosses.'

Word must have travelled quickly. 'I'm sorry we had to go over your head.'

Kinnear waved away Maggie's comment. He found a place on a bench, second tier back, so that seated, his eyes remained level with hers. 'Did you know I still perform? There's an amateur company in Red Hill. Gilbert and Sullivan, mostly.'

'Oh?' She'd heard those names before. Half-acting, half-singing? This was not why she was here. 'I've come to ask for your help.'

'I told you. We can't work on an Income until the powers that be—'

'I know you can't. But I'm going to Sydney, to sell the idea to Treasury.' Brij had asked her not to share this with anyone yet, but Maggie needed to offer something, to make sure she had his attention. Kinnear's eyebrows twitched, but he waited for more. 'And I'm new to all this. My meeting with you wasn't … great.'

'You're young.'

Maggie let this pass, making an effort to relax the muscles in her jaw. 'Not everything you said was unwarranted.'

'And so …?'

'There'll be more like you – no offence – at Treasury. I was wondering if you might be prepared to act as a sounding board. Maybe guide me a little.'

'What does Brij think about that?'

Maggie considered bluffing, but Kinnear had already had the better of their last exchange. It would have to be honesty, or nothing. 'She's got other stuff to worry about. I'm trying to be proactive.'

'What's in it for me?'

'Very little, other than the warm feeling that comes from making the world a better place. I imagine you don't get a lot of that, day to day.' Kinnear let his head loll, telegraphing his disdain. 'And ... I suppose that when we talk, you might learn things, incidentally, about what's happening over at Treasury.'

Hearing this, he sat up a little. 'I suppose I might.'

'So ... can you?'

He made a show of considering, taking to his feet and pacing down the empty row of seats, then pivoting to face her again. 'There'd be probity issues if I were to coach you. But you're a lobbyist, trying to get buy-in. It's natural that you'd check in with me from time to time.'

Maggie bowed her head, relieved. Kinnear could have refused. If he was feeling particularly officious, he could even have reported this conversation. 'That sounds sensible.'

They both took a moment to appraise the other. For once, Kinnear looked hesitant, as if he wanted to speak, but couldn't find the right words. He made a study of his hands, cracked the knuckles of his left by making a fist, the sound audible. An effect, but one that implied an obscene level of detail baked into this environment. Eyes still pointed down, he said, 'You've got a lot to learn, but at least you're trying. Everybody my age has given up. We thought that when it was our turn, we'd fix all the problems our parents left for us.'

She sensed that this was a gift, this opening up. To perform was to lie, but it seemed that here he had chosen to reveal something about himself. She clasped her hands together. 'I'll let you know how I get on in Sydney.'

'Good hunting.'

Kinnear terminated the call and the room dissolved, leaving Maggie standing in her personal lobby, a virtual holding area that was for her alone, that no one else would ever see. With voice commands and a few hand movements, she could have renovated. But since her last shroud upgrade years ago she'd hadn't found the time, so it remained a claustrophobic, off-white cube.

CHAPTER 7

What have you been missing??

A day contains more than 80,000 seconds. No one pays attention to them all, and that's why you need reCapp.

reCapp creates a 3-minute daily digest of the most significant moments from yr day. All we need is full read access to yr shroud, and we take care of the rest!

Just like more than 400 mil subscribers worldwide, you can use reCapp to:

-- Catch up on juicy IRL scenes that went down nearby while you were jacked in.

-- Re-watch the big moments from yr day – key info, D&Ms, laughter, love and tears – or catch up if you missed them in real time.

-- Stay in touch by sharing yr daily reCapp with friends and family, or publish on your socials to make your crew green when you live large!

-- See who's paying attention to you when yr not looking. Yr next lover could be scanning yr surfaces right now, while yr busy reading this. How will you know without reCapp?

Best of all, reCapp is completely FREE!* So what are you waiting for? If yr too busy living to notice every little thing, let reCapp give you the recap!

* Disclosure: reCapp shares your life data with select commercial partners to help bring you relevant information, news and special offers, for which reCapp receives commissions. For more details, read the full T&Cs.

– Digital pamphlet, collected at l:aus/beautySecrets, accessed 11:10:32 23-FEB-2058.

MAGGIE SPENT THE EARLY AFTERNOON AT NGANBRA Sports Park, a vast indoor complex, climate controlled for all weather. She dropped into a game of continuous Aussie rules and was assigned to the blues, who were winning by just over 700 points. She didn't have to do much – she tried to contribute positively when the ball came her way – but she tagged one of the opposing team's forwards and ended up running harder and longer than her usual target.

On her way home she swung by the shops, to pick up some extras she'd missed from her weekly delivery. When she arrived back at her apartment, bag in hand, she had a post-exercise feeling of earned weariness, and was looking forward to a shower.

When she saw her front door, she thought that the stain was paint, or maybe even shit. It was only when she got closer and smelled the metal tang that she recognised blood, congealed now into a dark brown against the olive-green surface, looking like it had been flicked or hurled from a bucket. Rivulets had run down from a splatter mark at head height. She started to reach and flick the air, to wipe the stain from her field of view, and then it hit her that this was real, not a projection. The smell, she realised far too slowly, left no room for doubt.

Placing her bag on the ground, Maggie stilled herself and made the necessary gestures to interface with the door, to access its camera, but all she got back was a message about a hardware error. The building would have footage of this corridor, but she wouldn't have the right permissions until she asked for them. She turned a slow arc, her eyes lingering over the darker spaces in the entryway she shared with three of her neighbours. Their doors appeared untouched. Whoever did this could be waiting, to vid her reaction, or—

No sign of movement, until Blake, her neighbour from across the hall, poked his head out of his apartment. 'You alright, Maggie?'

'Yeah …'

Blake was ancient, and gentle, and his presence allowed Maggie to breathe out.

'There was three of the buggers. They made a lot of noise, shouting and carrying on. By the time I could call up a view of the outside, they'd run off.'

With her foot, she nudged the bottom of her door, and watched, dumbstruck, as it swung inward. Impossible, since it locked and latched itself each time she exited, waiting to sense the digital signature in her wrist before it would permit entry. She glanced at Blake and he moved into the corridor, offering his presence. When the door to her apartment opened fully, she saw debris on the tiles, and beyond that, deep running gouges in her tatami, and more streaked blood on the far wall of the living room. What little furniture she owned had been upturned or smashed. Her clothing, which must have been pulled from the robe in her bedroom, lay scattered among the mess.

She couldn't bring herself to enter, but Blake roared, 'Anyone still in there? Cops are on their way!' Under his breath, to Maggie, he said, 'I doubt they would've stuck around, but I can go in, take a look for you …'

'Don't worry about it. And thanks for staying with me.' He could have ignored the whole episode. Many would have.

Still watching the door and her surrounds, Maggie started a vid call in her left eye.

Brij picked up, and wasted no time. 'You too?'

Maggie shared her visual field, showing Brij the view through her door and into her apartment.

'Come over to my place. Right now. Don't go inside.' Brij sent her address. 'Have you called anyone else?'

'Not yet.'

'Don't.'

It felt reassuring, having someone tell her what to do.

BRIJ LIVED IN A WHOLE HOUSE, A 1970S SPANISH revival bungalow, restored and retrofitted. Flanked by palms, centred in a desert of concrete and white gravel, the place was a jumble of angles and archways, finished in mustard stucco. It was so obnoxious, and so out of keeping with the rest of the neighbourhood, as to be a statement.

The only concession to privacy was the shoulder-height brick fence abutting the footpath. When Maggie presented herself at the front gate, it let her through with a chime. She hadn't been here before.

Brij greeted her on the front porch, and took her through

into an airy lounge that opened onto a verandah out the back. In the dusk, Brij's partner, Allie, was hunched over a dark patch on the tiles outside, scrubbing brush in hand. The handful of times they'd met, Allie had been friendly, if a little reserved. But now when Maggie came over to greet her, Allie looked up, scowled, and resumed her work.

'It's been a difficult day,' Brij said cautiously, her eyes flashing Maggie a warning.

'And now we need to go and live in a *hotel*,' Allie added.

Based on comments that Brij had made over the years, Maggie understood that Allie worked hard to support her partner on the domestic front, gatekeeping and managing schedules so that Brij's commitments did not overwhelm their lives. That was not such an unusual arrangement – with the scarcity of paying work, there was a resurgence in the number of single-income households, with the breadwinner supported by unpaid family members – but Maggie wasn't sure whether this was a role undertaken happily by Allie, or one that she'd assumed due to a lack of alternatives. Either way, Brij was candid about how much she relied on her spouse, and now it appeared she had her work cut out trying to keep the peace. 'The police say that's best. Just for a while.'

No one needed to ask how the vandals had found them. Getting information like that was trivial, once you knew who you wanted to target. And in the lead-up to the election, politicians on both sides had reported incursions into their personal lives. There would always be nutbags, but an attack on a home was unusual. Harassment in shroudspace was one thing, but this was an escalation.

In the living room, piles of clothes balanced on the coffee table, an open duffel bag on the ground nearby.

'Can I help?' Maggie asked.

Brij cleared one of the armchairs of debris and motioned for Maggie to sit. 'No. I told Al not to bother. We'll get a professional in this week.' Then, in a stage whisper: '*But it helps with her rage.*'

'It's ridiculous,' said Allie. 'How did you end up fronting this?'

Wearily, Brij took a seat, and began folding a lump of washing. To Maggie, she said, 'It's cow blood, not human, if that makes you feel better. Cass got the same treatment. Even Felix. He's enjoying the kerfuffle.'

'Was anyone home when it happened?'

Brij shook her head. 'Which means they were watching, waiting for the right time.' She looked disgusted, and then, abruptly, as close to despair as Maggie had ever seen her. 'This changes things.'

Maggie nodded. People would find out what had happened. There would be news drones here soon, buzzing darkly overhead. Perhaps that was why Allie was worrying at the stain.

'The meat eaters – they've forced the issue. We've got so much we want to do. But now this is all anyone will want to talk about.'

Maggie pursed her lips. 'You should step back. Gillespe supports this. Let him run with it.'

'Hmph,' Allie made a bitter noise.

'Gillespe's hard left, speaks for less than one per cent. We can't let this become a fringe issue.' Brij plucked at the shoulders of a blouse, trying to get it to lie flat on the coffee table along its seams. 'No, I have to account for myself. We'll take a hit, but

I need our grantors to understand why it's part of our platform. Why it's *not* that radical – it's just a common sense, progressive idea. Right on brand for us.'

'Meat reform's important,' Maggie replied cautiously. 'But don't let them make you single-issue, or you *will* lose support.' She thought, *Don't pick this hill to die on.* And then, *Cass has already been in her ear.*

It wasn't in Brij's nature to back down. 'It's finally our time. That's why they're being feral. If we let them bully us, how far do you think we'll get on anything else? Anything more nuanced?'

So many interest groups had been protected by the stasis of the last government. The oligopolists, and the rentiers. The aging tech bros who'd entrenched their vast fortunes at the beginning of the century. The religious, and the plain old-fashioned. By finding common cause, and lending their support to the conservatives, they had staved off reform for decades. On single issues, the polling usually found an appetite for change, but while the Liberal/Truvie alliance held, nothing had been brought to a vote. Now the beneficiaries of the status quo were chucking a tantrum, and the meat lobby was just the vanguard of a larger resistance. And Maggie could see that Brij was right. This attack would create a symbol, a rallying point.

Allie rested where she knelt, gave up the brush, and stood up. She shook out her hands, pink droplets flicking from her gloved fingers to the ground. 'Hopeless. I'm going to wash myself up. Will you stay for dinner, Maggie?' She looked down at herself. 'We'll have something simple before we leave.'

'Thanks, but no,' Maggie replied. Allie couldn't disguise her relief. Arms bent upwards at the elbow and held away from her body, Brij's wife quick-stepped through the kitchen and further into the house.

Checking behind herself to make sure that Allie had gone, and lowering her voice, Brij said, 'We'll accelerate. We can use this as cover for the Income. While everyone's distracted, you hammer out a program with the Treasury people.'

'I thought we might have more time to plan.' After the activity in shroudspace, and now this vandalism, Maggie supposed that Brij would have a full day of interviews, starting early tomorrow. But Maggie still wanted to map out a strategy, make sure that they were both aligned. If she succeeded with Treasury, and they made progress toward a bill, Brij would need to own the result.

But Brij demurred, reaching out to tug the duffel bag closer to where she sat. 'For your own security, you should get to Sydney as soon as you can. I've sorted a room at Homebush.' As she spoke, she placed a stack of shirts into the bag a little carelessly, the pile deforming as it found a new equilibrium. She looked sheepishly toward the hallway, and shrugged when she realised that Allie was nowhere to be seen. 'If you give me permissions to your door, I'll arrange a trauma cleaner once the police have finished up. Is there stuff in your apartment that you're attached to?'

Maggie considered, and realised that there really wasn't anything. The objects she cared most about, mementos and personal effects, were all digitised, and lived in the cloud. She shook her head.

'Good. I won't have time to get into the weeds on Income. And you know more about it than I ever will. You're going to have to take the lead.'

Brij wasn't wrong. Maggie had spent most of the last year becoming an expert. She'd written the paper that had become de facto OzProg policy, had spent evenings pestering economists about second- and third-order effects. Quite possibly, no one working in politics was better equipped to make the case. But it still felt like Brij was cutting her loose.

Brij looked outside through the bi-fold windows, to the stain, and then upwards to the darkening sky. 'When it happened, when OzProg won, we were unready. We can't get caught out again, you understand?'

Maggie nodded, annoyed. Even though she didn't disagree with the sentiment, it stung a little that her boss thought this needed saying.

'Good. There's no one else I'd trust to speak for me. You'll find a way.' She reached out and squeezed Maggie's forearm. The gesture was so halting, and so out of character, that Maggie almost recoiled. Brusquely, both women stood up.

On the way to the door, Allie pressed a bag full of perishables into Maggie's arms. A peach threatened to spill out, and Maggie juggled to keep everything together. She hadn't eaten fresh peach in years, and she wondered where Allie had sourced one, and how expensive it must have been.

'We can't take all of this with us,' Allie said.

'MUM.'

'Hello darling. What a lovely surprise.'

'I've got some news.'

'Are you pregnant?'

'Ha ha. I'm going to Sydney for a while. For work.'

'How long for?'

'I don't know. Until we have a bill, maybe.'

'Be careful. Sydney is dangerous.'

'I will.'

'You'll come back for Dada-ji's party?'

'Of course. I've got to go.'

'Love you.'

'Okay, mum. Stay clean.'

THE CAR FLED UP THE HUME. MAGGIE HAD BEEN sitting up, watching her feed, but fifty kilometres from Bowral she reclined until she was prone, looking through the vehicle's transparent roof at the dusk. Here, the road rose and dipped through scrub, more or less following the undulations of the hills. Near the road, parallel rows of concrete pylons lanced upward from the ground like the ribs of ancient megafauna. The remnants of a half-finished train line. After the roads had been reconfigured, the journey from Ngunnawal to Sydney only took an hour and a half anyway.

Earlier, on her feed, Maggie had scrolled through new footage of the protests at DHS. Through the week, the size of the virtual demonstration had swelled, and now the locals were complaining that it was hard to navigate their suburb without muting their shrouds. The protest was old news; it might not have made the nationals, except that someone had hacked the DHS building's projection system so that briefly, it appeared as if a huge banner spanning the width of the building had been unfurled, reading, 'OUT TO LUNCH.'

When Maggie had gone to visit Kinnear, the protest had retained the feeling of a carnival. There was evidence of hope, as well as performative rage. But now, with no tangible result, it appeared that the mood had soured. If she'd been in front of that crowd, she would have said: *Wait and see. Give us a chance.* She could have cast in right then from the car. But what reason would they have to listen?

A halo of light above the horizon was the first sign, and it brought Maggie back. She rode the overpass, watching as she rolled above the blocky social housing that dominated Little Cairns and Little Darwin, the new suburbs squashed south of the Toggerai, across the river from Long Point. Like the migrants below, it had been her choice to come; the only choice she could have made. The anticipation filled her up, and she didn't know which of her hopes to nurture, and which to set adrift.

AUTUMN

CHAPTER 8

First there was lobbying, then years of haggling between the states and the Commonwealth. But the end result of decentralisation is widely viewed as a success. Almost everyone has cause to believe themselves a winner: Health to Narrm, Treasury to Sydney. … Kaurna Adelaide picked up Defence; Perth was the natural home of Energy and Resources. With geography no longer a barrier, there was no reason for federal departments to remain concentrated in a single location. Only Ngunnawal-Ngambri suffered: retaining Human Support, it nonetheless entered a period of economic stagnation from which it is yet to fully recover …

      – [AlltFeed/aus_history/trends_decentralisation, accessed 13:17:24 26-FEB-2058]

'WE ARE MASSIVELY EXCITED ABOUT THIS. *MASSIVELY* excited. We're true believers.' From his position at the head of the boardroom table, Bradley Insalata, Deputy Director of Policy for the Treasurer's office, swivelled his chair to eyeball Maggie and Felix, ignoring the dozen or so other public servants on his side of the table, who had arranged themselves in a line from most senior to least. It was Maggie's first day at Treasury; Felix was casting in from Brij's office in Ngunnawal.

Each conference room in this place was named after an iconic Australian landmark. *Kakadu. Juukan Gorge.* This meeting was in *Blue Mountains*, and until she cancelled out, Maggie's shroud tried to replace the walls with an archival still-frame of the lookout above the national park, near the Three Sisters, before the die-back. It was too much like a staff picnic, since without exception, Bradley and his crew wore polo shirts and shorts. Unlike the Treasury boffins occupying the lower floors, these people were political appointees, and reported directly to the Minister. The casual dress was a statement: *the conservatives have left the building.* They kept the offices hot here, and Maggie felt stuffy and overdressed.

'Our job is to help you sell this,' Insalata continued. He was wiry, with carefully trimmed salt-and-pepper hair, and possessed of a nervous energy that appeared to leave his body unable to settle in one position for long. Behind his back, Maggie knew, he was most often referred to as Salad Boy. 'Sell it to the party,' he mused, 'and the harvesters. And to the public, of course! All your hard work will be for nothing if we can't get the votes.' Down the line, his entourage nodded as if this were sage wisdom.

'Thanks, we feel very welcome.' Maggie scanned the new faces across the table. 'You might be aware that Brij is tied up right now, so I'll be your point of contact. And Felix will be helping me.' She glanced at him. He flashed a broad, winning smile. Maggie hated that he'd been invited to this kick-off meeting, but Brij had been adamant. 'We're new at this, so we're grateful for your support.'

'We're all new at this. We'll muddle through together, okay? And as for support, the Minister has been very clear that she wants action. Every morning she calls me into her office, and pulls up a stream from the protests, and she says, *Why don't I have anything I can announce? Where are the announceables?* And I remind her she's only been in the job for a fortnight.' A nervous chuckle spread like contagion down the other side of the table. 'So we're all motivated to make this happen. But!' He turned his head to peer expectantly at Trish, his second-in-charge, a woman who might have been of an age with Maggie, but whose no-nonsense demeanour seemed borrowed from someone much older. Light-skinned like Bradley; in fact, now that Maggie looked, she couldn't fail to notice that the attendees became browner the further down the table they were sat, like an accidental gradient. She caught the eye of one of the juniors at the far end, who returned her stare but gave nothing away.

'Ducks in a row,' said Trish.

'Exactly right,' Bradley agreed. 'We need to keep control of how this gets presented. It's a new, complicated idea, and people scare easily. Even those who've cried out for change will turn on us fast if they don't like the specifics.'

'Checks out,' Felix replied unnecessarily.

'So the people in this room, this working group, this is where our ideas stay. Except for Brij Sutton, of course. You'll notice no one is recording, and that's the rule from now on. Absolute confidentiality.' Bradley turned to look at each person in the room in turn, waiting for some sort of acknowledgement. One by one, heads bobbed up and down, which struck Maggie as pure pantomime. Insalata must have known how difficult it would be to prevent leaks, or even identify the leaker, if someone was determined to share what was discussed here. Still, Maggie supposed, now he could tell his boss that he'd laid down the law. While Maggie herself had a strong interest in keeping things under wraps while they thrashed out the policy details, she was conscious of her last conversation with Kinnear, and the price she'd negotiated for the DHS man's guidance.

'We've all read Brij's position paper. Your handiwork, Maggie?'

'It was a team effort.' She couldn't entirely keep the pride out of her voice.

'So that will form the basis for our White Paper. The geeks will confirm the modelling, and do what's needed to make the economic case.' He said this dismissively, as if that were trivial. 'Our real work will be distilling the plan into concepts so simple that even a politician can understand. Talking points, so we're consistent and we stay on message. Once we've done that, we can start selling. So, Maggie: what's our message?'

'Well—' she stopped herself. 'Perhaps Felix would like to explain.' She wanted to show these people what he was: the absence behind the façade.

She'd expected him to be rattled, but he leaned forward, eyes flashing. 'Thanks, Mags. The way I'm thinking about it is, you can't be truly free if you're poor. We're making sure that everyone can choose how they contribute, to foster genuine self-determination. As a society, we have the means to do it, so it's a moral obligation.'

'That's ... well said,' Maggie allowed. *Someone must have coached him.* On the desk, Felix's fingers twitched, and his face transformed briefly into an emoji with an *aw shucks* expression of bashfulness. 'Felix is glossing over some details,' Maggie continued, 'but I could hardly have put it better myself. You said that it was a complicated idea, Bradley, but the strength of an Income is its simplicity; its purity. There'll be a temptation to play around with the settings, but as far as possible, we should resist. We're providing every dult with the means to live comfortably, and we'll do it by taxing the rich. We can't shy away from that.'

Insalata's mouth stretched into a taut line. 'I take your point, but we'll need to be more diplomatic when we reach out to business.'

'Then how about this: research has consistently shown that once basic needs have been met, experiences, rather than material goods, generate more happiness. So we're taking the benefits of productivity growth, and channelling that into increased leisure rather than consumption.'

Several members of the policy team winced, and Insalata made a low humming noise. 'If anything, that will make business types even angrier. It sounds anti-growth.'

'It *is* anti-growth.' This provoked a round of nervous smiles on the other side of the room, but Maggie wasn't joking.

Insalata pushed his chair out from the desk. 'Okay, that's probably enough for right now. We'll sort into sub-groups and plan for engagement with OzProg backbenchers. Thanks, everyone.'

Those that had cast in blinked off. Felix smirked in Maggie's direction, and then disappeared, too.

'HOW WAS IT?'

'I can't get a read. Salad Boy insisted they were all behind this, but when I explained what we were trying to achieve, he called time pretty quickly.'

Brij seemed attentive, but tired. She had called Maggie a few hours after the kick-off meeting, and now she paused to inspect the cramped booth that Maggie had found when her shroud had flagged the incoming call. Maggie appreciated the contact, but couldn't help wondering what it meant that Brij was checking in so soon.

Brij said, 'You need to remember what their job is. They're trying to get an early win if they can. And if not, they need to protect the Treasurer from embarrassment. They're not sure yet how this will turn out. In the meantime, you're there representing the public. Or at least our slice of the public, so they have to keep you onside. Use that.'

That was simple enough in theory. Easy enough for Brij to do, if she'd been here in person. Rather than say something she'd regret, Maggie asked, 'How are you going? Any more threats?'

'Nothing. Allie's calmer, although she detests the place we're staying at, and that's all she wants to talk about. I think the rabble will simmer down now they've made their point. I did the rounds on the panel shows yesterday and there's been some churn, but overall our numbers are holding up. In fact, we've had a net gain of almost 20,000.'

'How have our blasts about Income been testing?'

'Really well. Eighty-four per cent grantor approval, so about as popular as anything we ever do.'

Maggie smiled, relieved. Even so: 'I'm not sure if we've got enough sway by ourselves.'

'Then form an alliance. Don't wait for Treasury: get out there and get talking to other harvesters. Mackay has an office on King Street. Go see him.'

'I doubt he'd take a meeting with me.'

'Invite Felix.'

Maggie clenched the sides of her chair, trying to keep her expression neutral, but her irritation must have shown.

'Are you up for this, or not? He can be your bridge.'

MORE THAN THE DAYS, IT WAS THE NIGHTS WHEN she felt like she'd made a mistake. Maggie kept to her room, exhausted from being in a new place, too listless to engage with her feed. She'd been assigned an internal. No natural windows, so without augmentation the place felt claustrophobic. All hard surfaces, apart from her bed; too clean and warm, like a hospital room, an impression only heightened by the wet area set into the far corner, marked out by the guiderail for a missing shower curtain.

In the evenings she would procrastinate, and then finally acknowledge that she was hungry. She wandered the streets around the dorm, which had grown busier with the influx of government workers over the past decade, but she could never settle on a place. She'd left it too late: the restaurants were closed, or somehow too intimidating to dine alone in, and the fast-food joints were skeezy and unappealing. So she would stop at a convenience store, picking out meal bars and green tea from the multicoloured riot of real packaging and augmented recommendations and ads, while an attendant followed two steps behind with a shopping basket. It was always only her, the attendant, and the cashier in the store. She knew that the attendant would be on an unpaid internship. At the end of each week the two workers would swap, and the cashier would take the role of intern, both employees sharing one paid position and one salary, with the store able to claim that it paid the minimum wage. Over several nights they began to recognise Maggie, and she would offer them a smile as she departed.

Even though it broke with convention, she kept her bedroom door locked. From outside, she heard the susurrus of hallway conversations. There was a common area at one end of the floor, but every time Maggie approached, she felt like an intruder. These people lived and worked together, spent most of their lives held tight by this strange extended family that had grown out of the Department. Maggie was a blow-in, she wouldn't stay long, and so she felt like she had no claim to anyone's time.

More than that, Maggie was hoping to avoid the inevitable question that arose any time she made a connection with someone new. Of all the worthy progressive causes that could be advanced, why focus on a universal income? Maggie could only ever formulate a halting, hollow response that sounded disingenuous even to herself.

When she was lost in the detail of her work – the policy wrinkles, the machinations and charm offensives – her real reasons could be difficult to remember, and even harder to articulate. Maggie had spent most of her adult life learning how to identify the different moving parts of the economy, to understand how they interrelated. Once that had been achieved, the inefficiency of the current system struck her viscerally, like a personal insult. The status quo was so unnecessary and corrupt, so blatantly indefensible, and yet constantly defended. It took her years to correctly name what it was she felt, which was nothing less than moral outrage. Earnest, unironic, and therefore utterly cringe.

For Maggie, the connection between the pervasive brokenness of the wider system, and how that translated into wasted individual potential, was painfully apparent. Her thoughts often turned to her brother, but Tez was far from the only person she knew who'd been mugged. Childhood friends, contacts made at university, dorm-mates she'd lived with and loved: if pressed, the overwhelming majority would acknowledge that they were engaged in make-work, or under-utilised; in either case denied opportunity to reach their potential. Maggie ached for those people, even though she had been spared that fate for the time being. She felt a sort of survivor's guilt, and a queasy consciousness that, swaddled in privilege as she was, she probably didn't even know the half of it.

Rage, compassion, guilt: that's what it amounted to, but none of those things could be invoked in response to the question, at least not in a way that didn't leave her sounding unstable. So she usually mumbled something about her academic background and a keen personal interest.

Lying on her bed in the evenings, still too early to sleep, she kept telling herself that there was no point sulking. She had a mission, which was more than most could say. It had to be an Income. Income or nothing! Income or bust! She wished she had someone who could deliver this kind of pep talk, but Cass was far away, and ignorant of the very concept of self-doubt. Kei, meanwhile, knew hardly anything about her work, and was still learning to chart her emotional landscape. He wouldn't be able to give her what she needed, even if she'd felt comfortable asking.

Maggie was surprised to find herself missing Ngunnawal-Ngambri – didn't know it was possible to miss that place. She wondered if she should call her father, just to hear him prattle, which was the surest sign yet of some lack; some failure on her part to integrate with this cell-like room, her new colleagues, this strange and teeming city.

CHAPTER 9

Most commentators will tell you that the Cebu Incident, and the regime change that followed in Beijing, marked the end of Cold War III. But I reject this interpretation utterly. The war hasn't ended; rather, a pretence of rapprochement and opening-up has become convenient for everyone. Is that all peace ever is? Corporates, who chafed under the embargoes, can resume trans-continental operations, and Australians can pretend that we were never forced to choose sides.

> – Associate Prof. Sally Myrrh, 'The Unskewed
> History of the World' (2056; self-published)

'IT'S A REMINDER OF THE THINGS WE FIGHT TO protect. You know, for everything our nation has achieved, we lack scale. It wouldn't take much to lose everything.'

Like most people, Maggie had seen images of Howardville on her feed, but she'd never visited. The feeling of being here now was one of intrusion, like walking in on someone playing with themselves. This place was pilgrimage and sanctuary for the stalwarts of the Liberal Party, or what remained of it after the Truvies split away.

Mackay had ushered Felix and Maggie here, through the ID verification and the firewall. The proxy harvester was considered a reliable enough Liberal supporter to have been granted admin privileges, which meant that he could invite non-members. Beside her, Felix gawped.

They were on the crest of a gently rising hill, overlooking a strange hinterland. Below, vineyards ran to the edge of a bay, spanned by a replica of the Sydney Harbour Bridge. To her left, the Narrm Cricket Ground sat on a low rise, casting shade over a row of Queenslander houses, next to a scrubby beach marked by graves, which Maggie supposed was meant to represent the ANZACs. A lighthouse stood nearby. A ruin (Port Arthur?) – some of the landmarks were difficult to place, out of context and jumbled together. At the other end of the big bridge, office towers reared in a tight configuration, as if standing back-to-back to measure themselves: Centrepoint, Neon Crown, Palmer.

Maggie couldn't see any natural landmarks. That was probably just as well: the Libs weren't stupid enough to appropriate Uluru or Kumarangk-Hindmarsh Island, even in private.

The locale was almost deserted. In the distance Maggie could see a few avatars jogging through the vineyards or lolling on the beach. A stagecoach, pulled by horses, made its way between Old New Parliament House and an oversized facsimile of the Dog on the Tuckerbox. Above was blue sky, upon which the Southern Cross and the Union Jack had been faintly superimposed, like a watermark.

The overall effect was disorienting, but Maggie had to acknowledge that it was a slick job. The transition between sand, vines and city was almost seamless, considering everything that had been shoehorned into this vista. The juxtaposition of so many different structures created a collage effect, and it reminded Maggie of Soviet-era constructivist propaganda she'd studied at university. But she decided not to share that view with Mackay, who watched her, gloating, before turning to stare at the Bridge, which was glinting in the artificial sunlight.

[This is fkd] The text flashed above Felix's head in illicit purple – a private message that only Maggie would be able to read. She ignored him, and said to Mackay, 'We appreciate your time. And the invitation.'

'I thought you'd be interested in what we've built here, even if it offends your sensibilities. Classical liberals need a safe space, too,' he said, without a trace of irony. 'We're stifled by the thought police on the public feeds.'

Mackay was a relic; a stubborn vestige of the patriarchy. He was not so old that he had any excuse. He'd been president of the Young Libs in the early thirties, and an apparatchik after that, in a period when women had largely boycotted the party's org structure. Maggie had the feeling that those days would have suited him just fine. Now, face still youthful from the treatments, he wore a double-breasted navy suit, a white shirt and a baby blue tie, which in the open air could have left him looking like an insurance broker. But somehow, immersed in all this jingoism, he was a natural fit.

Brij had pushed for this meeting. Now that Maggie was here, she was determined to make it productive. She ignored the provocation in Mackay's comment, and came straight to the point. 'I'm wondering if you see any common ground on an Income.'

Mackay's mouth broadened. 'Absolutely.' When Maggie didn't respond, he continued, 'There are those on my side who contend that with the loss of government, we need to hunker down. That our role now will be to impede. But that kind of thinking will only lose us more votes. With change comes opportunity.'

'I'm glad you see it that way.'

'The right kind of Income could be palatable to my base, if I was to advocate for it. Of course, I'd have to be comfortable with the details of the scheme.'

'Mmm.'

'I'm sure we could work with you on the specifics,' Added Felix, when Maggie declined to say anything further.

'I'm very pleased to hear it, young Reeve. And please pass on my regards to your uncle.'

'Will do. He told me a story once, about you and him at The Refinery, before it got shut down …'

Mackay feigned embarrassment, but it was clear that this delighted him. 'We were wild lads back then.'

Maggie wasn't in the mood. With more impatience in her tone than she meant to convey, she asked, 'What exactly are you concerned about?'

Mackay looked down and grew still for a moment. A paper plane spawned in his hand, and he drew back and lofted it. All three of them watched it glide over the vineyards until, at the bottom of the hill, it came to rest at the feet of a bronze sculpture depicting four men laughing and patting each other on the back. Magnifying the area, Maggie could make out a concise inscription: *Lifters*.

Mackay said, 'Some of my benefactors see merit in giving people the means to afford the basics. But we don't want to be too extravagant, so setting the right level will be critical.

And then, of course, we need to work out how to pay for it. This would be the largest economic reform for a generation, so you want business onside, or at least not campaigning against you. The big corporates might be able to choke down a small impost, but most of the money required will need to be found elsewhere.'

This was impossible. *Elsewhere* would mean increased tax on individuals, which would never get up in a plebiscite, a fact that wouldn't have been lost on Mackay. He was playing with her.

Before she could tell him so, Felix interceded. 'That's super interesting, Mr. Mackay. Super interesting. You've certainly given us a lot to think about. We'll have a word with Brij and get back to you, but I reckon we'll be able to sort something out.'

Mackay winked at Maggie. 'I'm glad I could help. Now, can I show you more of the sights? There's a stunning tableau in the stadium of Ellyse Perry smacking a boundary. She was a cricketer. Want to take a look?'

MAGGIE DUMPED THEM BACK OUT TO THE LOBBY where she and Felix had met before transferring over to Howardville. She made no attempt to hide her anger. 'Don't ever do that again.'

'Do what?' Felix had the sense to feign confusion. Or perhaps he genuinely didn't understand why Maggie was taking him to task. Either way, it was unacceptable.

'You don't speak for me, and you don't speak for Brij.'

'I was just trying to help, and you weren't saying much at all.

It wouldn't have hurt to schmooze him a bit, you know what I mean?'

'Is that another way of saying, *you should smile more*?'

'Well, maybe you should smile more, Mags.'

'Don't call me that.'

'It sounded like he wanted to meet you halfway. If he could convince the Libs to support your plan—'

'He wanted to bastardise our plan. You said it yourself: an Income is about freedom. But an Income set at the poverty line, or below it, is more like slavery. And that's what Mackay was hinting at. The conglomerates want every dult to have just enough to be good consumers, but not enough to exercise any *real* choice about how they live. They want to use an Income to trap people in almost-poverty, to keep them dependent.'

'Mackay is old-school. I've been around guys like that my whole life. All they want is a bit of flattery. A bit of recognition.'

'You're very sure of yourself, aren't you?'

'I'm here for a reason.'

'Let's talk about that. Does your uncle support an Income?'

The bluntness of the question didn't throw Felix. 'He's interested, Mags. He likes what you guys are doing, so he asked me to check it out for him. Said it'd be good experience for me. And Brij thought so too.'

'Will he support it?'

'I can't speak for him, just like you can't speak for Brij.'

'What does he want?'

Now Felix hesitated, as if weighing his words. 'One of Chase's supporters is real big on vicarious liability, applied to AI. That's interesting to us.'

This was so off-topic that it took a moment for Maggie to process. 'What does that even mean?'

'Well, if you're a business and you have a human employee, you're responsible for their actions – up to a point. You're liable if they do something bad on the job. So, say, if you deal with a crypto pusher and they lie about asset backing, you can sue the business they represent. But if they go crazy and stab you with a knife, the employer isn't responsible, because there's no connection with the job.'

'Okay …'

'And for AI, we want the same thing. If an AI is deliberately programmed by the business to do something sketchy, then sure, the business should be held to account. But what about unintentional effects of programming? Like, what if, completely unintentionally, an AI becomes racist?'

This was not a hypothetical, Maggie knew. Like humans, algorithms that could learn autonomously often mixed up correlation and causation, using data to come to bad conclusions. A large part of human-led software dev was devoted to untangling these kinds of biases.

Felix was on a roll now. 'If a computer makes an honest mistake, and there's no malice, the owner shouldn't be punished for that. They'd only be required to apologise and correct the error moving forward.' He offered up his palms in a half-shrug. 'It's only fair.'

Maggie thought about her brother. How many of his job applications had been knocked back because his surname, Garewal, struck some half-smart AI as too ethnic? No one would ever know. 'You'd be letting businesses off the hook for testing, making sure their algorithms don't produce any perverse results.' No, Maggie realised, it was worse than that. 'You might even be creating an incentive *not* to do testing, so that businesses can stay ignorant about what their machines are doing.'

'That's something to consider,' Felix said, but his smile remained. 'Still ... it's what we want.'

There was something in Felix's tone. An entitlement; an assumption that things would be arranged accordingly. It was so alien to Maggie, who had needed to fight for everything – was fighting even now – that she felt wrongfooted. 'I don't know why we're discussing this,' she said, and she knew it sounded petulant. 'An Income is overdue, and Chase must recognise that. His support shouldn't come at a price.'

'I don't know how these things happen, Mags. I'm even newer at this than you are. I'm just trying to help you understand what my uncle is thinking.'

Maggie could feel herself fuming. 'We don't need his support.' And this wasn't exactly wrong: it would be technically possible to build a coalition of harvesters that did not include Chase Reeve. But to win a pleb without the self-described 'sensible centre' of Australian politics ... it would be much harder.

'That's not what Brij thinks. But I guess we'll see.' Felix wandered the edges of the small room, inspecting the generic texture of the wall, identical to hundreds of thousands of virtual meeting rooms used in shroudspace. Abruptly he turned back to Maggie, allowing his exasperation to show. 'Don't you get it? Chase and me, we're doing you guys a favour. Just having me with you in those meetings with Treasury, it makes it look like you've got clout. Do you really want me to stop coming?'

Maggie wanted to tell him exactly where he should go. With an effort, she tried to moderate her response. 'If you're going to be there, it has to be for the right reasons.'

'I'm not an idiot, Mags. I've read your paper. And I personally think an Income is a good idea.' The incredulity she felt must have been visible, because he blurted, 'You've convinced me! No joke. And I think we'd get further if you trusted me a bit.'

Maggie shook her head. 'Trust is something you earn.'

'Not always. Sometimes you need to give people the benefit of the doubt.' He morphed his avatar's face into that of a kitten, with exaggerated, pleading eyes.

With a swipe of her fingers, she cancelled the effect. 'You signed on with us as an intern, so start acting like one. That means following instructions.' After putting up with Mackay and his smarminess, it felt good to put this man-boy in his place. 'If you manage that, you can tag along. But this will happen with or without your uncle's proxies.' She double-tapped to end the meeting.

In the instant before the connection dropped, she heard, 'We'll se—.'

ON HER EIGHTH NIGHT IN SYDNEY SHE BUZZED KEI, and cast herself into the ramshackle townhouse he shared with his mother. The two Arakachis perched straight-backed on the family sofa, noodle bowls balanced on their thighs as they played an interactive quiz game with their shrouds. When Maggie joined them, she didn't know what to do with her avatar as they paused their game and turned to smile at her. The room was snug, crowded with old wooden furniture. Maggie positioned herself against the wall supporting the staircase, and offered a halting wave.

'Welcome to our home.' Kei's mother had a formal manner, even though Maggie had visited several times before, by shroud and even once in meatspace. But the warmth of the older woman's eyes softened her words. 'Why don't you sit down?'

Maggie crossed the room and found a place between mother and son. Kei seemed happy to have her by his side, even though her form left no indentation on the couch. She felt as if she should justify herself, to excuse her virtual presence when, after all, it would have only taken a couple of hours to deliver her body to this same location. She was here, with time to spare; but she was also in Sydney, required to remain in case something happened. Both things were true, and the superposition was hard to put into words.

She joined their quiz game. They were playing against a family from Western Australia, and so none of them talked about anything for an hour or more, except for capitals, and pop songs of the 20s, and Narrm Cup winners. After a full day spent with strangers, engaged in wheedling and persuading, it was a welcome distraction.

Later, she followed Kei up the stairs to his childhood bedroom, where, unable to touch each other, they undressed and touched themselves. Maggie's real body was in a claustrophobic room in a Sydney dormitory, and as her hands slid over her torso, her avatar mirrored her movements. Maggie missed the feeling of Kei's mouth on her, and she told him so. Closing her eyes, she tried to recapture what it was like. He was always closely-shaven and, she now remembered, smelled clean like soap. Counter-intuitively, she had the sense of feeling clean herself when he pressed his head between her legs. This consciousness, it didn't diminish the pleasure she felt, or the excitement; it was a separate layer.

She knew that as a rule, humans weren't clean, or even orderly. She had seen vids of water riots in South Africa. Photos taken in hospital wards of broken bodies, a product of the long-running Tatar-Bashkortostan conflict that had raged off and on since the disintegration of the Russian Federation. That morning she'd glanced at an image in her feed – a clinic somewhere in the tropics, showing the toll of the new wasting illnesses that had proliferated over the last decade or so. But those things were elsewhere. To achieve anything, to live her life, they had to exist in a compartment.

After they were done, Kei lay on his bed, and Maggie's avatar stood close by. Kei looked up at her. 'Do you ever think about the fact that one day you'll come for the last time ever? When it's my turn, I wonder if I'll recognise it as it's happening. Would that make it better?'

'That's kind of a weird thought to have,' said Maggie, appreciating him.

'You never think about weird stuff?'

'Never.'

UP, UP, DOWN, DOWN, LEFT, RIGHT, LEFT, RIGHT, B, A

TEZ GAREWAL, THE THIRTY-THIRD-RANKED B-FLY hunter in the whole of Australasia (he's dropped a few spots) is still running. He's left the fields and the forests of the beef hunting grounds far behind. He's running, but not toward personal achievement or professional success. He's found some new bullshit, a virgin grazing land of procrastination. Tez is on a manhunt.

The entity calling itself Hanabi exists. From that self-evident starting point, it must be possible to learn more. In the absence of anything more urgent, this is the mission that Tez has set himself. Hanabi and their associates doxxed Tez, and Tez wants to return the favour.

For the last few decades, a mouse/mousetrap race has been playing out between privacy stans and data junkies. With so many surfaces of attack, you'd think it might be easy to learn about a person on-grid, but for every exploit, there is a fix. Tez is reading up on IP sniffing, pattern matching, simulated voice fingerprinting. Hanabi's Flûttr profile is a dead end, but if they and their crew are badgering people in one MMO environ, it's a good bet they'll be active in others, too. Tez just needs to find the mind behind the kitsune mask.

He starts with what he knows. Hanabi and pals had been hung up about work: who has it, and who doesn't. Tez is aware, in a general sense, of the protests at DHS – they've been all over the local news. But politics is Maggie's thing. He learned long ago that there's nothing to be gained by occupying the same space as his brilliant younger sister.

Still, he reads up on the protesters' demands. Hanabi is trying to force him to front up at DHS for some special event. There's a feed with particulars, which teases that it'll be a day that will *change the course of Australian history*, which seems a bit hyperbolic. Tez does a deep dive into a linked manifesto. The analysis of the fundamental problem is so obvious as to be almost trite: massive inequality of opportunity, leading to entrenched poverty and a multigenerational underclass that has no choice but to fight for whatever scraps are available. Tez can't think of anyone who would dispute that. A trip to a physical shopping mall is enough to bear it out: floors of vacant space, occupied by unhoused and unshrouded squatters, seeking respite from the sun and the freezing Ngunnawal nights. On some level, maybe a tenuous and contingent level, Tez understands himself to be protected from that reality.

Where the manifesto gets a bit spicier is in claiming that this situation is not inevitable; nor is it the result of mismanagement on the part of the elites. Rather, the formation of an underclass is alleged to be a deliberate scheme to maintain precarity. Those in the comfortable middle can see what awaits them if they rock the boat.

At first, Tez doesn't buy it. In his family, it's Raman who is most receptive to a good conspiracy theory. Tez is more pragmatic, like Liv, and tends to believe that bad stuff can usually be explained by stupidity rather than malevolence. But he's in deep, now, learning about Matev, and f values. Legit economists, who study the social control benefits of poverty, who advise governments how to exploit it. It's on the record if you know where to look.

He wishes he'd listened to Maggie when she'd explained what she was pushing for. He knows the general outlines – not a guarantee of work, but at least making sure everyone has enough money to get by. That sounds like a good start; sounds like it would help give people more agency, but when he checks on the protest forums, most people are sceptical or even outright hostile to the OzProg plan:

[Nice idea, I guess, but they'll fuck it up somehow]
[Same leash, different colour]
[This is about meaning, not money. They can't buy us off!!!]

Mostly, what strikes Tez is how angry people are, a smouldering fury directed not so much toward individuals, but at the system itself. He feels like he can see the outline of something, massive but obscured. Something that would explain how things are turning out for him. Like, take the design comp he's been working on. There might be a couple of thousand entrants, from which the organising firm will pick three winners. Those winners will each get a year's contract, once they sign over all IP rights to their entries. The firm will take those designs, trim off any rough edges, and present their client with three options to choose from. The client will pick one, and the firm will rake in cash over the life of the project. In exchange for an investment of three grad salaries for a year, the firm has reaped the benefit of hundreds of thousands of hours of unpaid labour, and will claim the resulting spoils.

Competitions aside, there is no easier path to security. For the luckiest few, networking events might lead to an interview, which might lead to work experience, which might lead to an unpaid internship, which might lead to a trial, which might lead to a short-term contract and revenue targets, which might, one day, if attrition creates a suitable opening, lead to permanent work.

His failure to amount to anything is no one else's, but he begins to wonder if his failure might not entirely be his *fault*.

HE STAYS UP LATER, SLEEPS LESS. LIV TELLS HIM he must be working too hard, and for once she's right, as well as wrong.

It's time for an excursion. Lurking on the boards, he hasn't picked up on any references to an organiser calling themselves Hanabi. It's a distributed movement, but those doing the heavy lifting spend most of their time at the stockade, in front of DHS. Along with this focal point, there are local chapter meetings all over the country. Physical meetings, not for feedcast, which lends them a certain clandestine intrigue. Through some contacts he's made during his research, Tez finds one going down not too far from Ngunnawal.

Visiting real places and doing meat-type things is not Tez's style. Before leaving, he dresses and re-dresses, hunting through the bottom of his wardrobe to find a look that will let him pass as a downtrodden proletarian, but all his fibres are too soft. He settles on a checked cotton shirt that might pass as flannelette.

The ride to Goulburn takes forty minutes, just enough time for him to second-guess and start freaking out. The meeting is being held at a housing project, a commune of six-storey flats a few kilometres from the centre of town. His shroud informs him that the flats were originally built to accommodate police cadets. Now, in the glare of this early-autumn afternoon almost a generation since the law left town, there is less evidence of an organising force at work. Grubby-looking dults loiter in rows of vegetable gardens planted between the towers. There is no information desk, and his shroud has nothing useful to tell him about meeting spaces or common areas. His first error, he realises, is to roll up in the town car he's taken from Ngunnawal. It marks him as an outsider. The only other vehicles here are ancient, battered people-movers and utes. In ones and twos, others arrive on foot and by bicycle, and Tez attaches himself to the back of a small delegation as they file through the main entrance to one of the towers.

The lobby is crowded, and there are plenty like Tez who need directions. To his architect's eye, the space is an abomination. It's dingy in here, with the sun swapped for sketchy orange-white LEDs. The heat, sweat and uncertainty give the space an animal energy. There is no need: the footprint is generous enough, and the ceiling high enough, that with better access, acoustics, ventilation, it could feel safe and open. But the double doors that mark the entrance are pinched, and inside there are a series of waist-high counters that appear to serve no purpose other than disrupting any sense of flow. On the left-hand side of the room, people are trying to make their way down a steep concrete staircase, but they're blocked by the crowd milling on the floor. He can't see anyone who's cast in, which is fortunate, because there is nowhere for them to watch, and be, that would not add to the congestion. Tez experiences the sheer oppressiveness of this public lobby as a kind of psychic pain.

A dult starts motioning for people to use a second flight of stairs at the rear. Trying to look like he belongs, Tez descends into an industrial kitchen, just as large as the ground level. The floors are green-speckled cream linoleum, and a group of about eighty have crowded into an area flanked by refrigerator cabinets at one end, and stainless steel trolleys at the other. A rabble of boys stand on the trolleys, jostling each other and throwing their weight around to shift the worn rubber wheels, while adults who might be their parents face the front and pretend to be oblivious.

Tez gets the sense that most of the people gathered live here on the commune. Dressed like they've come straight from their couches, they have an easy way with one another. Some others are colour-matched and be-sloganned, or dressed less casually, and Tez figures they are from Goulburn proper, and better versed in activism. For the most part, these two groups sort themselves into separate blobs on either side of the room.

A balding, red-bearded man with a weary expression hammers his hand against a countertop until the clamour subsides. When he smiles, he exposes buck teeth. 'Okay, let's get started.' He is wearing a T-shirt that says *Proud Bludger*. Nearby, some of his mates try to hush the crowd.

'Thanks everybody for coming. Shrouds off please, I don't want any recordings tomorrow in my feed.' He pauses while a few people mutter or touch their temples. Reluctantly, Tez does the same, setting his shroud to do-not-disturb but leaving it on. For the first time, he notices that many of the locals appear to be unshrouded, and he wonders if they are weirdos or cultists.

'Cheers,' the organiser says. 'To kick off tonight, I want to ask a question that might be enlightening for some of our allies in town. So, all the Academy people here tonight, how many of you have steady work?'

In the whole room, only two hands shoot up.

'Right. Well Em's put her hand up because she's the Academy's government-appointed social worker. Thanks for coming, Em. And just between us, I know that Darug got his job at Dep-Culture because he lied about a having a post-doc in digital anthropology.' The locals grow raucous, and a man who must be Darug mutters something about having a certificate, but he's shouted down.

'So, my point is, we aren't here by choice, are we? Like, let's be real, we've been funnelled onto the old Academy 'cos we can't pay rent. We're a problem, to be managed by the same ruling class responsible for putting us here!' For a second it seems that he's gearing up for a diatribe, but then he reins it in. 'Anyway, preaching to the converted. I'm not gonna waste your time, even if the market thinks your time is worthless. We're here to support the movement. So, I want you all to tell me, what did you *want* to be?'

The speaker turns to his right, to a tall, dreadlocked woman in a khaki-coloured maxi dress. 'None of you cunts will believe this. But when I was little I actually wanted to be a cop. I knew they trained here, and I seen 'em around town. So it's kind of funny I live here now, hey?'

One by one, everyone volunteers something. There's a ripple of applause when someone expresses an aspiration that is particularly audacious or naïve.

'Vet, I guess.'

'I wanted to run a restaurant. Just make good food for people, you know?'

When it's Tez's turn, he says, 'I wa— I want—' He feels his face getting hot. Tez struggles when he's talking IRL, to anyone other than close family. Weirdly, he's never had a problem voice chatting in shroudspace. Most of the time, he forgets he even has a stutter, since he so rarely leaves home with his body. 'An architect,' he manages. 'I still want that.' He is surprised at the conviction he hears in his own voice.

He has revealed himself to these strangers. Not as Descartes the elite B-Fly hunter, but as Tez Garewal, the unemployed loser who lives with his parents. When the group responds with smiles and nodded affirmations, he doesn't misinterpret. No one here is trying to exhort him to be better, to embark on a journey of self-improvement. To Tez, it's unexpectedly sweet, a world away from the thinly veiled contempt he gets from his sister, or the cloying platitudes of Liv and Raman.

After everyone has shared, the facilitator rattles off theory. Tez half-listens, and catches parts of the manifesto, broken down and reconstituted for a live audience. But more than the ideas, he finds himself paying attention to the vibe in the room. He isn't sure what he expected, but most of the chat on the feeds and forums had an aggrieved tone which is absent here. There is a recognition that the current system is broken – that's almost taken as a given – but most of the talk is upbeat, about theories of political change, and practical strategies to advance the cause. Tez could never be comfortable with this many people around, but something about the energy here is supportive, like they're all on the same team. The quiet rage that Tez has nurtured for years: everyone in this room gets it. But they're not letting it block them; they're trying to change the game.

The facilitator is wrapping up. 'The most important thing is to show up at DHS on our day of action. If you don't have a shroud, get to a library and get on a terminal. We want this to be the largest demonstration in Australia's history. We need to let OzProg know that their promises count for nothing, if they're going to run the same rigged game.' Self-consciously, the speaker executes a small fist pump, and starts to move into the crowd, before pulling up short. 'Oh, and I've been asked to say, Capri's made a batch of Stroganoff for anyone who wants a feed. Thanks.'

A hubbub of conversation starts up again, and Tez, standing alone, remembers himself. He is here on a mission, after all. Approaching strangers makes him feel janky, but if he doesn't follow through, then this whole trip will have been for nothing. Trying to draw energy from what he's seen and heard, he tracks down one of the ostensible organisers, a bookish-looking middle-aged woman who's also wearing a *Bludger* T-shirt.

'Hey, sorry to bother you. Um, just— just wondering, do you know someone with the handle Hanabi? Active online, wears a red fox mask?'

She knits her brows, but doesn't seem put off by the question. 'No, doesn't ring any bells. Why?'

'Oh, they just … they introduced me to the movement. I'd love to talk with them a bit more about their take on … on what we're doing here.'

''K. Listen, if I run into them, I'll ping you. Give me your deets?'

'Sure.'

Forcing a smile, Tez makes himself approach a half-dozen others, from the commune and the town. Everyone's mingling now, and some of the kids have been conscripted to hand around cardboard bowls with rich-smelling stew. A bowl is pressed into Tez's hand before he can say no. Between mouthfuls – it's not bad, in an anaemic, bulk-vegan sort of way – he finds himself swapping stories. There are a few people here who've studied as long as he has, or longer. A paramedic; an art historian. And then there are plenty who saw the writing on the wall, and dropped out after high school. For the most part they have skills, though. There are self-taught electro-mechanics, and horticulturalists. As a collective, the people at the Academy are running an economy almost wholly off-net. For some, that's clearly a point of pride. For others, it's pragmatism, having been effectively shut out of the global, networked market that is the only one Tez has known up to this moment. In a strange way, he's not out of place at all. He finds himself laughing, responding with real personal details, as if this whole goose chase hadn't started with Tez being doxxed.

When the meeting wraps, he follows the crowd back out into the last of the day's light. Teenagers range along the rows of crops, calling boisterously to one another, collecting equipment and returning it to a nearby storehouse. Tez accepts the offer of a ride into Goulburn on an ancient minibus, figuring that it'll be less awkward to summon a town car there. A girl of eleven or twelve reaches into a hessian sack and hands a zucchini to each passenger as they board. In response to Tez's questioning look, she says, 'We got too many.' As consolation prizes go, it could be worse.

AT HOME, TEZ GIVES THE ZUCCHINI TO HIS MOTHER, and it fries, and he stews. Two more days pass slowly.

Tez has been lurking in an OzPol room, looking for a fresh lead after his excursion to Goulburn. He doesn't notice someone new entering the chat until he sees the DM.

[I hear U been asking round.] Now Tez scans the crowd in this virtual space, and picks out a familiar insouciant stance, a familiar mask.

[Yup.] Conflicting emotions jam Tez's signals. Hanabi is a jerk. Tez hates the way he was strong-armed; he can't get behind those kinds of tactics, however just the cause might be. Hanabi is the antithesis of the quiet, egoless optimism Tez found at the Academy. Still. He's been hunting this person. He wants this reckoning.

Through the random assembly of digital bodies, Hanabi navigates slowly, reducing the space between them. *[Well here I am.]*

Definitely a jerk, but there's no point dragging this out. Tez messages: *[I've learned about the protests. About your reasons.]* In meatspace, he winces. *[I don't think you're entirely wrong.]*

The painted rictus of the mask looks smug. *[You understand?]* *[I think so, yeah.]*

[If u understand, do more. U cant just rock up by yrself. Spread the word. Tell friends. Tell family. Make them get it too.]

[Or else what?]

Hanabi's avatar crosses its arms, throws its head back, and mimes a fit of laughter. *[Or else nothing? Ur one of us now. Just, dont let us down. Dont let urself down. K?]* And Hanabi reaches up to palm their mask, and draws it away. And the face below, which might be real, or might be another type of mask, but which is undeniably feminine, and gorgeous, and brazen, winks at him.

[K?] Hanabi asks again. *[K thx bye]* And they (she? They) are gone.

CHAPTER 10

I'm hearing word about a new bill coming up. A huge new tax, just so that the vegetables at OzProg can give money to bludgers. You've seen them. They skulk around the shelters, and they harass you at the shops. They slump on the footpath, staring at their shrouds. Gaming, wanking, whinging on the boards. There's a small army camped outside the DHS as I speak, complaining that there's no work. Bullshit! There's plenty of work. In cleaning, unboxing, elder management. They just don't want to do it.

I called it. I said: if you vote this mob in, they'll ruin the joint. And they haven't wasted any time. This is not what this country's about! We're about hard work and a fair go. If this comes to a vote, we need to tell them where to stick it.

– 'Mornings with Oskar', transcript of feed broadcast,
26 March 2058 [v:comment.au/Oskar]

MAGGIE HEARD THE DOUBLE PING AND WAS INSTANTLY awake. Her shroud had been part of her for decades, and it knew her more truly than a parent. Drawing on deep history, cycle after cycle of prediction, observation and subtle correction, it was alerting her to a message that it thought Maggie would want to read immediately.

[It wasn't me! Watch your back. – M.]

Something must be happening. She rolled on to her back to free her hands, tapped out the sequence for a mainstream news channel.

—*Free money? That's what the new government wants you to believe, but how will an Income really be funded? Details are emerging about a planned tax hike …*

Her shoulders pulled back in a momentary shiver, and she realised it had broken. For all that she distrusted Mackay, Maggie believed him when he denied being the source of the leak. There was no need for him to stoop like that. And in the background hiss of her semiconscious, she now realised, she had been waiting for coverage to start. An Income had been OzProg policy before the election, and between her efforts and Brij's, not to mention the mandarins at DHS and Treasury, the source could have been any one of a hundred people.

Distractedly, she showered, pulled on clothes, and joined her colleagues on the early train. By the time she arrived at Market Street, Tan had been rolled out to make a statement. Yes, it was something that the Government was considering, they'd been up-front about that before the election. No specifics yet: they would go about this in a careful and considered way, to get the best outcome for all Australians. Yes, Tan had seen the commentary, which amounted to misinformation and fearmongering. No dult would see their taxes rise.

Maggie sat watching with the Payments working party, one eye on the Minister at their podium, crowded by the full suite of Australian and Indigenous flags, and one eye on her colleagues. When Tan made the assurance that there would be no tax rise, there was a collective tightening. Maggie ground her molars together. While she didn't think that any changes to individual rates would be required, Tan had just committed them to raising any new money from corporate tax. She thought about Mackay, and about Felix, who hadn't bothered to join them that morning, and the conference room felt small. Her shroud, sensing her elevated heartbeat and the tension in her neck, played a soothing melody, and for an instant she felt impelled to dig her fingers into her brow and rip the thing out.

'Come on, we've got a job to do,' said Maggie, too quietly. The Treasury staff on either side turned toward her, blinking away their own feeds. The members of the Payments team tended to anxiety, Maggie had found, pursing their lips and twitching their fingers too often, like they were strung out, conscious of being one careless error away from causing a disaster. Their work, concerned as it was with the mechanics of identifying and transferring money to millions of recipients while preventing fraud, was important but deeply unsexy. Their project lead, a sour-faced veteran named Pia, took palpable satisfaction in the flagging of problems. Her inclination to prepare thoroughly, and to try and get things right the first time, was obstinately old-fashioned.

'For this to work, we'll need to de-risk the government's forward obligations,' said a bearded dult, one of the econometricians, in a monotone that managed to both convey boredom and foreshadow an apology. 'Income payments will have to be made in Aussies.'

Maggie recalled what Brij had said about leverage. 'That won't work. The payments have to be in Standard Basket, otherwise we can't guarantee a decent standard of living.'

With the explosion of virtual, corporate and hybrid monies, every dult had become an unwilling currency speculator. Holding all of one's cash in dollars issued by the Australian government was a gamble. To buy a shroud upgrade, for instance, you needed to pay in ToshiBucks or E-Won, and the Aussie could fluctuate wildly against those kinds of coins. To hedge, most people held cash in a diversified 'standard basket', a spread of crypto, corporate-issued, and government-issued money. Most employers paid wages in Basket, too. Government workers received pure Aussie, which they usually converted automatically on payday to a less volatile spread.

'How can we model the cost of this when we don't know what Basket will cost in a year's time?'

'You make assumptions,' Maggie replied. She would have expanded, but a message blinked at the top of her field of vision. It was her father. Surreptitiously, fearing some sort of family emergency, she opened it with a twitch of her index finger.

[WHAT ARE YOU DOING RIGHT NOW I AM HAVING MORN-ING TEA?]

'Treasury models the Basket cost of programs all the time,' said Maggie. 'Supply contracts, foreign debt—' Under the table, she tapped out a response against her thigh. [Busy. In mtg.]

'This is different. Maggie, this is vast. The government can't carry that kind of risk.'

[DRIED APRICOTS MOSTLY AND SOME HEALTHY NUTS]

She would have to revoke Raman's popup privileges. Trying to focus, she said, 'So you want recipients to bear the risk? These aren't government workers, these are unsophisticated … I mean … you know what I mean.'

[ARE YOU COMING TO DADA JI'S PARTY?]
'You mean that the average dult might not employ a sensible hedging strategy.'

[I told you already, yes. V. busy!] 'Yes.'

Pia brushed her thumb over her bottom lip. 'I take your point. We'd be funnelling them, by default, into a high-risk portfolio.'

[THATS GOOD. ABOUT THE PARTY I MEAN]

Maggie nodded, trying to focus. 'Not everyone would convert to a better spread.' She was sure this would be borne out by an asset class analysis. The best thing about working with Treasury was the unexpurgated data access. The level of granularity was something completely different to the public feeds Maggie had based her preliminary work on. With her new credentials, she could track individual dults longitudinally; peer into their tax filings and monitor income over time; match against census household summaries, address records, health information, and the flow of funds between successive generations. It was staggering what a complete profile she could build – albeit on a no-names basis. She was formulating case studies about how specific Income settings might affect people of varying life stages, including with respect to currency risks. On nights when sleep was elusive, she drifted in these vast subterranean reservoirs of information.

'But hold on,' one of Pia's lieutenants was catching up. 'If we can't trust people to manage their currency exposure, isn't that like saying we can't trust them to manage their money?' Pia smiled indulgently, glancing sidelong at Maggie. 'And if we can't trust recipients to manage their money, doesn't that mean there's a more fundamental problem with an Income? That if we give people money, they'll just blow it?'

Now Pia frowned in apparent concern. 'Well that's a very cynical view to take, Arlo.'

They'd skewered her, scored a point on some meaningless tally board these people kept in their own heads. Suspending her frustration, deferring her regard of it, she said, 'This is about giving people dignity. If we empower them, they'll make good decisions. But we have to set them up for success.'

[I'LL LEAVE YOU ALONE NOW]

The smug curl of Pia's mouth reminded Maggie of Kinnear, and she knew she'd lost face. She didn't care, as long as she got her way. Giving people pure Aussie was reckless.

[LOVE YOU MY DAUGHTER]

[Not now dad!]

The meeting lasted another twenty minutes, but everyone with a clue could see that it was just for show. No one's mind would be changed, but Pia would be able to report that she'd heard Maggie out. Maggie would lobby, and Pia would offer up her own view, and the decision would be made elsewhere. As long as it stayed off Brij's desk: this was exactly the kind of wrinkle that Maggie had been put here to manage.

Toward the end, Insalata dropped by, apparently on a mission to reassure. He hovered in the doorway, leaning with his hands clutching the frame so that only his head and shoulders were in the room. 'It's full steam ahead. I've just spoken to the boss, and she says we'll need to get our message out quicker than we'd planned.'

Pia made a snuffling noise. 'Bradley? There are some finer points here that we could use your thoughts on.'

'Absolutely. Not now, but ... we'll make a time later.' He jogged in place, and mimed flicking sweat from his brow. 'Gotta keep moving. Gotta have a plan we can announce. The media abhors a vacuum. Stay clean!' He was out the door before anyone could protest.

THE COURTYARD WAS OVERRUN WITH POSSUMS. Maggie had stepped out with the idea of trying to find a late lunch, the humid conditions bringing a strange kind of relief after the dry heat of the Treasury office. Scores of animals zipped along the stone pavers between the brush box trees, and clambered up a trellis set against the concrete wall of the neighbouring tower. An activist group had set up signs and a card table in the middle of the yard, next to a cart serving gelato. Even though she knew that the possums were only projections, it was hard to move quickly among so much activity. Several times, Maggie checked her stride to avoid the appearance of stepping on one of the creatures. They looked and sounded too real to ignore. They were reacting to the physical features of the courtyard, so they must have been clever simulations, rather than a simple projection of stock footage, but there were the usual giveaways. One large specimen ran along the spindly branch of a tree and hung suspended from its tip. But the possum had no weight, so the branch didn't sag like it should have.

She stopped to watch a mother with a baby on its back. The mother was sniffing the air, its head turning constantly, trying to catch an elusive scent. An older woman left the activists' stand and approached.

'Cute, right?'

Maggie nodded. 'They sure are.'

'Sad to say, these little guys are extinct IRL. They're Leadbeaters Possums. But we're trying to bring them back.'

Maggie smiled cautiously, not wanting to become embroiled. 'Good on you.'

'We could really use your donation to help fund our research.'

'Not today, thanks.' Maggie stepped to the side, intending to skirt by the mother and its child.

'You're a heartless cunt.'

Maggie stopped in her tracks. As an expletive, the word had lost its sting decades ago, and fallen out of favour. It was so incorrect, so old-fashioned, that she wondered if she'd misheard. 'What?'

'I said you're a hypocrite, heartless cunt. You pretend you care, but you privilege humans above other life. I'm recording this. I know who you are' – a pause, probably for a database lookup – 'Maggie Garewal. We'll put your name on our stream, message your friends ... unless you're ready to discuss a giving plan?'

'Leave me alone.' Maggie turned and walked briskly back toward the entrance of the Treasury building, where there were protocols. The activist shouted after her.

'Everyone will know who you really are!'

That should have been the end of it. As shaken as Maggie was, she knew that the threat was probably empty. It would be self-defeating to doxx everyone who refused to donate. But as she approached the security line she heard other voices raised, and when she turned back she saw two police, in black balaclavas and tactical gear, converging on the activists. When the older dult who had harassed Maggie broke away, one of the cops pointed at her and she dropped to the ground, rolling and clutching the sides of her head.

Maggie couldn't help but wince. She knew that the police could do this – jam a dult's shroud to make it spit out disorienting lights and sounds, overriding the usual safety limits. But she'd never seen it happen firsthand, and from the way the woman was writhing, it didn't look pleasant. The three other activists had submitted, arranging themselves facedown on the ground.

With order restored, one of the officers approached. Close up, Maggie could see how small they were. They only came up to Maggie's nose, with what might have been a petite frame under all the body armour.

'You okay?' the officer asked, and then, without waiting for a reply: 'We've been monitoring these freaks. We'll take sound and vision from your shroudlog... Maggie Garewal. That should be enough to convict, but we'll be in touch if we need anything else. Thanks for your cooperation.'

The cop positioned themself between Maggie and the scene unfolding behind. With a dismissive flick of their head, they let Maggie know that it was time to move on, and it didn't seem wise to argue.

CHAPTER 11

DAVIS: Our top story tonight: the new government has moved swiftly to implement one of its election promises, guaranteeing all dults freedom of movement. Regionals have been put on notice that travel bans will be illegal from the first of July. Sharni Dent has more.

DENT: Eddie Collins grew up in Narrm's outer eastern suburbs, and dropped out of high school during the recession. Unable to find work, he started sleeping rough, working a series of low-paying gigs.

COLLINS: The best one was laundromat delivery, before the trikes took that over.

DENT: Eddie had never left Victoria. But when he was twenty-four, the City of Narrm offered to pay his bus fare to the Gold Coast, and gave him four thousand Aussie. The catch? He had to agree that he'd never return to the greater Narrm area.

COLLINS: I had debts. It got so bad that couldn't jack in, with all the collectors after me.

DENT: As Sydney, Brisbane, Perth and other large centres adopted similar lockout policies, Eddie moved back and forth across the country, staying in a neighbourhood until he was made an offer. For the last few years, his choices have been limited: head to the bush, or choose a free town like Newcastle, Yass or Kaurna Adelaide.

COLLINS: I've been in Newy for six years. It's bad here. But the cars won't take me past the edge of town.

DENT: Now, things are changing. By a narrow margin, the government has won a pleb that will restore the freedom of Eddie and thousands like him to travel, if they can find the money for a fare. Experts predict that many will return to our largest cities.

COLLINS: I've still got friends in Melbs. It'll be good to see them again.

DENT: Not everyone agrees with the change. The councils of Greater Sydney and Greater Narrm have joined forces for a legal challenge, asserting a right to control their borders. A preliminary hearing has been scheduled for June. Sharni Dent, NewsCult.

DAVIS: Times are changing. I hope Eddie doesn't end up on my street!

LENG: Ha! Me too. And now, the latest forecast in your location...

– 'NewsCult Late Bulletin', transcript of feed broadcast, 18 April 2058 [v:NewsCult]

SOME NIGHTS, AGAINST HER BETTER JUDGEMENT, Maggie would plug in to one of those streams designed to do nothing more than trigger the release of dopamine and serotonin. No plot, just shifting blobs of colour and a sound-scape designed by some anonymous psychotechnician in a studio somewhere. Boring, but as she lay on her cot, she could feel the muscles in her neck and shoulders unclench. For most of the following day she would feel better than well, the object of a gentle cosmic affection, until the crash arrived. When it came, slow like an iceberg against her hull, the only thing she had to turn to was the work.

'It's muggy here,' Maggie told Cass.

'Sydney? Never been.' This was delivered in a drawl that suggested that Cass's blood sugar was low. They'd been working together long enough that Maggie could recognise her friend's mid-afternoon slump. Hoping to shake off a sense of stasis, Maggie had scheduled her body to menstruate in a few days' time. But for the time being she felt scratchy, and so the shared energy on this call was hardly convivial.

Cass stretched her arms upward, her neck cracking audibly as she turned her head to the side. Their avatars sat in high-backed chairs, facing each other over a coffee table. This locale was designed for casual team meetings, with the same semi-bland decorating scheme that augmented Brij's physical office in Ngunnawal. Maggie found it comforting. Since anyone could go anywhere, or summon a view, there seemed to be no reason not to surround oneself with beauty and spectacle on all sides. Most people did exactly that.

'It's just up the road,' said Maggie. 'You could come up this afternoon.'

'What's the point? It's probably just like here, only bigger and uglier.'

Maggie knew that she could lose fifteen minutes trying to rebut this. 'Speaking of big and ugly, how's the meat business?'

'Not quite so bonkers. OzProg is giving the mob time to settle down before they bring on a bill. Hey, Garry, you're at Treasury, right? We need them to rubber stamp our voucher scheme. Convince them we're not trying to blow up the industry. Would you squeeze them for me?' Her hands groped lewdly at the air in front of her.

'I'll see what I can do,' said Maggie.

'That's what people say when they're about to do fuck-all. If you're gonna brush me off, at least admit it.'

Sometimes talking to Cass was difficult. 'I'm not the right dult for the job. I haven't got that much sway, Cass. I feel like I'm barely in the room with these people, like they're just humouring me and then having the real meetings once I've left. The Income has to come first.'

'So much for teamwork. You should try thinking about other people once in a while.'

'You can talk.'

'I don't need to be nice. I've got other qualities.'

'Cass ...'

'Hang on.' Her avatar winked out, leaving an empty chair. Seconds later, she was back. 'Boss wants to talk to you.'

Brij materialised at the edge of the room, an awkward distance away from Maggie and Cass. She didn't bother to approach. 'Maggie, some MPs have asked to see me. No cast-ins. Can you get back to Ngunna by seven?'

Maggie had only spoken once with her boss in the days following the meeting with Mackay and Felix. She was still trying to decide whether the quiet rage she felt was justified. All along, Brij must have known what the Reeves had been angling for, but she'd kept Maggie ignorant, even as Felix had been let loose to spy for his uncle. But now wasn't the time or the place for that conversation. 'If I leave now ... should be fine.'

'Good.' Brij signed out.

Cass squeezed her chin against her neck, one eye shut, one eye bulbous, and bared her teeth. And then she disappeared, too.

THERE WAS A WAIT FOR LAND CARS OUT OF SYDNEY, and Maggie was delayed. She'd tried the interchange at Minto, which she guessed might be less hectic, but the natural order of the place was fraying. Most dults appeared to be losing a battle with some combination of an oversized bag, a child, and a companion animal, and the ushers had their work cut out. As she shuffled through the dim hall, dodging obstructions as they presented, she received a call from Insalata, which she answered voice-only. 'Hi, Bradley,'

'Hey, Maggie. Just thought I'd touch base, see how you're getting on with the working groups.'

This was the first time that Salad Boy had proactively reached out. He mostly cultivated the impression of having too many other urgent commitments. Cautiously, Maggie replied, 'To be honest, we're getting bogged down. The Reserve Bank liaison crew are sinking time into problems that might never arise. Either way, they're issues better dealt with by regulation after the bill passes.'

'Oh, man, I know! Those guys are the actual worst. I try not to talk to them at all, if I can help it.'

Maggie kneaded the handle of her carry-bag. 'So why don't you do something?'

'Eh. Like everyone else we've inherited, most of them were brought on by the Libs decades ago. But they're the cattle we've got! They do know how to work the gears. No time to turf them, recruit, and train up replacements if we want to get an Income passed this decade. Anyway, while I've got you ...' He trailed off, as if waiting for Maggie's consent. When she didn't respond, he ploughed forward anyway. 'Trish has been getting some reach-outs from Human Support. Nothing unusual in that, I guess. But they seem to have the scoop on what we're doing, like, hour by hour. You wouldn't know why that is, would you?'

Maggie tried hard not to think about Kinnear, and what she'd been sharing with him. 'Nope.'

'Cool. Just asking around, 'cos leaks. You've seen what's getting out to the news wraps.' The phrasing of his speech took on a curliness. 'I guess whoever it is that's sharing with DHS, they might have their reasons. Maybe they think they're building cross-departmental consensus, or whatever. But they're not helping, you know? They're just making it harder to get a draft bill, something we can sign off internally and present to the Minister.'

'I'll keep that in mind,' Maggie replied, almost at the front of the platform now and eyeing off the cars that were coming down the ramp. 'Though, as I say, nothing to do with me.'

BY THE TIME SHE MADE IT TO BRIJ'S OFFICE, TEN minutes late, the place was already besieged.

There was no one in the bullpen, and no sound until Maggie pulled open the thick door to Brij's room. Counting Brij and herself, there were nine bodies, and the air felt close, like there ought to have been smoke and the smell of stale pizza. Brij was installed behind her desk, her face a mask of detached amusement. The MPs, three masc-presenting and four femme-, had claimed what purchase they could. There were two chairs for guests in front of the desk. The other visitors stood, or slouched against Brij's bookcase, or perched on the windowsill. Some of them wore thoughtful expressions, and others looked angry. Maggie noticed that no refreshments had been offered, no extra chairs borrowed from the conference room.

A few heads turned when Maggie closed the door, but there was no other acknowledgement. As Maggie weaved through the bodies to stand behind Brij, one of the MPs, a younger man, said, 'It's the lack of consultation, as much as anything.'

Brij shook her head. 'You and I talked before the election, Toby. And this is OzProg policy. It was hardly a secret.'

One of the other politicians cut in. 'It's the policy of the Australian Progressives to look after those in need. Will it do that? Do you even know?' There were murmurs of agreement. Maggie knew the speaker – she knew all of the MPs in the room; that was part of her job. But this dult, Sabra Dean, was lean and athletic, a former Olympic pole-vaulter, and her striking appearance had helped her build a stronger personal brand than the rest of her colleagues gathered here. Together, they formed a loose faction on OzProg's left flank. They weren't crazies, and historically, their disposition was one of resigned disappointment. Now, with the election win, with more proximity to power than they'd enjoyed in their entire parliamentary careers, they were riled up.

Brij stared ahead, not bothering to return her inquisitor's glance. 'Maggie here is working with Treasury on the details. They'll put together a white paper, and then Cabinet will consult with the parliamentary wing of the party.'

'You mean, once everything's already locked in? That doesn't work for us.'

'I've got a responsibility to my constituents,' said an older dult near the door. He took a wheezing breath. 'I'm here to give voice to their concerns, which I can't do if we're excluded from real decision-making.'

'Randall, *I'm* your constituent,' Brij responded, the half-smile never leaving her face. 'You know as well as I do that it was me – me and four or five other harvesters – that delivered your seat. So put a sock in it.'

Standing next to Brij, Maggie stiffened. She expected Randall to bite back, but he just folded his arms across his chest and looked at the wall.

'At least give us an outline,' Sabra said, with an edge of impatience.

'What do you want to know?'

'For a start, this Universal Basic Income. Exactly how universal will it be?'

Brij glanced at Maggie, inviting her to jump in. Maggie said, 'Just like it says on the box. Universal means universal. If you're a citizen or a semi-perm, you're eligible.'

'Means testing?'

'No. It's universal.'

Randall made a guttural sound. His voice shook as he spoke. 'Then explain, would you please, why you are intent on handing out government money to the extremely wealthy.'

'Because they're a part of this country, too. And they pay far more in tax, one way or another, than they'll receive as an Income.' She drew a breath, tried to channel some of Brij's assertiveness. 'But that's beside the point. If we start talking about who *deserves* to receive an Income, we fall into the same old trap. Our side says that the rich don't need more. They're greedy; they already take too much. And the conservatives whinge that the poor shouldn't get more, because they're lazy, or they're wicked. And straight away, we're having the same fight we always do. About morals. And it's a fight we always lose, because we're the ones trying to make change happen. Deep down, most people think that only others like themselves have earned a break.'

Maggie couldn't see Brij's face, couldn't tell if her boss thought that she was saying the right things. No one else spoke, and Maggie had been around politicians for long enough to know how rare that was, so she pressed. 'An Income isn't charity, and it's not a reward for individual merit or good behaviour. Think of it like a dividend. Collectively, we have built a society with extraordinary wealth' – at this, she detected a bristling – 'but that wealth isn't fairly distributed. With an Income we say: everyone deserves to share in what we've created. Everyone gets their dividend cheque. Some people will save that money, or invest it. Some will convert that money into time, by choosing to work less. And, yes, some will fritter it away. Spend it in shroudspace on virtual crap. Or buy specCoins. And that will be their decision.'

'Dividend ...' muttered someone up the back. 'Sounds capitalist.'

Maggie would not be deflected. 'If you take the U out of UBI, if you introduce qualifiers, then it becomes just another welfare scheme. Something the Libs will chip away at or dismantle when they get back in. But a true Income would be like Medicare was, once upon a time. What it might be again. People would come to see it as something like a right, a part of what it means to be here.'

'I don't know if I'll be able to vote for this,' said Randall. 'In all good conscience, I don't.'

'Have fun explaining that to FWE,' said Brij. In addition to her role as Treasurer, Freya Ward-Evans served as whip in the lower house. Since the merger of Labor and the Greens back in the thirties, OzProg MPs could vote against the party line in exceptional circumstances. But Randall would be radioactive to the leadership if he carried through with a dissenting vote on a key plank of the party's election platform.

'Don't forget,' Maggie said, 'we still need to get this past a pleb. It's got to be simple, and most people need to feel like they're benefiting. If we drop universality, then we create losers, and things get complicated.'

'Maggie's young and optimistic,' said Brij. 'She thinks we can bring the public along as we execute the broader program, and perhaps we can. But consider this for a moment: we don't know how long our turn will last. If we can do this, it will be a true legacy. It may not be perfect, but an Income is something we could achieve. *If* we all play it smart, and play as a team.'

'Much incrementalism,' said Sabra, in a gently mocking tone. 'Wow. It's good that we've got you here, a sensible pragmatist, to explain the limits of what we can achieve.'

Now Brij deigned to look straight at her, fixing Sabra with a cold smile. 'Always a pleasure. Now, I have a dinner booking with my wife, who I'm sure will be keen to offer her own list of the ways in which I've been a disappointment. We'll be in touch.'

When the rabble had cleared out, Maggie folded into one of the chairs across the desk from Brij. The fabric was still warm from the parliamentary bottom that had recently vacated it, and Maggie fished around in her bag for hand sanitiser.

'You'd think they'd be happier,' Maggie said.

'There's no pleasing those people,' Brij replied.

WHEN MAGGIE GOT BACK TO HER PLACE, SHE STOOD for a while in the frame of her newly repaired and repainted doorway, hesitating. But the cleaners had finished and, she'd been told, her damaged effects had all been replaced with near substitutes. A brochure for the new security firmware installed in the room assured her there was nothing to fear. Slipping off her shoes, she called Kei, explaining that she'd found herself in town for the night.

Just after she ended the call, a distinctive triple-chime sounded in her ear, meaning that one of her family was trying to reach her. In her overlay, she saw that Tez was trying to initiate a call. This was unprecedented, and Maggie almost accepted just to find out what was going on, but after the day she'd had, her reserves of patience and empathy – both vital qualities for any conversation with her brother – were depleted. Thirty seconds after the call rang out, she got a meeting request instead, fixed to take place in Tez's personal lobby in about a month's time. Intriguing. Maggie resolved to follow up as soon as she had the headspace.

Kei rolled in twenty minutes later. Together, they found ingredients for a Thai curry in the building's communal store. Run as a co-op and replenished daily by machines, it kept essentials for purchase by residents, to minimise reliance on individual deliveries. Whatever Maggie took was added to her next rental payment.

Arriving home, Maggie had felt drained, and she'd considered not letting Kei know that she was in town. But the thought of sharing a meal was appealing after so many nights spent by herself. She enjoyed watching him move about the kitchen, doing things differently to the ways she'd been taught. Maggie made a mess when she cooked, using superfluous bowls and utensils, not worrying about the clean-up until afterwards. But Kei stepped more lightly. He rinsed and re-used measuring cups, and cleaned up small spills as he went, brushing aside stray lemongrass husks and coriander to make room for serving bowls. It made him slow.

'What were you up to tonight?' he asked.

She told him about the meeting, and he listened sympathetically. She'd never really probed him too deeply about his own politics. She got the sense that he didn't have strong opinions, or, perhaps, that the opinions he did have were somewhat inchoate. Not for the first time, she wondered how he'd voted in the election.

'Which pollies were giving you a hard time?'

It seemed an oddly specific question to ask, if he was just trying to feign interest. 'Sabra Dean and Randall Fünf, mostly. But Pickering, Johannesen and Quan pushed back, too.' Seeing his blank expression, she teased him. 'You don't really know who any of those people are, do you?'

'… Not really.'

She got a call halfway through dinner, as they sat together at Maggie's small dining table. Maggie had already wolfed down her curry. The message in her feed was from Sydney; the Treasurer would be appearing on one of the morning wraps, and needed talking points in case she was asked about an Income. Maggie was relieved that she'd been asked to contribute. The Treasury folks could easily have decided to prepare a brief by themselves, and who knew what that would have looked like.

'I need to go dark,' Maggie said. 'Not sure how long I'll be, so you might want to go.' She stopped, thought about what she was saying. 'Sorry to muck you around.'

He swallowed his mouthful of food. 'No dramas. Just tell me what's going on.' Kei must have sensed her discomfort, and he wore a tolerant half-smile.

'I might be twenty minutes, or a couple of hours.'

'I'm already here, aren't I? I can check my feed. It's what I'd be doing if I was at home.'

Wiping her mouth with the back of her hand, she squeezed his shoulder and walked to her bedroom, closing the door behind her.

Insalata was mid-flap when Maggie cast in. 'Parameters,' he kept saying. 'She's got to be able to talk about the broad parameters. What we're ruling in, what we're ruling out.'

Maggie agreed, and pushed for Ward-Evans to confirm that the scheme would not be means tested; that it would be funded primarily by a corporate tax; and that it would be set at a level that would fund a dignified, if frugal, existence. 'Tell them that the Income will be pegged at sixty per cent of the median full-time wage. Those are the primary settings we've been modelling.'

Perhaps these were not the specifics that Insalata was looking for. 'Too risky,' he said. 'We need flex, at least until we've consulted more widely.'

They went round in circles for an hour and a half, Insalata looking for something concrete that the Treasurer could announce, without locking them into anything substantive. By the end, they managed to scrape together some talking points about fringe issues. The scheme would be administered by DHS. And it would replace unemployment benefits, but not family payments or other means-tested concessions.

'Ward-Evans should talk about *why* we're doing this,' said Maggie. 'Why it's the right thing for a wealthy, compassionate society to do for its people. Something like this is overdue, by about two decades.'

'Sure,' Insalata replied. 'Good thinking, Maggie. Thanks for your help tonight.'

When she came back, she found Kei on the couch, chuckling softly at something only he could see. He'd gathered and stowed their used dishes for collection, and wiped the countertop. She nudged him and they prepared for bed, getting in each other's way as they navigated Maggie's small ensuite. He took up a lot of space, and once ready, she retreated, sitting at the foot-end of her mattress. When he came to join her, already naked, she said, 'It's been a while.'

'It sure has.' His expression gave nothing away.

'We should have sex. And I want to, but … I don't really want to.'

'Oh.'

'Sorry, Kei.'

They lay down, and Maggie could feel the space he'd been careful to leave between them. 'It's okay,' she said. 'I'm just— my brain is jammed. I'm sick of people tonight. But not you.'

She held him until his warmth became too much, and then she rolled over and closed her eyes. In the morning they woke together, and it felt easier. They sat and shared the same feed of Ward-Evans' press conference.

When asked about an Income, the Treasurer said, 'It's an important reform that we're very keen to get done, and we're taking a prudent approach. We're consulting widely, and we're considering all the options. That's all I can say for now.'

CHAPTER 12

The measures we are announcing today are a culmination of almost three years of negotiation and cooperation, with tremendous amounts of goodwill and compromise on both sides. We should feel enormously proud of what we have accomplished here ...

Some have called this outsourcing, but nothing could be further from the truth. These arrangements represent the closest, most integrated, mutual military cooperation of any two nations in modern history. The measures counter the threat from the north, and recognise the reality that for decades, the matériel and know-how of our closest ally has been vital to Australia's warfighting capabilities.

Under the arrangements, The United States will maintain and operate Australian infrastructure, strictly for the purpose of defending Australian interests. Australia will make periodic financial contributions to support this arrangement, and American forces will continue to be stationed at Darwin, Broome, Cooktown, and Townsville, among other sites, but in an expanded capacity and role. With a corresponding diminution of Australia's own active roster of military personnel, we will see substantial efficiencies and savings ...

– Speech by Prime Minister Roy, 11 August 2043.
Transcript extracted in 'After the Thaw', Healey, 2052

ON SUNDAYS, TREASURY CLOSED AND THE OFFICE
was locked to all but senior management. Maggie used the time
to explore downtown Sydney, a task she undertook methodi-
cally, like a mollusc scraping a patch of sea floor. Ngunnawal
suffered from extremes of heat and cold, but at least it was
reliably dry. She was fascinated by the oppressive texture of
the air in the Harbour City. Her shroud told her to expect a
relieving storm within hours, but until it arrived, heat wept
from the roads and the concrete. On Pitt Street, she passed
a scrum of tourists pawing at their slick foreheads and pant-
ing as they struggled uphill from Circular Quay. The locals
parted for her, eyes pointed down, executing a compact scut-
tle as they plotted courses between air-conditioned lobbies
and arcades.

It hadn't always been such an inhospitable place, her parents
had told her. A generation ago, the sea walls still held and it was
more temperate, except maybe for a few weeks in summer. Even
now, after all the slow/quick change, Sydney had fared better
than the old coastal cities further north.

It was after midday. Even as she paced, a charity dinner was
taking place on the other side of the globe, in New York. In a
Q&A session, the guest of honour, the US Secretary of State,
had been asked about the new Australian government's plan to
introduce an Income.

It wasn't until Monday morning that a transcript lodged in
Maggie's feed.

*I tell you what, I'm surprised. An Income, that's like commu-
nism, right? They've got some new folks down there, they've been
out of power for a long time, and they've got all kinds of ideas*

[laughter] but I think this one will blow over. And if they're serious, they should remember the Alliance. Our two nations have a special relationship, and that's built on values. A shared economic philosophy. If the Aussies move away from that, we might need to rethink a whole lot of things.

Reading as she ate breakfast in her room, Maggie put down her bowl. Without thinking, she shook her head, which was a mistake, because the words hung fast in front of her eyes no matter which way she turned, and the effect was disorienting. Holding her temples, she cancelled out of her feed. The Secretary's comment had sounded scripted, workshopped. It was a deliberate effort to send a message.

Even worse, when she could bring herself to log back in, another item blinked for attention. DISSENT IN THE RANKS. An anonymous source had briefed a journalist about a meeting between Brij and a posse of disaffected OzProg MPs.

Maggie put a vidcall in to Brij. 'Do you want me to come back?'

'No,' Brij said, looking strained. 'We need eyes, now more than ever. Cabinet will assemble, and we've got to know what Ward-Evans is thinking.'

'I'll see what I can find out.'

'Good.' Brij paused, as if weighing her words. Perhaps she was deciding how much she thought Maggie was ready to hear. 'We knew there'd be resistance from the US, but I didn't expect them to be so blatant about it.'

'… Yeah.' Maggie was shaken.

'The PM will need to make a statement …' Brij trailed off, staring at her desk. When she looked back up at Maggie, there was resolve in the set of her jaw. 'You didn't tell anyone about our meeting last night, did you?'

Maggie thought about her conversation with Kei, what she might have let slip. She was glad that her avatar would not telegraph the heat rising in her face. 'No,' she said.

'Thought not. It'll be one of those idiot backbenchers, trying to work their way in with the content spinners.'

Maggie murmured noncommittally. 'If you hear anything about which way the government's leaning on this, let me know, okay?'

'Will do.'

AT TREASURY, THE CORRIDORS AND THE SPRAWLING, open-plan desk farms were unusually quiet. Most of the staff kept to their assigned workspaces, and the few that moved between offices trod with grim purpose. She had been working with these people for weeks now, but Maggie remained an outsider, and she sensed her colleagues drawing back, avoiding eye contact, as she moved about, looking for intelligence.

In the end, it was Felix that found her. He was here in person this time. 'Mags,' he said solemnly, but he couldn't quite disguise his excitement. 'Bloody Americans, am I right?'

'Why are you here. Like, *here*?'

A look of hurt swept over his face. 'We're in this together. I'm just trying to help.' He led her to a side room.

Insalata and Trish were already there, swapping whispers. Trish wouldn't meet Maggie's eyes, but Bradley said, 'I'm glad we caught you. We're all just waiting. But if the decision is what we expect, then I want you to know that we'll keep working closely, to make sure no one is embarrassed by the change of direction.'

'What do you mean?' asked Maggie. She knew well enough, but she wanted to make Insalata say it.

He kept his tone conversational. 'There are a few options. Brij could say that she's polled her grantors, and that there isn't as much support for an Income as she'd thought. Or a strategic leak could come from this office. Treasury has done modelling, and the scheme is projected to cost more than originally thought. Regrettably, it can't be done. Something like that.'

Felix sat in the corner, watching. Maggie turned to look at him straight on, inviting him to weigh in. He must have been in contact with Chase, and she desperately wanted to know whether the Reeves would back away, now that it was clear that the Americans disapproved.

'Pause,' Felix said, flashing a determined expression at Insalata and Trish. 'I know what that American lady said, but an Income is OzProg policy. And some important harvesters have tied themselves to this. No one can afford to give up.'

'This won't pass a pleb, now,' Trish said mournfully. 'Forget about the Chinese; the bloody Kiwis could invade us if the Americans withdraw.'

'Like it or not,' Insalata added, 'We're a protectorate. We never should have allowed outsourcing. It was the middle of the Cold War – maybe we never really had a choice. Either way, Australia listens when America speaks.'

Maggie shook her head. It was exactly what she'd expected from these bureaucrats, but to hear it confirmed left a bleak, tight feeling in Maggie's chest. Whatever his deficiencies, Salad Boy knew how to read the wind. Still, Maggie protested. 'I don't accept that. There's a way to steer this.'

'Maybe,' said Insalata. 'But that's not what Ward-Evans thinks.'

SHE LEFT THEM WITHOUT ANOTHER WORD. IT WAS abrupt, but she had to go. Everything Maggie had worked for was slipping. She found an empty darkroom, buzzed Kinnear. Five minutes later, he opened his private room to her.

She didn't have time for pleasantries. 'What are you hearing?'

He tutted and shook his head. 'You first. What's the mood on Market Street?'

In her need, she felt no compunction, and she related what Insalata had said almost word for word. 'He thinks we're cooked.'

Kinnear rolled his eyes. 'Insalata,' he intoned, 'is a chihuahua. He's been promoted above his station.'

'But do you think he's right?'

'He knows where his loyalties lie. And Ward-Evans is on Team America. She'll be pushing hard to abandon an Income and issue a grovelling apology.'

'You're not reassuring me.'

Kinnear's avatar vaulted upwards from where he stood, somersaulted three times in the air, and landed in the centre of the room on one foot. It was a crude effect, something a child might orchestrate. Outside of fantasy and roleplaying spaces, it was crass to do anything in shroudspace that shattered the illusion of reality. But this was Kinnear's room, and his rules. 'You're forgetting,' Kinnear said, showing his teeth, 'that Freya Ward-Evans is detested by most of her own party. The Left, in particular, resent what's become of our country at the hands of an ostensible ally. *My* minister will be arguing that now's the perfect time to chart a more independent course.'

'Tan? Does he have enough sway?'

'He'll have support around the Cabinet table. The real unknown is which way the PM will break. Notionally, he represents an old emerald-green electorate, but the pressures of office ...' Kinnear shrugged. 'We'll know soon.'

'What can I do in the meantime? There must be a way to nudge this.'

'Your boss will be working her contacts,' Kinnear said languidly. 'But I doubt even she can change anyone's mind at this late stage. People think what they think. For you, best to find shelter and wait.' He cocked his head, as if a thought had occurred. 'I know a few people up past Cairns, in the Surrender. The kids of conservationists, who found a way to stick it out, after their parents' warnings came to pass. If you want to take some time, drop off grid, I could make a call.'

The suggestion was ludicrous. More than ever, Maggie needed to be where the action was. 'Thanks, but I'm not looking to escape.'

'Not escape, just a reset. Keep it in mind. The way we live, it's not good for you. Or me. Or anyone.'

THAT EVENING, THE PRIME MINISTER SPOKE. MAGGIE
and Felix had spent the day with Treasury people, and now a
large group had remained in the breakroom, wanting to be
together as they learned the fate of their project. It brought
home to Maggie that despite their differing allegiances, despite
the fact that she still felt alien, many in this building had been
working hard in service of her project. The lights had been
dimmed almost to black, the better for casting, and they waited
in silence, physically together but each watching from their own
preferred vantage point in shroudspace.

The PM favoured an intimate format for public announce-
ments. Every dult tuning in found themselves in an old-fashioned
sitting room, a facsimile of a real room at The Lodge, the Prime
Minister's Ngunnawal residence. The vantage point was fixed –
there was no moving about the room – and showed the view
from an armchair directly opposite where the PM would sit once
he arrived. Everyone watching in real time would be afforded
the same position, as if they'd been granted a private audience. Of course, not every dult could ask questions and expect
a response, so two hand-picked journalists occupied seats off
to the side to act as interlocutors once the PM had finished his
opening remarks.

There was an art to this mode of communication, and not
all politicians had mastered it. It had something to do with plain
speaking, while providing just enough detail to present credibly.
Warm, but not patronising. Jack Alpin, the new Prime Minister, was a virtuoso. Brij had told Maggie that in the old days,
they used to talk about politicians who dog-whistled, which
meant sending a message that would only register with a specific

target group. Brij said that Alpin could harmonise, by which she meant that he could deliver multiple, almost mutually-exclusive messages in a single sound-bite. Since OzProg had won the election, he'd been feted by his party as some sort of political savant. Riding a post-victory wave of approval, he had capital to spend. He was too smart to spend it on a lost cause.

Maggie watched as he materialised in the chair across from her. They were so close that it felt like she should be able to reach forward and put a hand on his knee. By this stage, after a long campaign, she had watched him in this setting so many times it felt like dropping by a close friend's house for a chat, an impression Alpin did nothing to discourage. He smiled as if delighted to see her – even though he couldn't see her – and said, 'Thanks for coming, I've got something I wanted to talk to you about.' His brown eyes searched, commanding her attention. Slim, in his early fifties, with thick, close-cropped chestnut hair, he'd won the androphile vote by a thumping margin. Maggie was a professional; she understood the tricks he was employing. Even so, she was not immune to his appeal, and despite all she had riding on this, she felt herself settle into a posture of still attentiveness.

'Let's talk about Income,' he said gently. 'It's an idea that we took to the election. It's very popular, but it's also complicated. I'll try and give you the outline.' He flashed a self-deprecating grin, as if unsure whether he could remember his lines. 'It's about giving people freedom, true freedom, to flourish and make a contribution. Whether that's through paid employment, volunteering, or family support. Everyone who pitches in should be recognised for that, and a humane society doesn't let anyone fall through the cracks.'

The PM leaned forward, as if sharing a confidence. 'Sounds great, right? And we want to make it happen, if we can afford it and also maintain a strong economy. So right now, a team at Treasury are trying to work that out. They're checking if this is doable, and making recommendations about what the details should be. Once they're done, I'll look at the findings and share them with you.

'I've had some questions today about how our allies feel about our plan. No—' he held up his left hand, index finger raised. 'I should be specific. There was a comment out of the United States overnight, and I want to respond to that.' This would all have been scripted, so the hesitation would have been a confection.

'The OzProg platform is clear,' Alpin continued. 'The US is Australia's friend and steadfast ally. And Australia has an absolute right to determine our own domestic policy, and the US has always recognised and supported that. And we'll be consulting very closely with our American counterparts on this, like we would any major new initiative.

'I hope that answers some of the things you might have been wondering about. I think Cate and Rahim might have some more questions,' he turned to the two journalists waiting to his right, 'so, over to you.'

A half-muffled yell brought Maggie back to her body. A scattered burst of applause swept the breakroom before faltering, as these public servants remembered that they were meant to be apolitical. Still, the sentiment was clear.

'—talking about *us*. Did you hear?'

'What was that stuff about making a contribution? Does he mean some kind of work test?'

'He wouldn't have talked about how great an Income is if he wanted to kill it.'

Several people came up to Maggie and bumped fists, or clapped her on the shoulder. It felt like camaraderie, like she was finally part of this strange team.

From across the room, Insalata caught Maggie's eye and shook his head in thankful disbelief. *We're on*, he mouthed to her. In her eye, a message from Brij arrived: *[There's still a path. It's narrow, but there's a path.]*

Felix found her as she headed for the elevator. 'Congratulations,' he said.

She was so relieved that she forgot, momentarily, how much he annoyed her. 'Thanks.'

'Looks like you'll still be needing Uncle Chase.'

'We'll see. Either way, you might as well stick around.' She was too relieved to let him bring her down.

TRISH CAUGHT UP TO MAGGIE ON THE GROUND FLOOR, just before she passed the exit gate. 'Hey.'

'Hey,' Maggie replied, curious as to what Trish might have to say that couldn't wait, or couldn't be said in text.

'Um, a few of us are getting together tonight in the rec room back home. For a party.' The halting way Trish spoke conveyed her meaning clearly enough.

'You mean, like a tryst?'

'Yeah.'

'How many's a few?'

'Oh, probably ten, twelve or so.' Her eyes shifted around

the lobby. 'There's, ah, a couple of people who were hoping you'd join.'

Sex wasn't mandatory at these kinds of gatherings, but it was the usual outcome. Trysts were common among work teams, notoriously so in the insular world of the public service, and some managers advocated the group-cohesion benefits of regular sessions.

Maggie was flattered to be asked. It was a signal that they trusted her enough to want to include her. She wondered if Felix had been invited. Probably not, or Trish could have approached them both earlier, when they'd been speaking by the elevator. She was conscious that if she turned down this invitation, Trish and Insalata might take it as a slight. And then there was Kei. She'd told him she didn't want to fool around; had insisted that he should also refrain. Then again, if she called him up, told him that she'd had a change of heart, and released him to explore other possibilities while she remained in Sydney, she didn't think he'd object too strenuously.

After the first crash of conflicting thoughts, she pulled back, tried to determine what it was she wanted. It had been a long week, and being alone gave rise to certain frustrations. But that was something she could take care of herself; that was what holos and toys were for. As for intimacy, she wouldn't find it at a tryst. Her feeling of being an intruder among these people would only be stronger in that kind of setting. At some basic level, the idea of taking part turned her off.

Trish was waiting for an answer. Maggie said, 'I'd love to. But I'm kind of in this committed thing. I know that sounds prudish, but ...'

'No, not at all. They must be a catch.'

'They are. Have fun, though.'

In a complete inversion of the no-nonsense persona she cultivated during work hours, Trish flashed a lascivious smile. 'We will.'

CHAPTER 13

Matev's insight was to realise that in fact, wealth *does* trickle down from the wealthy to the poor; but that through influence over policy, anti-competitive collusion, and efforts to prevent workers from organising, the ultra-rich have almost perfect control over downward flow, and the rate of recovery via consumer pricing ...

In her second treatise, Matev expanded the idea to posit what is now called the 'Matev Contention': Let f be the minimum rate of trickle-down wealth transfer at which the general population can be maintained in a productive, quiescent state. It can be shown that f is a function of the costs of keeping citizens fed, healthy and reasonably content. The latter element can be optimised through a variety of strategies including diversionary entertainment, promotion of a shared purpose and culture (via, eg, nationalism or religion), and active suppression of dissident elements. Matev demonstrated that real returns to capital via corporate profits can slightly exceed the trickle-down rate, effectively indefinitely, such that social stability can be maintained even while most people experience sustained negative wealth accumulation ...

No major national government has ever pursued *f* overtly as a policy goal. But seminars on Matevian economics continue to be well attended by decision makers and senior public servants ...

> – Extract from 'Subterranean Homesick Government: The Hidden Agendas Driving Modern Policy', Sharpe, 2054

THE PATHWAY HAD RAISED EDGES THAT CAME UP TO Maggie's knees, as if she stood in a large gutter. There were no other railings or supports, and when she looked over the side to the canyon far below, she had to fight back a wave of vertigo. Ahead, the path curled to the right as it ran, exposing arched columns beneath, like an old Roman aqueduct. The whole structure was made from white brick, white mortar, showing no sign of dust or wear, and only shadows cast by a light overhead marked the edges of each component. It was uncomfortably white. Where the canyon ended, kilometres away, a massive spire jutted like a fang from a gum.

Something was wrong with the horizon. The ground bent upward as it went, like the base of a mountain, but there was no end, and as her head tilted backward, her mind finally made sense of the input: she was inside a gargantuan sphere, with a pale sun at its core. When she focused on a group of large structures protruding from the inverse side, like stalactites, the effect was more than a little unsettling.

Tez's lobby. She had never been here before.

He faded in directly in front of her. 'Ready?' he asked.

'What exactly are we doing?' The meeting request, sent weeks earlier, had been curt. *[Something you'll want to see.]*

It was so out of character for him to extend an invitation, to include her in anything that he was involved in, that she couldn't ignore it.

His mouth settled into a smirk, aware that he had her interest. He looked around, upwards and over his shoulder. 'What do you think of the place?'

'It's ... stark,' she said honestly, and then realising that this sounded harsh, she hurried on. 'I mean. It's wonderful, grandiose ...' She thought of the warmth and reassuring imperfection of Kinnear's environment, his well-trodden theatre stage. 'Doesn't it make you lonely? If you can do all this just for yourself, why don't you get into environment design?' She didn't mean to nag, but she couldn't help herself. Ever since Liv and Raman had given up on him, she was the only one that would even try.

His self-satisfied expression dissolved. 'Do you know what the tensile strength of bamboo is? Pine? Carbon nanotubes? I spent years learning that shit.' His eyelids drooped, like he'd found himself stuck in an old rut. 'Which was pointless, because those are all things that a bot can know, and recite with less error. My point is, shroudspace is for pretenders.'

She shrugged an apology. He had always been prickly, and a near decade spent alone in his room hadn't improved matters. She remembered him as a child of ten or eleven. She had idolised him, with his quiet proficiency and his self-possession. Back then, it was Maggie who'd set the agenda, deciding what game they should play, or how they should explore the walled gardens of kids' shroudspace. In the intervening years, he hadn't lost his preference for someone else to provide direction.

'Let's just go,' he said, extending his arm. She offered her hand, or at least the shroudspace replica of her hand, supplying the finger pattern that would grant him a temporary right to control her avatar's location.

Tez's lobby dissolved, and she found herself peering into glare, toward a setting sun, standing on a grass-covered embankment above water. When she turned and saw the crowd, she recognised their location: the edge of the occupation outside the DHS building. Scattered camps and fires ringed the lake, but most people had packed in tight along Soward Way, tighter than they could have managed if they'd all been here in meat form, crowding the bridge and thronging in the gardens. There were vastly more people here now than there had been when Maggie visited Kinnear IRL, three months prior. Awed, she called up a window showing a live aerial view. The protest ringed the DHS for almost a kilometre in every direction – there must have been hundreds of thousands. Impressive, even for a mostly virtual event that might disperse at a moment's notice. For now, there was a weird energy, with most avatars facing the same way, toward the building, like iron filings pointed at a magnet.

'What are we doing?' Maggie asked. She'd been hassled last time she'd come here, and returning made her uneasy.

'I heard something on the boards ... made me think of you. Come on,' he said, setting off toward the main body of the crowd. She hadn't yet cancelled his permissions, so her avatar followed obediently.

There was still plenty of cosplay, ample evidence that the people assembled had spent too long tweaking the look of their avatars. There were swamp creatures and fire twirlers and goths and anthropomorphised kangaroos. But the levity she'd noticed last time, the carnival atmosphere, seemed brittle. In its place was agitation only just held in check, like the feeling at a concert the second before the band takes the stage. As she was pulled deeper, she caught snatches of conversation:

'… heard it was tonight.'

'But that's the problem with these distributed movements …'

'… don't think anyone has laid out demands, exactly.'

'We got them. We got them scared.'

Hands still linked, Tez pulled Maggie to a stop on the flat cap of a virtual rampart bisecting the front garden. Last time there had been a wooden stockade acting as the focal point for the occupation, but it must have been deleted, and now there was a clear view of the building's entrance about forty metres in front of them. She could see stiffly-dressed public servants filing out at the end of their shift and into an assault of augmented vision and noise, doing all they could to ignore the weird sensation of moving through projected humans as they joined queues for transport. Below and all around her the shifting mass of avatars jiggled as server farms around the world tried to map positions and simulate virtual collisions.

Tez turned to her, motioning outward at the crowd. 'Do you ever feel … like you're watching things from a distance? Like a tourist?'

Maggie absolutely did, but it was a strange question to ask while they were hemmed in on all sides. 'In what way?'

'Just that most of these people, they're living this in a way that you and I don't. They're really out of options. I've met some of them recently, like IRL, and—'

It was getting difficult to hear her brother. Starting somewhere behind, and rolling forward around them, a chant gathered volume like a rumbling belch: NO MORE TIME! NO MORE TIME! NO MORE TIME!

This didn't feel right. 'Tez, seriously, what's going on?'

'Just wait. I think whatever it is … should happen soon.'

A white fabric sheet slid down the side of the building. An effect: all the movement and sound assaulting her senses was augmentation, a product of shroudspace. Still, the blooming of this vacant field commanded attention.

An image was projected onto the sheet – a screen, Maggie saw now, like people used to watch cinematograph films on. Dropping her gaze to the front entrance of the building, Maggie could see that it was an expanded live view of a bot standing by itself. Humanoid, ash-skinned, it was a rudimentary virtual envoy, dispatched here and now to deliver a message, which it would do in a polite, affectless tone. Corporates sent them as reminders to pay bills, and the unscrupulous used them for light harassment, since the sender's anonymity could be preserved.

'OzProg could have stopped this,' it said, sounding almost human, a tightly framed shot of its head and shoulders replicated at massive scale on the screen above, its words amplified and synchronised. 'But they hold you in contempt. They could make enough work. Honest labour, environment and community projects – they've admitted it. But instead they want to bribe you. Turn you into a quiet, obedient consumer. Well fuck that,' it relayed without feeling. 'They are out of time.'

A hush descended, as those assembled took in the message and the messenger. But then came a roar of approval. Incoherent shouting resolved once more into organised insistence: *NO MORE TIME! NO MORE TIME!*

'We create our future. We need clear ground.'

Message delivered, the bot executed a curt bow and vanished. Maggie glanced at Tez, who was watching with rapt attention. She had never known him to engage in this way; could not have said what part of this had reached him.

Because her eyes were on Tez, Maggie heard the blast before she saw it. The sound was so loud that back in the room where her body was located, reclined in a chair as she engaged with her shroud, limiters tripped, protecting her ears from damage. A ringing distortion lasted for less than a second – and she turned back to the DHS building.

She couldn't feel the explosion. And surely there would be nothing to feel, even if she'd been there in meatspace. An effect, like all the other stunts the protesters had pulled. Around her, dults overcame their initial surprise and started to laugh, gesturing obscenely toward the huge office as ejecta rained on the garden and the street.

The debris was a finicky detail. Metal shrapnel, lumps of concrete and splintered glass, thrown from the site of the blast. What had been the right-hand corner of the building, a few floors up, was now obscured by smoke. It had been a brief, sharp bang, loud and concussive, and now it was over. The designer probably should have added a large orange fireball, flaring upwards into the sky with a deep bass rumble. This was almost an anticlimax.

Half a minute passed before DHS workers, shaken, some bleeding, emerged from the doors. Those that could still run did so, cradling themselves. The demonstrators closest broke off their chanting, looking here and there, hands touching temples to mute all overlays. Tez did the same, and without thought, so did Maggie. Everything fake receded, but the smoke, the debris, the victims – those things remained. And Maggie saw what was in front of her, again, for the first time: this was violence.

Around her, a scattering of lights blinked on as avatars started to record. But most of the demonstrators wished themselves away. She could hear the spoken safe word, *Sever!*, rolling through the crowd, until the garden began to empty, and she felt exposed up on the rampart. As the smoke began to clear, she got a better look at what was littering the ground: stationery, fake plants, tattered items of clothing. She saw a mangled portrait of an old balding man, and she remembered stepping out of that first meeting with Kinnear, and into the soulless hall where the picture had hung. From somewhere on the other side of the lake, sirens blared. As bodies gave way to absence, she turned to look at Tez. His face was naked with horror.

'Tell me what you know.'

'I didn't— you don't understand,' he stuttered. And before Maggie could reach out, her brother was gone.

WINTER

CHAPTER 14

The True Values party was established by former Liberal and independent politicians on 17 December, 2033. We represent people of faith, character and conscience.

Our Values:

Freedom of religion

Tolerance of traditional practices

Strengthening of tax exemptions for faith-based organisations

Promotion of a clean and good lifestyle

– 'About Us,' True Values Australia

[n:tva.pol, accessed 18:19:54 15-MAR-2058]

The True Values split was an expression of supreme pragmatism. None of the factions – the Pentecostals; conservative Jewish, Muslim and Buddhist sub-groups; the Scientologists – had much love for their fellow travellers. But, as one of their leaders noted on that boiling night in December, 'The enemy of my enemy is my friend. Our enemies are legion, but so too is the brotherhood of everyone who lends us strength.' Another responded: 'Jewish halakha and Muslim fiqh can never be compatible. But both share more with each other than with the degenerate creed of the Liberal Party.' Disdain for the irreligious has proved a powerful binding force: the Truvies have been more united, and more effective, than most could have imagined.

– H. Barry Zimmerman, 'Sounding the Trumpet',

[n:essay/hbzim/truvies, accessed 18:43:09 15-MAR-2058]

MAGGIE AND FELIX BLINKED ONTO A PLATFORM abutting the exclusion zone around Ulu̱ru. Maggie was tired of spectacle, but she'd had no say in the location for this meet. Beside her, Felix rolled his head from side to side, as if his neck was stiff.

The True Values Party had agreed to dispatch a triumvirate. If they were planning to dismiss her out of hand, they surely wouldn't have done that. And while privately, Maggie shared the view of most progressives that the Truvies were irrational at best, and hypocrites at worst, ignoring these people was out of the question. More than any other political organisation, they owned their flock. Almost without exception, their aligned harvesters and grantors voted in lock-step with party leadership, with practically no leakage on individual plebs. While they didn't pose a threat in the new House, Maggie was all too aware that unless she received benediction here, the Truvies' base, representing more than fifteen per cent of the voting public, would default to opposition when the question of an Income came up.

To the discomfort of the A̱nangu who owned and cared for the land, the red rock had been co-opted by the True Values Party as a symbol of religious freedom. For their part, the Truvies had taken it upon themselves to keep the monolith and the surrounding sacred sites clear in shroudspace, by doxxing the trolls and militant atheists who, in deliberate disregard of the local custodians' wishes, cast themselves on to the summit. As assistance went, it was useful but unsolicited, and the Anangu no doubt remembered prior occasions on which help had been imposed from outside, and the legacy of intervention. The extent to which the Truvies should be tolerated, and what form any resistance might take, were topics of continuing debate.

The bluestone pad Maggie and Felix had spawned on was octagonal, about the size of a tennis court, and they found themselves alone. When Maggie focused on Uluru, a popup informed her that it was 1.2 kilometres south-southwest from where they stood. With no other structures to offer comparison, its gargantuan scale was hard to process, giving rise to a sensation like mild vertigo. As a child, Maggie had felt the same way when she'd looked at the full moon and attempted to truly internalise the distance and size of that object. The rock interrupted a white-blue horizon line that deepened into rich azure as her gaze drifted upward. There were no clouds visible in any direction, and the sun shouted over Maggie's right shoulder, lancing rays at the concrete they stood on, and at the spinifex, mulga and desert oaks beyond. The variety of green in this landscape, dark and dusky and vivid, set against the soil and the sky, took Maggie by surprise. A patch of white daisies bloomed on the far side of the platform – there had been early rain this year. Her shroud informed her that the ambient temperature was twenty-two degrees, not so different to where her body lay back in her room at Homebush. She wished she could take a lungful of the dry, clean air.

Maggie had done her homework, and when the trio materialised, it was not difficult to guess who was who. Spiritual leaders of their respective communities, turned to the squalid business of politics: the long-limbed blond with the wispy moustache was an evangelical Christian named Saul; smiling, bearded Nasir al-Ouda, a Salafi Muslim from the activist tradition, had arresting, gentle green eyes; and Prak Yav, a Theravāda Buddhist, was fine-featured and almost skeletal, head shaven. All three wore white business shirts and black trousers, a uniform borrowed from the Witnesses and, by Truvie custom, deployed when attentions turned from the spiritual to the secular.

Felix took it upon himself to handle the introductions. Perhaps he thought that a display of chauvinism was called for. When he'd finished, Nasir leaned past the kid and spoke directly to Maggie. 'We're very interested in your idea, and we'd like to know more.'

'We have concerns,' added Prak.

'Of course,' said Maggie, internally bracing herself for another round of justifications. In the few days since the bombing, she'd grown thoroughly sick of talking, to others and most of all to herself. It had been difficult to keep her thoughts in order, to not let herself be derailed by memories of the attack which came to her unbidden at all times of the day and night. She wasn't exactly feeling eloquent, but for the sake of the cause she put on her game face. 'I know that True Values and Australian Progressive platforms can seem far apart, even opposed. But sometimes I think we forget the intersections. OzProg conceives of itself as a party of compassion.'

'No one has done more for the working poor than us,' Saul announced, and as sanctimonious as that sounded, he may have been right. The Truvies had fought hardest against creeping automation of the service industries. In the process, they'd become the natural home of the trade union movement, or what remained of it.

'Do you have faith?' Nasir asked Maggie.

It was hard to know if any response could please them all, but Maggie didn't hesitate. On this matter, at least, she knew herself. 'I'm not religious. I have hope that we can leave a better world behind than the one we've inherited. As for what happens after we die, I don't think we can know.'

Nasir looked over at Felix. 'And you?'

'Plus one to what Maggie said. Many paths up the mountain?'

They gave Maggie time to sketch the outline of the Income scheme. She tried to emphasise how it would give people freedom to set their own course. With their material needs secure, dults would have more time to think about higher matters, including the spiritual. Maybe she was laying it on too thick: Saul and Nasir didn't give much away, but Prak didn't bother to hide his disdain. As she spoke, the five of them shifted instinctively to stand in a ragged line, each facing more or less southward, as if the monolith would deliver its own judgement.

Speaking in this place made Maggie feel mercantile, like she was trying to sell crypto. It was cynical and gross to use this place to conduct politics, but the Truvies had their reasons. Despite everything, the land had its effect, juxtaposing all things said and done here with a presence that was profound, substantial and slow; a temporal mode dissimilar to the way she had always lived. When she trailed off, Felix started to add something, but Maggie silenced him.

'You know that we favour a jobs guarantee,' Prak said abruptly.

'With respect, an Income will provide the same benefits, but it will be more far-reaching. Some people can't work, and some would prefer not to. We can look after those people, too.'

'What does this policy mean for you?' asked Nasir.

'Sorry?'

His eyes sought hers, holding her gaze. 'How does this benefit you, personally?'

'Well ... it won't have much impact, since I'm working thirty-five hours. I'll probably have to pay more tax, directly or indirectly, than I get back through the Income.'

Saul intervened. 'Nasir isn't suggesting that you're financially self-interested. But when we evaluate any complex proposal, we like to know who we're dealing with. How do you *feel* about this idea?'

'I support it. I'm passionate about it.' Judging by quizzical expression Nasir returned, Maggie suspected she'd missed the mark. Prak raised an eyebrow, his avatar's slightly hunched posture suggesting that in meatspace, his body was tapping out a private message to his colleagues.

Saul cleared his throat, and tried again. 'You must have worked hard to earn your place with Harvester Sutton.'

'Yes ...'

'And your work gives you purpose, and recognition. It's hard work, right? Believe me, we know! So you deserve to be recognised.'

'I don't ...' She stopped, and thought about what Brij might say if she'd been here. 'I'd like to think so, yes.'

'You are ambitious,' Prak said flatly.

'That's not a criticism,' Nasir added. 'We're all ambitious, or else none of us would be here, with the honour and burden of representing others.'

Saul picked up the thread. 'So, you believe in merit. Some people achieve highly, and that should be encouraged.' Maggie could tell that he was building to something, but nonetheless she inclined her head, conceding the point.

Saul turned to glance at his colleagues, silently checking in before he continued. 'My father was a delivery driver. One of the last. He brought home a pittance. When even that was too much for the corporates to pay, when a trike could do it cheaper, we all suffered. And so, after my outreach year, I joined the party, because I don't want any other family to live through that experience. I feel it in my heart.'

Maggie nodded, trying to show him that she got it. 'I've seen how the system treats people I love. It's capricious.'

'You know it in your head. But your heart is mute.'

Felix took a half step forward. 'Wait up. I've been working this with Mags for a while now. She's all in, and so am I.'

'It's difficult to hear you,' Prak replied. Smoothly, he edged past Felix and came to stand directly in front of Maggie, too close for comfort, their eyes almost level. Unsmiling, taking his time, he scrutinised her, as if he could see into her soul. Maggie wondered if he really thought this would yield some insight. More likely, it was mystical theatre that the Truvies employed to spook lobbyists. Either way, Maggie returned Prak's stare, willing herself not to blink as the seconds crawled by.

Finally, he snorted and backed off. 'I think you're full of shit,' he announced.

There was little else to add. Maggie and Felix quietly traded looks. After a moment, Nasir said, 'If you'll give us some time, we'll discuss and return with a response.' Not waiting for affirmation, the three Truvies blinked out.

Conscious of the semi-public locale, and that anyone could be listening, Maggie kept her thoughts to herself. She disliked fundamentalists, with their perfect certainty born of spurious evidence. And the whole True Values arrangement, a marriage of convenience between incompatible faiths, felt grubby. She'd just spent half an hour trying to mask those feelings under a layer of polite formality, but maybe her distaste had been apparent, after all.

Felix paced around the viewing platform, crouching to inspect the rust-coloured sand at the edge of the stone, but unable to take it in his hands. Bent over like that, facing away from her, his avatar's cherry red underwear riding up past the belt of his trousers, Maggie was briefly overcome by an impulse to aim a kick at his rear. But for all his lack of substance, he'd at least tried to lend his support.

The triumvirate was gone for a full ten minutes. When they returned, Saul wasted no time, stepping out in front of his associates. 'This is a formal statement on behalf of the True Values Party,' he said in the practiced way of someone reciting a well-learned script, 'which I will deliver and which I call on my brothers to witness and record.' Prak and Nasir bowed their heads.

'We have discussed and reached a consensus that reflects our principles and gives due regard to our diverse traditions.

'You suggest that freeing humans from the need to work will lead to a flourishing. We do not share your optimism.

'You speak of dignity, and freedom, as if those things are the same. We say, there is dignity in work, even menial work. Even exploitative, degrading work. The value of work is inherent, separate from its fruits. You may not understand that.' Behind Saul's shoulder, Prak grunted his support.

'In explaining our reasons, I find myself reaching for what I learned as a child. "The poor you will always have with you." I believe this to be the word of God. My brothers agree with the sentiment, at least. Indeed, we go further: the poor we *should* always have with us, as a lesson. They are part of the natural order, and if you find yourself facing resistance,' he looked directly into Maggie's eyes, 'You might ask yourself whether you are trying to impose something that cannot be. Our duty is to offer consolation where suffering occurs. To believe that we can eliminate suffering is hubris.'

When it was clear that Saul was done, Felix cleared his throat. 'Okay. We can respect that,' he said, though it didn't sound like he meant it. 'But I know you guys. Whatever else you are, you're political animals. You might hate the Libs, but you've propped them up for a long time. To get what you want, you've done deals that would make the Antichrist blush. So let's be real: what's your price?'

Instinctively, Felix's bluntness appalled Maggie, but she could see the sense in it. It was what Cass might have done. They'd tried the respectful approach and got nowhere. Maybe it was time to be transactional.

But Nasir shook his head. 'No price.' Though his voice did not suggest anger, it was firm. 'There are no terms on which we could support this, especially with so much attention. That said, we would welcome the support of Bridget Sutton, and Chase Reeve, for our jobs guarantee.'

Returning Nasir's gaze, sensing that this was her final chance to sway them, she threw caution to the wind. 'The poor and desperate are your *base*. If their lives improved, maybe they wouldn't need the Truvies anymore. Is that what scares you?'

Nasir pursed his lips. 'You fight, and you doubt, and you lie to yourself. An Income means professional advancement for Maggie Garewal, personal achievement for Maggie Garewal, and you crave those things because like most godless people, you have no centre. My counterpart,' – he motioned toward Saul – 'quotes often from his holy book, sometimes flippantly.' Saul gasped in mock offence.

'But here it seems apt,' Nasir continued. 'Why do you attend to the speck of sawdust in your brother's eye, and pay no attention to the plank in your own?'

COMING BACK, FINDING HERSELF ALONE IN A DORM room, felt like the cutting of some wire that had been holding her upright. Maggie felt a sadness she couldn't place. It was early afternoon, and the hall outside was silent. She sagged against the wall at the top of her bed, half propped up by pillows, and felt the ache in her back from slouching too long. She should check in with Kei. Jesus, she should call her mother. Instead, she tried Tez again for what felt like the hundredth time. But he wouldn't pick up.

He'd been dodging her ever since the bombing, nine days earlier. Maggie couldn't escape the news, and at work they'd had a series of crisis meetings about what it might mean. Five killed, scores injured. And, somehow worse: mere hours after the physical attack, the digital lives of the dead had been comprehensively erased, potentially forever, and no one could identify the culprits. It should have been impossible, to disappear information so extensive and distributed, leaving hardly a trace. Those left mourning could build no shrines, could not use chat logs and government records, images and sound, to construct a simulation of their loved one. It was unthinkable, to lose five people so totally from the world, like they'd never existed.

No one had claimed responsibility for the violence or subsequent erasure, and yet it had been widely construed as an escalation of the pro-work protests. If Prime Minister Alpen would just come out with something strong, that the government wouldn't be cowed by terrorists, that they would redouble their efforts to provide income security, Maggie knew they'd win people over. Some good could come from this, if it were handled well.

Physical attacks were almost an impossibility. Everyone with a shroud knew that their location was being tracked. And everything was a camera: people, walls, doors. So how had someone manoeuvred a loitering explosive – a self-destructing drone, picked up later in replays as a dark blur lancing into the side of the building – without being identified? The police would be working through a list, Maggie was sure, of everyone who'd been there, in meatspace or by shroud, when it happened. Maggie's name would be on that list, and so would Tez's. What would she say when she got the call? What *could* she say, other than that her brother had invited her? What if the press found out that someone on Brij's staff had been there? What would Brij make of it when *she* found out? Her boss might conclude that Maggie had become a liability to their own cause.

She had been present at a mass-murder. She repeated that fact to herself, deliberately, like she was trying it out. It still didn't seem real, didn't carry the emotional payload that those words ought. When Maggie forced herself to think about it for any length of time, she just felt tired, like she wanted to crawl under a heavy blanket, but that was unhelpful. Until she could corner Tez, or until she was cornered, the only thing she could think to do was swallow the fear and the stress and keep working. Hence the Truvies.

The poor you will always have with you – how pathetic. This was precisely the attitude she rejected, the kind of blithe defeatism that spurred her on. Could she only explain her mission when confronted with its opposite? Surely that was not so unusual, but perhaps, this late in the game, it was irresponsible. For the rest of the afternoon she chewed this over, kept asking herself whether her lack of self-knowledge, of faith – funny to use that word – might be thwarting her.

In her short career as a policy advisor, Maggie had paid careful attention. She made a study of the kind of people who succeeded, and they had found a way to jettison all self-doubt. Like Brij: Maggie tried to imagine her boss pacing her office back in Ngunnawal, beset by uncertainty. The notion was absurd.

To be simultaneously thoughtful and confident was a logical impossibility, or a magic trick. She held a deep scepticism of anyone who didn't question their own motives, and Maggie couldn't become Brij, but perhaps she could emulate her mentor's stubbornness. Return to pick over her own misgivings at some later time. If she didn't back herself, no one would, so she rolled out of bed and straightened her clothes. Public servants loved to gossip, and someone on Market Street would know more.

CHAPTER 15

FRESH DEBATE has resurfaced about kiddyZap implants, after a clandestine shroudspace locale was found teaching parents how to hack the devices for use as a behavioural control.

When used according to default factory settings, kiddyZap only triggers when there is a risk of serious harm. In their ubiquitous advertising, the manufacturer raises the terrifying prospect of children heedlessly running into traffic, or reaching forward to put their hands into a fire. The kiddyZap implant, which can be installed as part of a standard juvenile shroud rig, sends a brief, harmless but arresting electrical pulse through the child's body, which is often enough to avert tragedy.

Now, however, The Monitor Lizard has learned of a thriving subculture in which parents share tips for reprogramming the trigger settings for the devices, so that shocks can be administered for non-life-threatening infringements, such as rudeness or failure to follow parental instructions.

'I saw a post by one dad who was raising – he claimed – a pair of future Olympic swimmers,' recounted Monique Bulling, a parent who says they browsed the site, but did not engage in any modification. 'He had the kids on muscle gel, round the clock. Made it so that the kids got buzzed if they tried to eat or drink anything that wasn't on the meal plan.'

KiddyZap was the source of significant controversy when introduced six years ago. At the time, many felt that there was no justification for subjecting children to even temporary pain, and that the potential for psychological harm – from children apprehending unpredictable, inescapable threats from within their own bodies – outweighed any potential safety benefits. Since then, however, several documented instances have emerged in which kiddyZaps appear to have prevented accidents, and outright opposition to the devices has waned, even as take-up rates have plateaued at around forty per cent.

A spokesdult for the company said that 'The kiddyZap platform is a last line of defence to prevent serious injury', and is not intended for disciplinary purposes. 'Changing the trigger settings is a breach of the end-user licence agreement, and will void your warranty', they said.

– 'SHOCK HACK AS PARENTS AMP UP PAIN',
The Monitor Lizard [n:mon.itoro/kz,
accessed 22:03:19 28-MAY-2058]

THE NEXT DAY WAS GALLIPOLI DAY, AND SO WAS LOST to productive work. Maggie recorded her pledge after breakfast, not bothering to do anything interpretative, or to post-produce her vid with backdrops, music or effects. Still, it was four takes until she was satisfied with the delivery, followed by some mucking around to format the clip before it could be posted on her public profile.

She knew the words off by heart:

I pay homage to those who fell at Gallipoli, and I promise to uphold their spirit in defence of Australia, against all who would threaten us. Together we embody the spirit of mateship, the fair go, and having a dig.

Like all children, Maggie had learned about Gallipoli at school. The self-guided history modules had been light on detail, but the gist was that the Aussies had won a hard-fought victory against the forces of oppression, helping to turn the tide of the war in the Allies' favour. She wasn't sure why they needed Gallipoli Day as well as Anzac Day, Remembrance Day and Western Values Day, but she supposed it was important for people not to forget the sacrifices that had been made to keep them secure. It wasn't necessary to go overboard for the pledge, as long as you recorded yourself saying the words, and posted it to your feed so that others could see. Anyone who forgot was called out, and those few who refused were swiftly cancelled.

When she was done, she cast in to Brij's office. 'You done with yours?'

Brij sat easily behind her desk, and let out a scornful laugh. 'Did it last night. What a saga – three-and-a-half hours of make-up, lighting, the works, all to make me look natural and spontaneous. Allie enjoyed watching me squirm, started making faces at me out of frame. Last night I was repeating the words in my sleep: *I pay homage to those who fell …*'

Her lack of patriotism put Maggie on edge. Brij was privately cynical about this stuff, she'd said as much before, but Maggie didn't want to deal with the fallout if something got overheard or caught on-mic. She was most surprised at Allie: Brij's wife had always presented as serious, even humourless.

'Anyway, don't mind me,' Brij continued. 'I'm grumpy because we're stuck on plate reform. It's been referred off for another feasibility review, and you can imagine how Cass has taken the news.' Maggie had a clear enough idea, and was privately glad that today, she would not be sharing an office with her friend. 'But enough chit-chat: how did you get on with the Truvies?'

As always, there was nothing to be gained with Brij by deflecting. Steadily, Maggie replied, 'I gave it a good shot. And Felix tried, in his way, to back me up. But they won't support it. It isn't their idea, and they've spent too long in the pocket of the Libs.'

Brij's mouth settled into a well-worn pout. 'I see. I've started a tally.' Her glance was a question and a challenge.

Dreading exactly this, Maggie nodded. Brij's fingers danced above the desk, and part of the interior wall of the harvester's office transformed into a collaborative document, sectioned into three columns, labelled *For*, *Undecided*, and *Against*. At the top of the wall: *Economic Transformation (Universal Income) Bill 2058 (Cth)*.

The *For* column was populated with names that Maggie knew well: Keller, Yang, Smyth and their ilk, along with Brij herself; the font size of the names getting smaller as the list descended, to indicate relative numbers of votes spoken for. Stalwarts of OzProg, Maggie knew that their support was assured. 'Yang and a couple of other Green traditionalists still have misgivings about universality,' Brij said, following Maggie's eyes. 'But they'll fall into line.' A tally at the base of the column read, *For: 7,119,328 (18%)*.

The final column contained a similarly familiar cast: Bell, Sheppard, Bernardi, Jones. Harvesters comprising the backbone of the Liberal party's conservative base. Together they spoke for a full twenty-two per cent of the vote. 'We've got nothing to offer the Libs,' Brij announced. 'We can pretty much write them off. Which leaves ...' she foregrounded the central column. As Maggie watched, a bloc of Truvie-aligned harvesters shifted out, and re-appeared in *Against*. Turning back to Maggie, Brij asked, 'Any more luck with Mackay?'

Maggie shook her head. 'The only way he'll support a bill is if it's an Income in name only. Mackay wants to look open-minded, as long as nothing really changes. He's exactly what the voters rejected. It would be suicide to do a deal with him.'

Eyes widened at the conviction with which Maggie delivered this assessment, Brij duly shifted Mackay and a few minor hangers-on into the final column. With the Truvies and Mackay, the total now read *16,870,451, (41%)*.

Top of the central 'Undecided' column now was a familiar name: *Reeve (8%)*.

'Ah, shit,' said Maggie.

'He's no fool. He's exactly where he wants to be.'

'According to Felix, he wants us to support a vicarious liability standard for AIs.'

'Then I guess that's what we'll have to do.'

'An Income is a good idea on its own terms.' Maggie could feel herself glowering. 'It's popular, and we've just won an election. We have a mandate.'

Now Brij looked impatient. 'Yeah, well, I don't know what to tell you. You're seeing what I'm seeing? We need Chase's eight per cent, and he knows it.'

Maggie could hardly dispute that. Chase Reeve knew how to count as well as anyone. But it rankled, this outsize influence that he could wield by claiming to be the sensible centre.

Brij pressed, apparently in no mood for soul-searching. 'I pay you to advise me, Maggie. So what should I do? Or are you too close to this now?'

For a moment more, indecision threatened to spill over into panic. Maggie thought of the people they might be screwing over: those harmed or swindled by AI, who would find it hard to get justice if Chase had his way. Was it this easy to write people off? But she remembered what it was she wanted, remembered that she'd resolved to back herself. No one better was waiting to take on the job.

'Do it,' Maggie said through gritted teeth. 'If we get the Income bill passed, we'll have some wiggle room to add in safeguards when the AI thing comes up.' Cynical, perhaps, and a bit underhanded, but Maggie wasn't feeling charitable toward Chase or his nephew.

'Right, then.' Brij shifted Chase into the *For* column, boosting it to twenty-six per cent.

The central column still retained a sea of smaller names, centrists who could be bought or bullied, plus the ten per cent or so of the public who hadn't bothered to grant a proxy, and who could theoretically cast a direct vote on the Income pleb. Near the floor, the subtotals told the story: 26% / 33% / 41%.

It was not encouraging. 'The undecideds will need to break hard our way.'

Brij nodded. 'And there's no good reason why they shouldn't. That would reflect the public mood, and the support behind the new government. But you know as well as I do,

Maggie, that harvesters can be swayed by, shall we say, extraneous considerations.'

'We need to make it hard for them to say no.'

Brij nodded, waiting for Maggie to step it out.

'Which means we need the public to get vocal. We need to make the case on the feeds, remind people why they voted for change.'

'And.'

'And … with respect, Brij, everyone knows you, knows what you'll say. There's no virality there. It needs to be a fresh face, someone with an inside scoop. It needs to be … it could be me.'

Brij nodded. 'It will have to be.'

'It'll piss off Treasury.'

'I wouldn't lose any sleep over that.'

MAGGIE AND KEI HAD ARRANGED TO COLLECT MAGgie's parents on the way to the party. As they neared Liv and Raman's place, Kei edged away from Maggie in the back seat, withdrew his hand from where it had been resting in her lap.

'Are you … nervous?' Maggie asked. She'd never seen him like this. He'd dressed formally, in long trousers, closed-toed shoes and a button-up shirt.

'Nah,' Kei said. 'It's just, you know, meeting the parents …'

'I'm not worried about *you* making a bad impression. I've told you what my dad's like.'

'I'm sure I can handle him. How was your day, anyway? You had a meeting?' He grimaced, perhaps with a sense that he ought to be able to recall more specifics.

Maggie smiled, amused at his momentary discomfort. 'With the Truvies. They were as stubborn as we expected.'

'What did they say?'

Kei was staring at her, and self-consciously she thumbed at a wrinkle near the hem of her almond-white cocktail dress. He often asked about her work, but she usually got the sense that he didn't care too much about her answers. Perhaps he was just trying to distract himself from the evening ahead.

'They claim to be all noble and pure, but they're just protecting their own racket like everyone else. If an Income is introduced, what would be the point of the unions?'

'What's the point of them now?'

'And they're a party for the miserable. They make a lot of noise, but genuinely improving people's lot would be bad for business.'

Kei's eyes grew wide. 'They said that?'

'No.' His interest felt incongruous, given what she knew of him. He loved his work at the co-op, reality shows, eating. 'They said ... um. They said, *The devil finds work for idle hands*. It's a Bible thing, I think.'

He mouthed it silently to himself. 'So helpful.'

'They were never going to go for it.'

They both swayed forward as their car found a stopping point outside the Garewal family home. Liv was waiting on the footpath, looking cross. When the door opened and Maggie stepped outside, Liv glanced back toward the house and tutted. 'I told him you were on your way, but he's fussing.' She searched for something in her purse, and then noticed Kei as he rounded the car to join them. 'Oh, hello.'

'Mum, this is Kei.'

'Lovely to meet you, Kei. You look very smart. Maggie's never brought home a … what's the right word, the taxonomy's difficult these days …'

Kei appealed to Maggie with his eyes. Maggie said, 'Partner will be fine.'

'Oh, good, that'll be easy to explain.' Liv paused, and then something must have occurred to her. 'Not that I'm judging! When Raman and I were young we tried all sorts of things before we settled down.'

'Mum.'

'Trysts, poly, throuples … There was a carpenter in Belconnen we both dated for about a year,' Liv's eyes had grown dreamy; Maggie thought she was enjoying this reminiscence far too much.

'Mum. Kei doesn't want to hear this.'

Ignoring her daughter, Liv leaned toward Kei. 'Maggie can be a wet blanket sometimes. Are you expanding her horizons?'

'I … don't know how to answer that,' said Kei, but his eyes sparkled as he returned Liv's gaze.

Maggie had had enough. Confident that this would derail Liv's attempts to flirt, she asked, 'Where's Tez tonight?'

'He's busy, but he'll be at the party later. Yes, in person. Don't look sour.' Maggie realised she probably was looking sour, but she needed to speak with her brother.

From the darkness came the sound of keys jangling. Raman jogged out from the side of the house to meet them. 'My hair was unruly,' he said by way of apology. He wore a plum-coloured suit jacket over a white-and-plum check shirt and jeans. His glasses dangled precariously from his shirt pocket.

The boyish way that Raman was shifting himself, together with Liv's reminiscences, made Maggie imagine the pair as twenty-somethings, which was always a disconcerting exercise. She knew academically that they had been civic-minded, and active in the organised and frequently violent resistance efforts of the early thirties. By then, practically every Australian had come to recognise the importance of mitigating and adapting, but actual reforms had continued to lag.

Maggie had always found it hard to understand why her parents' generation took so long to do the obvious work, while so much harm was being locked in. But with the benefit of recent experience, Maggie was developing a sense of how slowly the needle moved.

Once everyone had folded themselves into the car and it slid from the curb, there was silence. Maggie realised that although she'd discussed the logistics of the party many times with her parents, she'd never heard her father acknowledge the meaning of the event itself. She studied Raman as he fidgeted with one of his cuffs. 'Do you think Dada-ji will really do it, when the time comes?'

Raman smiled. 'I am sure that he will. He is becoming a sage, I think.'

'What does that mean?'

'He is bored of everything – his family, even – but he's trying not to be a dick about it. We have had many differences over the years, he and I. But in this matter, I respect him.'

Vasur Garewal had been an important, wealthy man. A surgeon for nearly half a century, and a volunteer and philanthropist after that. None of his family begrudged him his place in the finest assisted living facility to be found in Ngunnawal. Raman had always predicted that his father would insist on remaining in the old house, alone after the death of his wife a decade earlier from a sudden stroke. But after that seismic event in the life of Maggie's family, some of the stubbornness appeared to leave Vasur. He had become more pliable, more open to suggestion. He'd been living in this community for three years. And now this party: arranged in the common hall at an old folks' home. The man Maggie had known as a child would never have suffered it, and she felt sad for him, even putting aside the reason for this celebration.

Maggie's image of Vasur could not be untangled from the place he'd grown old in alongside his wife, a sprawling stone cottage with – luxury of luxuries – a private lawn tennis court. Intellectually, Maggie knew that this was obscene wealth, reified. Leaving aside everything else, the water required to maintain it would have been prohibitively expensive. But still, her memories were of him on the weekends, running the roller over the turf, and carefully painting the lines, his surgeon's hands keeping the line marker straight as it tracked down the side of the court.

They arrived right on time, which was effectively late, since Raman had promised to be there in advance to help set up. They found the hall in the centre of this campus for the old, wealthy retired, who had made their money in the last days before strong AI. Some attendants were still hanging physical decorations, gold and metallic purple streamers that looked crinkled, like they'd been rolled out and packed away again and again. Maggie thought it was tacky. Vasur had an implant, so it would have been no bother to project something more elegant, something more personal to *him*. She was surprised to see her grandfather in the middle of it all, beaming at the sight of them.

'Dada-ji,' Raman began formally. 'Congratulations on your five-year.' Maggie had seen it before, but the way Raman's usually casual demeanour changed in the presence of Vasur made her almost embarrassed on her father's behalf.

'Thank you, my son. Liv.' Vasur inclined his head. 'And—' his eyes sparkled, 'My clever granddaughter.' He took Maggie's hands in his. 'And welcome to your friend.'

Maggie made the introductions. Vasur was diminutive, the silver hair on his head sitting in line with Maggie's chin, but he stood straight and possessed the hale, alert look of someone who never skipped a treatment. He was dressed modestly but immaculately in a bottle-green blazer over a black turtleneck. Maggie felt sure that he would still be capable of living by himself, if that had been his preference.

Kei said, 'I think it's a wonderful thing you're doing.' He looked around at Maggie, Liv and Raman, as if retrospectively seeking permission.

Vasur was not perturbed. 'That's kind of you to say. I have been very blessed. You see?' He spread his arms to indicate Maggie, Raman and Liv. 'Happy.'

No one really knew how long life could be extended. Those that had received the first, crude versions of the treatments in the late thirties were dying off, having achieved a span of eleven or twelve decades. But Vasur had benefited from the later refinements. If he'd wanted to, he would be around to access the more sophisticated options that were being developed even now.

Another sixty years was not out of the question; but Vasur had signed the pledge. And so, on this occasion of his eighty-fifth birthday, Maggie's grandfather was renewing his commitment to end his life when he turned ninety. By custom, this five-year party was meant to be a celebration of a life well lived, and a timely, purposeful end.

Raman's two sisters and their myriad children and grand-children arrived, and for Maggie and Kei, the next half hour was a sequence of introductions and small talk. Maggie wasn't par-ticularly close with her cousins or her aunties. When Maggie was growing up, Raman had experienced a slightly strained rela-tionship with his older, more successful sisters, who had each moved to Narrm in early adulthood.

Now that he was here and in the middle of it, Kei was polite, assured and warm, like Maggie knew he would be. She was grateful for him, and guiltily she realised that if they stayed together, he could be an asset: the perfect, dutiful wife to drag along to fundraisers and dinners.

In this setting, Kei was a welcome novelty, like a B-list celeb-rity. After she'd proffered names, he did most of the talking, answering with good grace all questions put to him, both tact-less and polite. He was not Jat, not even Indian, and Maggie supposed that when her parents were growing up, that would have caused tension. Raman's choice of a white woman had raised enough eyebrows back in the day, Maggie knew; and back then it would have been even harder for a woman to choose a partner from outside the community. But with time and the erosion of standards caused by prior transgressions, Maggie had it far easier.

When she had a chance to look around, she saw that the party had started in earnest. There was no mistaking that it was a celebration for an old man: almost everyone was here in person, and Maggie and Kei were several decades younger than the average age of the guests. Along with his new neighbours at the community home, many of Vasur's old surgeon buddies had made the effort to travel. Maggie watched her grandfather listening intently as one of his former colleagues told a story, accompanied by what could only have been a mimed incision and subsequent eruption of viscera. Vasur's eyebrows crinkled and his mouth pursed slightly, in a way that Maggie could read as disapproval.

Her eyes wandering, she spotted Tez near the buffet table, talking to one of her cousins. She turned to Kei, who was speaking to an old family friend, explaining why his mother had decided to come to Australia. Maggie put her hand on his shoulder, interrupting him. 'Are you okay here?' She motioned with her head to indicate that she wanted to leave him.

'Sure,' he said.

She made directly for her brother. He spotted her coming, and he glanced around like frightened prey, looking for an escape. When Maggie drew near, she punched him in the ribs, partly to double-check that he was meatspace-present. 'Ow,' he complained. 'Rude.'

She turned to her cousin. 'Nina, hi. Would you mind giving us a moment? Tez and I need to talk.' Nina got the hint and moved off quickly, perhaps glad to have witnessed an exchange that would become grist for the always-turning family gossip machine.

Maggie grabbed Tez by the sleeve and marched him away, finding a tiny side room that felt too bright after the dim of the hall. She grabbed him by the shoulders. 'You went dark. Why?'

He stepped back, shrugging off her hands. At least he looked abashed when he replied, 'I thought you'd be pissy.'

'Of course I'm pissy!' With a supreme effort, Maggie tried to calm herself. 'I was worried, you idiot. Has anyone else tried to contact you? The police?'

'What? No.'

'Tez, five people died. And, not to minimise that, but—' there was no way to express her next thought without sounding self-centred, but she'd left Kei by himself and she didn't have all night. 'You know what I'm working on. Can't you see that when they check the logs, and confirm that I was there, that I'm going to look suspicious?'

'I— I was just trying to help you. For once, I thought I could actually help.'

The naked defeat in his expression was disarming. With less heat, Maggie asked, 'Did you know that there would be a bomb?'

'No! Jesus, no, of course not.'

'Then why did you take me there?'

'I was ... just messing around on shroudspace. And then this lurker started teeing off about how no one had any work. Said the system was rigged, and that something really, really massive, a protest, was going to happen at DHS. I did some reading, even went to a meeting.' He looked at her expectantly, as if Maggie might approve. 'And I thought, *you know who'd be interested in this ...*' He trailed off.

Even when he was trying to do the right thing, Tez was exhausting. Maggie felt like there was nothing inside to sustain her, no reserves of patience or tolerance that remained for her to call upon. 'So this lurker, they knew who you were. And they found you …'

'No,' Tez waved his hands in negation. 'Or … it didn't go down like that, exactly.'

'Okay,' said Maggie. It all sounded decidedly suspect, but there was no point burdening Tez with her own misgivings; her worry that Tez had been a vector to engineer her own presence.

Tez looked pale, and his mouth grew slack as a thought occurred. 'If the police do call, what should I say?' A sardonic smile formed on his face. 'I guess … I'm out of work, I'm disaffected. It would make sense that I'd join the occupation, right? Like, on my own initiative? And you were just there because you'd decided to tag along, because of your work stuff?'

She could see he was trying to shield her. 'No. It doesn't hang together. You've never been to a protest before, and you rock up half an hour before things get violent? No,' she repeated. 'I don't know what's really going on here. So *when* the police call, safest to tell the truth. They'll have questions for you about this lurker, and more questions for me, I'm sure. And there might be leaks and stories, but we'll just have to deal with that when it happens.'

'Mags, I'm so sorry.' His voice had grown husky. 'I've fucked up my life, and now I'm fucking up yours.'

Despite her defences, and all the rage she'd held on to for the past week, this undid her. 'You were trying something. It's good to see.' She kissed him on the cheek, and stood aside so that he could escape back to the party, for once a place of greater comfort for him.

She found Kei dancing with one of her aunts, kicking his legs to an up-tempo pop song from the forties, and clapping his hands in delight when his dance partner started to find her groove. When the song cross-faded into something else, he and Maggie went to find food. He looked flushed. 'It's so weird,' he said. 'Growing up, it was just me and mum. Your family makes so much noise.'

Maggie had to laugh. 'We don't get together very often. You're witnessing a rare natural wonder: the convocation of the Garewals.'

Sharing a plate of daal baati and churma, they were drawn into a conversation about real estate, and the price of apartments in Queanbeyan. Maggie tried to pay attention, but really, she was working over what Tez had said. The more she mulled it, the more convinced she became that someone had used him. To embarrass her, perhaps, or to falsely implicate her? She fumed, picking at their food, while Kei did the talking for them both.

It took him another fifteen minutes to notice that she'd gone quiet, and when he did, he pulled her aside to check in. 'I'm fine,' she said. 'I'm just … I just need a walk and some air.' She left him holding their almost-empty plate, knowing he wouldn't complain.

She wandered the room for a while, trying not to get pulled into any conversations, scrutinising all of these people that her grandfather loved, in the act of celebration. She saw Raman dancing with Liv like they must have when they were young.

In Maggie's current state of mind, the scene struck her as distasteful. She knew that this was an overlay entirely of her own making, and she wished she could be better at enjoying these moments. They were rare enough.

When her grandfather noticed her, he excused himself from the group he'd been standing with. Approaching Maggie, he said, 'Would you come with me.' He led them out the rear of the hall, past the kitchens and a wire-screen door that swung shut aggressively when they'd pushed past. Outside it was a frigid night, the lawns heavy with frost. Vasur reached into the pocket of his coat, pulled out an inhaler, and took a drag.

'Dada-ji ... you're vaping!'

Vasur laughed heartily, enjoying her surprise. 'This is very bad for the health, and you must never do it. But I have decided to try some new things.'

'Your five-year ... are you really going to? I know we're not meant to be sad, but you're so ... not young, but *not old*.'

He smiled kindly. 'After your grandmother passed, there was a time when I simply existed. There was no salt. But since I made the pledge, everything is interesting. These last five years will be very good. I will travel, likely to Ahmedabad, the birthplace of your great grandfather.'

'How long has it been?'

'Almost forty years.'

'Was that the time Dad went with you?'

'Yes. He didn't understand, couldn't really *see* the place. That is my fault.' For a moment he was far away. 'Yes, Ahmedabad. And I have always wanted to visit France, and perhaps I will, for half a year. I will be content. Besides,' he said, a glint in his eye.

'When I am eighty-nine years and eleven months, I may change my mind, eh?' But Maggie knew him better than that.

They stood for a while in silence, looking at the rows of single-storey units, each with a privacy screen and a scraggly native garden. Eventually, Vasur said, 'You are upset?'

Maggie nodded. 'I don't mean to be, not on your birthday. It's just stupid work stuff.'

'Not stupid, I'm sure.' Vasur packed his inhaler away. 'I remember what it was like. I was vexed, and wished for a way to escape. But tolerating unhappiness is service. Raman never understood that, but you do.' Maggie nodded, recognising the truth in this.

'I don't know if this thing I'm doing will work out.'

He grunted in sympathy. 'That is why reasons are so important. If you are working for others, for something greater, and you give your utmost, you will be content.'

'Easy for you to say, Dada-ji. You're a hero to everyone in there.'

'That doesn't matter. In a few years I will be gone, and all that will remain will be the stones I disturbed, and the trees I planted. I am head of this family, Maggie, and for the time being you must listen to me: do as much as you can.'

CHAPTER 16

I think I'll love you
>I'm almost sure that I will love you
>Oh … Oh …
>Oh!
>Yes! Yeah … yeah … I'm gonna love you
>But maybe not the way that you expect.
>>– '74% Match', The Bad Balloons,
>>© 2055 Malpractice Records

SHE JUMPED A CAR BACK TO SYDNEY WHEN THE party wound up, hugging Kei goodbye and leaving him to negotiate a ride home with her parents.

The following morning, after a night of fitful sleep, she wasted no time in linking up with Brij's part-time media consultant. They canvassed options for Maggie's debut as a talking head, but for maximum impact there was only one choice, if they could land a spot.

The original Oskar, back in the early forties, had been a new spin on a well-worn trope. The character of Oskar, played by a real person named Oskar Allen, drew inspiration from comedians of the early twenty-first century, who would create caricatures of right-wing demagogues. But Oskar wasn't played merely for laughs: he was the last pan-Australian television experience. You could watch him with your hippy sister and your racist uncle. Conservatives saw straight news, reportage and commentary that affirmed their own beliefs. Progressives detected a grim, subtle satire, laying bare the logical inconsistencies and absurd biases underpinning Oskar's rants. Content to act as a political Rorschach test, the performer behind the phenomenon had never let on one way or the other where his true allegiances lay.

Just as importantly for the longevity of the show, everyone wanted to be interviewed by Oskar: right-wingers sensed a fellow traveller and a soft touch; leftists who could hold their own would look like a voice of reason in contrast to the bombastic host. After Oskar Allen retired in 2049, a succession of new hosts took up the mantle for a season or two each. The current Oskar was a petite blonde named Yasmin Porter. She'd come up through the theatre scene, and had a knack for hinting at the mannerisms of a large, older man without pushing it too far and collapsing into crude impression.

By lunchtime, a slot had been booked for Maggie on the morning show the following day. The Income proposal was perfect fodder for Oskar, and more than half of the hour-long episode would be given over to a discussion between Oskar, Maggie, and a guest yet to be determined, the latter arguing the case for the negative. Maggie spent the rest of the day prepping, trying to anticipate how Oskar might try to tear her down. Brij and her media manager helped Maggie stage a mock runthrough, and Brij seemed to relish playing Oskar. She would stab questions at Maggie and not wait for a response; mischaracterise details of the Income plan, and editorialise over the top of Maggie when she tried to speak. The trick was to remain composed. If Oskar got under your skin, it was all over.

After hours of practice, Maggie's head was a muddle of statistics, talking points, rebuttals, and the nonsense she'd absorbed from Brij-as-Oskar. When Maggie started a sentence with, 'Sometimes a slippery slope can be a shortcut to opportunity …' Brij called time.

'Enough. You're as ready as you're going to get. You know your brief, and what to expect. You'll give a good account of yourself.'

Grateful, Maggie let her shoulders drop. 'How do you do this every day?' she asked.

'It doesn't come naturally, at least not to me. But you get used to it. Things will move quickly now, one way or another. Either the Income plan will falter, or momentum will build fast, and we'll need to rush to get a bill pulled together and force it to a vote while the cats are herded.'

'… Okay. I'm ready, I think.'

'I've seen how you've worked this, Maggie. Whichever way this plays out, there's a future for you in this game, and a job with me for as long as you want it.'

Coming from Brij, this was positively effusive. Maggie blushed, stood up, and embraced her. 'I'll get it done. I will.'

THAT NIGHT, SHE CALLED KINNEAR. HE RESPONDED audio-only, so that she couldn't see his face. Maggie reciprocated, killing her avatar and getting up from her too-soft dormitory bed where she'd been reclining. She paced the floor.

'I'm glad you're okay,' Maggie began. She had texted Kinnear soon after the attack, to confirm that he hadn't been hurt, but this was the first time they'd spoken since. She could only imagine how chaotic the aftermath would have been at DHS, with staff restricted from gathering in person and all branch offices shuttered, just in case the attackers sought to continue their campaign. Sensitive to the likely demands on Kinnear's time, and not wanting to explain that she'd been in the crowd, she'd left him alone for more than a week.

For his part, Kinnear seemed relatively unperturbed. 'I had a medical appointment that morning, so I was casting in from home when it happened. One of my juniors was on the top floor, though. They had to dig out metal from his thigh. To be honest, I'd rather not dwell – there's more than enough of that within the Department. Was there another reason for the call?'

She brought him up to speed, and when she'd finished, he said, 'Oskar. Are things really that bad?'

'We've run the numbers, and we'll need a lot of undecideds to break our way.'

There was a pause, and without a visual, Maggie assumed that he must have been doing a rough count in his own head. 'Truvies?'

'I tried. They refused, politely but smugly.' After a carefully calibrated pause, she added, as if an afterthought, 'Their spokesman said something that keeps playing in my mind. *All that glisters is not gold.*'

Kinnear wheezed a laugh. 'That's a bit esoteric. It's not even scripture, it's Shakespeare.'

Maggie kept her voice flat. 'Is it? I'll take your word. Anyway, Oskar might be our best hope to change some minds.'

'Good hunting, then. And listen: I'm sure you've been counselled to keep your cool. That's good advice. But do you remember the first time we met?'

'I try not to think about it, to be honest.'

'Despite everything, you left an impression. Don't be afraid to show how much you care. People respond to that.'

SHE WAS OUT OF BED BY FOUR. LIKE AN AUTOMATON she dressed in a modish indigo blouse and cream sailor pants that had been purchased for her, and delivered to the dormitory. The outfit would have been appropriate for a church fundraiser, and was hardly to Maggie's taste, but she supposed the idea was to appear non-threatening, like she was part of the establishment.

The studio was in Haymarket, and in the pre-dawn she watched the crowd on the early train, so different to the professionals that packed out the carriages just before nine. This lot tended to wear uniforms: the dusky greens and blues of cleaners, the high-vis of construction, and the hyperactive reds and yellows of iron-free cafeteria attire. A lot of these people would be coming in for a brief shift, preparing the city for the day, and then departing as the knowledge class rolled in. Three or four hours might be all the work they could get; might be barely enough to live on.

Clouds loomed over the city like a dim ceiling, and drizzle buzzed the air, forming beads of moisture on the outside of the glass windows and misting everything up inside, so that the swaying carriage felt like its own submerged universe. For the most part, the occupants emitted the zombie gaze, heads lolling in time with the undulations of the rails, heeding their own private distractions. Inadvertently, Maggie caught the eye of an older woman a few seats away, and they swapped silent acknowledgements.

She arrived at the studio clammy from the rain and her own nerves. A fortyish, harried-looking man, face puffy like a shift worker, introduced himself as Archie and bustled her through security to a cramped dressing room. 'Someone'll be in to do make-up, and then you'll wait here until it's time to bring you on,' he explained.

'I thought I might meet the other guest,' said Maggie. 'And Oskar, to go over the format.' She felt anew how unprepared she was. She had no idea how these things worked. Her escort just shrugged, already on his way to some other task.

Maggie set her comms to blackout, to hold all incoming messages. The last thing she needed was for Raman to start texting her while she was live. Soon enough, a pair of make-up artists descended upon her, running fingers experimentally through Maggie's dark hair. As they stuffed greaseproof paper around her collar, they chatted over Maggie's head.

'Her top is wrong for her colouring.'

'At least it's not stripes. Access this: it's a guy I worked last week.'

'Bah! He's like a zebra crossing.'

'You have nice skin,' one of them said, finally catching Maggie's eyes in the mirror. 'But it will look too dark on shroud, especially when you're sat next to Oskar.' Without waiting for assent, the outer edge of her palm hovered over Maggie's brow and started swabbing her forehead.

To Maggie, the result made her look like a cancer patient. But as a neophyte, Maggie didn't know enough to challenge them, had to trust that they knew their craft, and that under the lights of the studio, filtered through a shroud, she would look right.

They left her alone. Maggie checked her clock app, and realised with a jolt that the show would have started a few minutes ago. Her segment would be the closer. She brought up the program in her shroud, and inset it so that it occupied the bottom right-hand corner of her visual field. It was hard to believe that the Oskar she saw was speaking these words live, a few metres from where she sat. A pang of nausea rolled through her guts – she hadn't eaten. And her bladder felt full, but there was no one around for ask for directions to the bathroom. So she waited, trying to follow Oskar's opening rant, which was about the wickedness of public subsidies for urban rehabilitation.

The next twenty minutes passed in fits of lost time. She ran through some key lines they'd rehearsed the day before, but Oskar's strident opinionising made it difficult to collect her thoughts. When she tried to recall the costings for their preferred Income model, her mind went blank. She'd architected the position paper on this. She knew it better than anyone. But she couldn't remember.

'Mx Garewal? Two minutes. Follow me.' Archie had returned, still looking like someone had condemned him to serve at this studio for a cursed millennium. Maggie walked floatingly behind as he led her through a zig-zag of bleach-tiled corridors. He stopped in front of a nondescript door with no handle, pushed inward hesitantly and stuck his head through. Satisfied, he swung it wide and held it open for Maggie. Inside, she could see the reverse of the thick maroon curtain she'd been looking at moments before, draped behind Oskar. She stood, perched on the edge of the set, hesitating. A clacking sound of shoes came from the corridor behind her, and she turned.

The program's other guest wore a self-satisfied smile. 'Maggie. Such a pleasure to see you again.'

Her stomach dropped, and she tried to form a response. 'Mackay. Did you know it would be me?'

He looked amused. 'Of course. Didn't they tell you I'd be here? Oskar *is* a rascal.'

If Mackay was her co-panellist, that must mean he would be coming out against an Income. To her surprise, the realisation calmed her. She and Brij had all but written him off anyway, and she was already braced for a hostile reception.

From the other side of the curtain, a voice barked, 'Come through, we're back in a minute.' Mackay and Maggie were ushered around and guided to chairs on either side of Oskar, at the fat end of an egg-shaped desk. At the point of the egg, a single empty chair had been placed to signify the vantage point that each viewer would assume when they cast in.

Once Mackay had taken his seat, he and Oskar leaned in air-kissed each other's cheeks. The host was even smaller in the flesh than she appeared on feed, and Maggie noticed that Oskar's chair had been raised so that her legs dangled off the floor. She wore her straw-coloured hair in a shoulder-length bob, parted on the side and swept back behind her ears, emphasising her sharp jawline. Maggie felt acutely aware of her own dimensions.

'Em,' Oskar cooed at Mackay. 'So good to have you back, how's Charlotte?'

'She's well,' Mackay responded chummily. 'She still talks about that weekend at Hotham.'

Oskar looked like she was about to reply, but held up a finger and swivelled her chair to face Maggie. 'Maggie Garewal,' she announced, as if remembering a key piece of information. Then her expression softened. 'You look nervous, babe. First time?'

'Yes.'

'Speak up. You'll be fine.' For a second her expression was encouraging, and only a little patronising, and then she must have got a cue. She turned to nod to Mackay, and then assumed the tight, infuriated look that Maggie knew so well from the vids, of someone who has planned an expensive function that is not living up to expectations, who is demanding to speak to the manager.

For six seconds, everything was still, and so silent that Maggie could hear her own breathing. And then Oskar began.

'Welcome back. I'm joined now by Maggie Garewal, some kind of advisor or spokeswoman or fixer for that hopeless bleeding heart, Brij Sutton. And this man beside me needs no introduction. Good friend of the show, influential harvester and backbone of the sensible centre, Mr Mackay.'

'It's a genuine pleasure, Oskar,' said Mackay.

'Thanks for having me,' said Maggie, and her voice sounded insipid to her own ears. In the corner of her eye, she could see herself in the picture-in-picture, see how blanched she looked. Twitching her fingers beneath the desk, she banished the image.

'Depending on who you ask, the letters UBI stand for universal basic income, or utterly batshit idea. Miss Garewal here' – despite herself, Maggie bristled at the gendered honorific – 'thinks that we should strip wealth from those who produce, those who make a contribution, and throw it up into the air, and let it rain down on the indolent and the stupid. Now, I've been getting reports about shady backroom deals, and secret meetings at Treasury to try and get all this locked in before the people even have a chance to consider it. Perhaps Maggie can tell us more about that in a moment. Meanwhile, the Prime Minister has been slipperier on this issue than a buttered cane toad. We need to sort this out, right here, right now. Mackay!' She turned to face him. 'Has anyone tried to sell you this vapourware?'

'Yes,' replied Mackay, matter-of-factly. 'As it happens, Maggie here came to see me a few months ago. She tried to persuade me that an Income would be good for the poor. Maggie is very young. Very … compassionate.' The word dripped condescension. 'And she is sincere, I believe, in her desire to make society, as she understands it, kinder and gentler.'

'And did you tell her where to stick it?'

'I kept an open mind. After all, we do have a new government. I like to believe that I can work with all sorts of people in good faith, so I told Maggie I'd give her idea due consideration.'

'Did she offer you any incentive to back an Income? Some sort of sweetener?'

'Not overtly, no. I wouldn't go so far as to say she offered anything specific.'

For the first part of this exchange, Maggie had sat stunned. It was all so congenial, like two parents swapping stories about their misguided children. But with this soft, qualified denial, Mackay made it sound like Maggie had tried to bribe him. 'I can assure you—' Maggie began, but Oskar wouldn't have it.

'We'll get to you in a moment,' she snapped, turning back to face Mackay. 'And now you've had time to chew it over, what do you reckon?'

'In good conscience, I can't support it, Oskar. I want to be constructive. It would certainly be advantageous for me, personally, to work with the new government and the harvesters representing the majority. But one must sometimes take an unpopular, principled stand. Some of this scheme's backers are delirious with envy, some of them may be well-meaning. Either way, an Income would ruin us.'

With an obviously contrived innocence, missing only a wink to the viewers, Oskar supplied the necessary Dixer. 'Oh? How do you mean?'

Mackay leaned forward over the desk, and his tone grew solemn. 'We're fortunate to live in a country where everyone who wants it, who puts in the effort, can succeed.' He paused to offer a sorry shake of his head. 'Everyone else is, by definition, unwilling to prosper, or simply incapable. To give those people a large handout, unearned, is to tell everyone that it's okay to just give up. That's unsustainable.'

Oskar's faux-rage was starting to bubble. 'More than unsustainable. It's a bloody joke! It's un-Australian!'

'I'm afraid so.'

Now Oscar pivoted, swinging in her chair to stab a question at Maggie. 'Would you call yourself a proud Australian?'

'Yes.' She knew she should elaborate, take the opportunity to turn the conversation her way. Yesterday she had work-shopped a personal story, in case it was needed. But Oskar was a seasoned cross-examiner, pausing just long enough to get the answer she wanted before pressing on.

'A patriot?'

'I … I suppose so, yes.'

The host let that hang for a beat, giving the viewers a chance to draw their own conclusions. 'What would you say to the pro-testers at the DHS, who watched, who *applauded*, when that drone hit? As government workers were blown apart, as others emerged from that building with horrific injuries. What do you say to them?'

Maggie had the feeling of leaving the ground and drifting free of her body, anxious in only the most distracted way about what the landing would be like. Why would Oskar ask this? Why ask this of *her*? She knew there could only be one reason.

'There's no evidence that anyone at the protest knew what was about to happen,' Maggie started. Oskar glanced over at Mackay, incredulous. Mackay responded with another despair-ing shake of his head, and hastily, Maggie continued, 'Those people feel let down, but until the attack, there had been no vio-lence. Not in shroudspace; certainly not IRL. Still, I think the people in that crowd need to reflect on their strategy. Correctly or otherwise, they are now associated with whoever carried out that attack. For the first time in a long time, they have a government sympathetic to people who can't find enough work. Now more than ever, we need to be constructive. To work together to make change.' It was an equivocation. She needed to be more direct, but she didn't want to blunder into whatever trap was being set for her.

Oskar's eyes grew narrow and calculating. Here it was: here was where the hammer would drop.

The two women stared at each other. It might only have been a second or two, Maggie couldn't be sure, but it was dead air. Mackay cleared his throat, but he was ignored. Finally, as if it was what she'd meant to ask all along, Oskar blurted, 'Where is all the money going to come from? Are you going to take people's houses? Their retirement savings?'

The change of subject was a reprieve. And deliberate, Maggie felt sure. Perhaps Oskar was toying with her, and would reveal at the very end of the segment that Maggie had been at the DHS bombing, leaving her no time to explain. Either way, Maggie realised that she'd been asked a question to which she could give a substantive response.

Before she missed the chance, she summarised the revenue measures that Treasury had worked out. She was probably giving more detail away than the Department would have liked, but that was a second-order problem. If she couldn't bring the public with them, then her plan would never even be brought to a vote.

The more she spoke, the more her passion found its way into her words, and she stopped worrying about how she was coming across to her audience. At first, Oskar and Mackay interjected frequently, speaking over the top of her. But in this room, she was the expert. Patiently, she stepped through the main objections to the scheme, explaining what they'd done to avoid unintended consequences. 'I'm convinced we've got the model right,' she said. 'But once it's implemented, if something needs to be tweaked, we'll tweak it. If, as Mackay contends, it's unsuccessful, then there will be a pleb and it will be repealed, right? That's how our system works.'

Her dealings with Kinnear and the Truvies, even Mackay himself, had prepared her for this moment. Once she'd addressed the risks, she started talking about the benefits, which would flow to all dults, not just the less fortunate.

'Maggie,' Mackay said, 'You're a nice girl, but you're out of your depth. Why are you here, fronting this? I'll tell you why: it's because no one in OzProg with any sense wants to touch it. They know it's toxic, and it won't pass a pleb. Still, it's sad that they're making you wear this just because they're scared.'

There was no sense engaging with the merits of this. After the show, Maggie would have time to think about whether Mackay had touched a nerve. But at that moment, all she could feel was cold fury.

She drew herself upright in her chair, leaning toward him. She looked him right in the eyes, ignoring Oskar, and Maggie said, 'I'm young, that's true. But I'm here because you're killing us. You and all the plutocracy apologists. Even if you won't admit it, you're poisoning a future you won't be around to see. We're the ones who live in it.' She beat her open palm against her clavicle, careless of the lapel microphone attached to her blouse. 'Get out of the way. Lock yourself in your hilltop mansion, delete your socials, pay some fucking tax, and let us get on with fixing the mess you've left.'

Maggie took a half-breath. Before she could register what she'd done, before either of the others could interject, she started up again, talking about how existing social programs would be replaced or harmonised, reaping efficiencies that would help fund the scheme. Mackay watched on sullenly, and so it fell to Oskar to play defence, throwing up doubt and fear like puffs of smoke. But the balance in that studio had shifted, and now, even in the midst of the flow state she'd achieved by some external act of grace, Maggie could sense it.

From off to the side, a producer gave a two-minute warning. Having come to this, it was Oskar's duty to run the same, feeble argument that would always, always, be served up like day-old leftovers. 'We've got so much,' the host complained. 'We can't afford to risk it. We'll lose everything.'

Now it was Maggie's turn to wear a sad, condescending smile. 'If we can't adapt, if we can't improve, then we've got nothing. We've had twenty years of stasis, Oskar, and look where that's left us. A country bitterly divided. Half of Australia languishing. We can do more than survive – we can flourish, all of us. People have done the hardest part already by voting for change. This is what it looks like. We need to see it through.'

AFTER OSKAR HAD WRAPPED THE SHOW, MACKAY made his displeasure known. 'You soft-balled her,' he growled, his petulance showing in his eyes and at the corners of his mouth. He tugged off the jacket he'd been wearing. 'Where was the aggro?'

'Where was yours? You went missing for the last ten minutes, mate,' In her mode of speech and her mannerisms, Oskar was still in character. Perhaps it was hard to drop after an hour of performing. 'I just provide a platform: you're meant to make the case.'

'That's bullshit and you know it.' Mackay stood up, folded his coat over his arm.

Oskar smirked. 'See you next time.'

'Yeah, yeah,' the harvester muttered, stalking off toward the stage door.

The two women traded sardonic grins, enjoying the sight of this man in a huff. 'I haven't introduced myself properly. Yasmin.' She offered a hand, and the pair brushed fingertips.

'Maggie. You're very ... convincing. When you're in character, I mean.'

'Thanks. Hey you're doing some ask-me stuff after this, right? I've got a thing, so I'll leave you with Arch.' Yasmin/ Oskar motioned toward the older man who'd shown Maggie in. 'I've got to run, but you were okay. Better than okay. We'll need to get you on again.' She started to move toward the exit, and Maggie kept pace.

'Hey, before you go.' Maggie had to know. 'I feel like ... you had something. But you didn't use it. Why?'

Yasmin turned to look back. 'I'm a journalist,' she said, and then her mouth twisted. 'Kind of. Anyway, we got a tip. About you, the protest, the bombing.' Maggie's heart sank. 'But what we got was anonymous and unsubstantiated. It could have been a smear, and even asking you to deny it would have made you look suss. So our producer reached out to your boss, who said that if we ran with it, we'd never book any more OzProg-aligned talent, ever.'

'Oh. Well, thanks for your restraint, I guess.' The studio felt too hot. Maggie hadn't been proactive, hadn't warned Brij of the trouble she might be bringing down on them – and now Brij had needed to run damage control, without even having the facts.

Yasmin frowned. 'Listen, Maggie, you need to sort your shit out. If I heard that rumour, then others have, too. It's not going away.'

'I know.'

MAGGIE WAS GRANTED A TEN-MINUTE BREAK BEFORE being hustled to an adjoining darkroom where she fell into shroudspace, and a lobby that had been organised by the show. The space had been set up to look like an old-timey pub, with Maggie perched on a stool next to the bar. Viewers, pre-vetted by the show, could approach and ask Maggie questions about the segment they'd just watched. Brij's media manager had explained the day before that she didn't have to answer anything she didn't want to; and had correctly predicted that many of the questions would be impertinent:

[Which charity are you giving all your coin to, if you love sharing so much?]

needlessly personal:

[Will an Income bring forward your plans to start a family? Are you looking for a donor?]

and not obviously related to the topic at hand:

[Will this affect opening hours at Bulimba Library?]

Maggie's objective was not to persuade these super-fans, but rather to stick to her talking points and avoid saying anything that could be used to discredit her.

Even though she knew her job, it took focus to stay on task, and it was exhausting work. After two hours, she dropped back out into meatspace. Archie, who'd doubled as one of the moderators in the chat, finally cracked a smile. 'Not bad for a first-timer,' he said, and walked her outside to find a car.

On the ride back to Homebush, she turned off her shroud blackout, wanting to check the initial reacts. An alert told her she had three hundred and seventeen text and voice messages. Ignoring those, she scanned the headlines of one of the mainstream feed aggregators, searching for takes about the show. Mostly, responses ranged from begrudging respect through to full-throated enthusiasm for the Income plan she'd described, and for once, Maggie let herself enjoy the moment. She felt herself smile, and self-consciously let out a laugh. Why not? She was alone, and this thing was finally building.

Even as she scanned the headlines, a new story was posted to the feed by an old-school tabloid. And in real time, with mounting horror, Maggie saw the counters tick over, watched it build eyeballs and reactions.

EXCLUSIVE: TRUVIES TURN AWAY DESPARATE INCOME LOBBYIST

Harvester advisor Maggie Garewal, who appeared earlier today on Mornings with Oskar, *will do whatever it takes to get her Income bill over the line – even if that means sweet-talking those she'd consider enemies under any other circumstance.* The Southerner *has*

exclusively learned that Mx Garewal recently approached a delega-
tion from the True Values Party, seeking support for the bill sponsored
by Garewal's boss, Brij Sutton. It is not known what inducements
the harvester rep might have offered. But a source close to Garewal
claims that the Truvies rebuffed her, insisting that 'The devil finds
work for idle hands'…

The article continued for another thousand words or so. It
had been posted so quickly that it must have been pre-prepared,
ready to go once Maggie's spot on the show had ended.

She felt sick. She needed to talk to Kei.

ON THE RIDE BACK TO NGUNNAWAL, SHE KEPT GET-
ting calls from Cass. But she couldn't speak to anyone else, not
now. She kept trying to come up with some other explanation.
Something besides the heavy truth in her gut. But there was
nothing.

She didn't let him know she was coming. Didn't know if
he'd even be home, but when Kei answered the door in response
to Maggie's persistent knock, and ushered her inside, the pair
found themselves alone in the lounge.

'I saw you,' he said, still standing, a puzzled smile plastered
on his face. 'You were brilliant.'

Maggie didn't move when he motioned for her to sit. 'Yeah,
thanks. Read this for me.' She threw the article in the direction
of his shroud, and he reached out so that it would open in his
feed. 'Oh.' His eyes darted left-right, reading quickly. 'Bummer.
Still, you must be getting some good press, too, after the way
you tore that chump a new—'

Maggie held her arm up to silence him. 'Did you read the quote from the Truvies?'

Kei looked bewildered. 'Uh ... here it is. *The devil finds work for idle hands.* So what, that's what they said, right? I remember you telling me.'

'Yes. That's what I *told* you they said.'

Now Kei sat on the edge of the couch, not allowing himself to sink fully into it, his movements more deliberate as he began to register her tone. 'I don't get it. I can see you're upset, but—'

'I told *you* that's what they said, but it's not actually what they said. They told me, *The poor you will always have with you.* But these leaks, Kei – out of Brij's office, things only a handful of people know – they had to be coming from somewhere. First it was details of the Income Bill. That might have been Felix, or even Cass. Then there was a report about Brij's meeting with some OzProg backbenchers. I was there, and it got me wondering: have I been careless? Who have *I* been talking to? So when you kept asking about my work, I fed you a line, just in case, never really thinking—' abruptly she stopped speaking, shook her fingers out, took a breath. After what Kei had done, she was determined not to let him see her break. 'I fed my contact at DHS something different: *All that glisters is not gold.* But it was you – you were the only one. The devil. Idle hands.' She gave a rueful laugh. 'Seems about right.'

Kei's expression set hard, indignant. 'Wait. Are you accusing me? Of, what, telling journos about your work?'

Maggie held his gaze. 'Did you?'

For a few seconds he couldn't bring himself to talk, and his jaw worked silently behind pursed lips. When he spoke again, it was slow, like he was figuring something out in real-time. 'Your job has made you legit crazy, you know? If you never trusted me, why tell me anything? It's not like I really wanted to know, Maggie. You were so bummed about your project; I was trying to help you process.'

'Are you for real?' Her voice cracked, and she knew she was losing control. If he'd lied, she wasn't going to let him manipulate his way out of trouble. 'What other explanation is there? Tell me how this could be anyone but you.'

His eyebrows knit, and his hands gripped a couch cushion. 'I don't have a clue. This Income thing sounds like a fairly shitty idea if you really want to know my opinion, which you don't.' He was looking at the floor now, and there was something plaintive in his tone. 'I guess it's good this didn't go any further.'

Despite the logic, the knowledge that it could only have been one person, she hesitated. If it *had* been him, as it must have been, was it forgivable? Would it be possible to continue, and shut him out completely from that part of her life? Without meaning to, she'd come to view him as a source of stability, of comfort – but he was right. Kei and her mission had become incompatible.

With deliberate movements, desperate not to let him see the fury and pain he'd provoked, she closed the distance between them. From his place on the couch, he wouldn't meet her eyes. Her hand moved toward his sullen face, but Maggie couldn't have said why: she didn't want to embrace him or touch him in any way. There was nothing more that could productively be done, so she stepped clear. By the time she made it out the door, a car was already cruising slow along the street, waiting to take her.

CHAPTER 17

You'll get what's coming to you. You all will, everyone. And so am I!

> – Concession speech by Jeremy Buck, failed candidate
> for the federal seat of Katter, 9 February 2058

THAT EVENING, SCROLLING THROUGH LOGS OF missed calls – from journalists, Cass, Felix, Cass, her mother – Maggie decided that nothing good could come from interaction. Against her better judgement, not knowing where else to go, she'd retreated to her apartment in Bruce. She ordered in a meal. There was nothing much left in her fridge, in her cupboards: the cleaner Brij arranged after the break-in had been thorough.

Undertaking the usual household routines felt weird. The place was as quiet and still as a dry paddock. Her loose-leaf tea had been put back in the wrong place, and when she finally located it, she sat down on the floor, back pressed against a cabinet, and cradled the jar against her stomach.

Not quite forty-eight hours earlier, she'd surprised herself by thinking about Kei as someone like Brij's Allie, a caring spouse who might remain with her for years. When she'd served him up that fake quote from the Truvies, Maggie had been attempting to rule him *out* of suspicion. Even now, the nature of his betrayal violated every idea or concept or insight she'd accumulated about Kei Arakachi. To be so epically wrong might mean that from Kei's perspective, the relationship had always been transactional; that her own growing feelings, of not-quite-love-but-one-day-perhaps, had never been reciprocated. It terrified her, to entertain the possibility that she might be such a poor judge of character.

The following morning, Maggie procrastinated for hours, knowing full well the backlog that waited, blinking, in a sub-menu inside her right eye. It would be draining work. She wanted her Income – wanted it more than ever; it was what was left – and she knew that once she started, there would be no stopping until she'd caught up.

After she had dressed and re-dressed, and pinned her hair, she decided that it would be best to settle at the office in Barton, where there would be fewer distractions and more bodies around to keep her on task. Besides, she owed Brij a face-to-face conversation. On the drive in she caught herself raking her fingers against the armrest, and was overcome with self-disgust. As forcefully as she could manage, she shouted to release some of the pressure inside, but the cushioned surfaces of the cabin swallowed the noise.

Arriving, as soon as she was through the stairwell door and into the office proper, it was clear that something had gone wrong. There were too many human bodies, and they were too animated. To double-check, she killed all her overlays. Yes – no mistake, almost every single member of Brij's staff was physically present. There weren't enough chairs.

'The fuck have you been? Is your shroud busted?'

Maggie turned at the sound of Cass's voice. She was huddled with three data analysts, all of whom were recording. Cass waved them away. 'Follow me,' she told Maggie.

Falling in behind, Maggie trailed Cass through the open-plan space and into Brij's office. Their boss was absent. From habit, Maggie went to take one of the guest chairs. Without hesitation, Cass made for the seat on the other side of the large desk.

Red flags everywhere. 'What's going on?'

'Are you for real?' The look Cass shot back was scathing.

Maggie glanced toward the door. Testily, she said, 'I've had kind of a rough night. I turned off my notifications.'

'So you don't know?' Cass's face took on an almost pensive look. Her voice grew quiet. 'Maggie, Brij is in hospital. The med staff have put her in a coma.'

From the moment she'd arrived, some part of Maggie had been sifting theories, trying to find something that would make sense of what she was taking in. But this input was so perpendicular that, for an instant, she had to fight an impulse to laugh. Studying Cass again, Maggie could see the results of a night and a morning of crisis.

'It was a cardiac arrest, but they don't know what caused it. They're still running tests. One possibility is that she ingested something.'

'So … like an overdose? Of *what*?'

Cass shrugged, and leaned forward so that her arms rested heavy on Brij's desk. 'They're trying to work it out. But it there's no family history of heart disease, none of the usual risk factors.'

'And Allie?'

'With Brij. She's shattered, as you'd expect. I visited last night. Brij was on a ventilator, and it's too soon to tell whether she'll be okay, brain-wise, once she wakes up. So Allie's dealing with that, and there's all these cops running round trying to organise a security detail—'

Now Maggie felt herself catching up. 'Oh God, the media.'

'We're drafting a statement now. We're saying that an incident has occurred, Brij is in a stable condition, and it's being investigated—'

'Wait. Back up. Who's driving this if Brij is unconscious?'

Cass hesitated, choosing her words more deliberately than usual. 'Turns out Allie has a power of attorney for situations like this. So, for the time being, Allie can cast all of Brij's proxy votes. And. Allie's appointed me to run the office. Until Brij gets better.'

Later, Maggie would recall that her colleague at least had the good grace to look uncomfortable. Cass turned in Brij's chair, letting her gaze settle on the virtual bookshelf that had been projected against the far wall.

'How did she come to that decision?' Maggie asked, keeping her voice level.

'It was pretty simple. You and I have the best understanding of the Sutton policy platform. Can you believe that? And you weren't answering your messages.'

'And you've explained this to everyone outside.'

'Yep. They needed to know that someone's in charge.'

Someone, yes. Cass had assumed command. Maggie wondered how it might have gone down if she hadn't turned off her shroud. Would they have flipped a coin? Forged a power-sharing agreement? Maggie suspected that nothing much would be different. She admired many things about her friend, but Cass had a hunger that surfaced during moments like this. Maggie was ambitious, but she was programmed to wait until recognised, until her case became so compelling that no reasonable person could deny it. Cass was a street fighter, and now, in this moment of chaos and opportunity, she would take what she could.

Unable to keep the bitterness out of her voice, Maggie asked, 'So what's the plan, boss?'

Cass ignored the barb. 'We're going to pull back on most of our initiatives. At least until the dust settles.'

'Most. But not Income, right? I've just bought us the momentum we needed. This thing is building, we can't step away from it now.'

Cass shook her head. 'It's too complicated. At least while Brij is out of play, we need to streamline. Focus on one achievable thing.'

Ah. 'And let me guess what that is.'

Cass returned her stare, unashamed. 'Meat reform is our most advanced proposal. It's popular with our grantors, and it's not hard to understand.'

Some buried part of Maggie, irrational but canny, raised its hackles. In that moment, Cass presented like a threat, or worse: an enemy. Maggie couldn't let Cass's single-mindedness spoil everything that they'd done, everything that Brij had done. Speaking softly and slowly now, aware of the danger, she said, 'Cass, the carnivores broke into our homes, trashed them. What if it turns out Brij has been poisoned? This is not simple, and we – you – should not be making any rash decisions.'

Cass stood, turning away from Maggie, shifting restlessly until she came to lean against the far window ledge. She took to her feet again and resumed pacing. 'Guessing won't get us anywhere. Personally, if we're looking for threats, I'd probably start with the pricks that blew up DHS. They seemed to be pretty upset about the idea of an Income – but like I say, speculation doesn't help. Right or wrong, I've made the call.'

Maggie couldn't fight Cass, and Allie, and the whole office. She wasn't strong enough, even at the best of times, and certainly not while she was trying to process so much loss. The most Maggie could do right now was defend. Thinking fast, she said, 'At least— at least let's keep our options open. Brij could be back on deck next week, you know what she's like. So don't do anything to make it look like we're backing away. Let the reactions from *Oskar* play out.'

Maggie watched her counterpart bite back her first instinctive reaction. Perhaps the responsibility was tempering Cass, because she said, 'Alright, Maggie. I won't get in the way. But you need to leave it alone, too. You've taken your shot, and now the moderates will either get on board, or they won't. You need to drop out for a couple of days.' There was a moment of silence as both women considered the politics, and the practicalities. 'Huh,' Cass barked. 'It's not safe to stay in your apartment, not by yourself ... crashing at Liv and Raman's might bring trouble down on them. Kei?'

'Not an option,' Maggie said, willing Cass not to enquire further. 'But ... I might have another idea.' As much as she hated to admit it, Cass was right that they all needed to lay low. Following up her appearance with any more media work, while Brij was lying in a hospital bed, would make Maggie look callous. The problem was knowing how much trust she could place in Cass. With Maggie out of the picture, Cass would have total control over the office, and all of Brij's votes. She could change her mind again, give Income a quiet burial. 'You've got to give this a couple of days of full support, publicly and through our networks, to see where it lands. If you won't do that for me, do it for Brij, okay?'

Cass turned her head and gave Maggie the bird-eye. 'I already said I would!' Maggie nodded and started for the door, but Cass wasn't quite done. 'And, you know,' she muttered, 'be safe. Take the time you need. I'll keep things going here.'

MAGGIE'S EXPRESSION MUST HAVE BEEN INTENSE, because it was enough to send two of her co-workers scrambling out of the casting room. Once she was alone, she called Kinnear and he answered immediately, audio only.

'Hang on,' he said. 'I'll find somewhere to be.'

When he'd settled and turned on his avatar, so that it appeared, seated, in the armchair opposite, Maggie said, 'I'm sorry to call you like this.'

'You're at your work?'

'Yes, but I don't know for how much longer.'

'What do you mean?'

'Something's about to break,' Maggie said.

Kinnear hadn't leaked her meeting with the Truvies, but that didn't mean he was trustworthy. Still, with everything in flux, she felt like she had little to lose. She needed an ally, and intentionally or not, that was how she'd come to think about Kinnear, how he'd presented himself. He would have to do.

Speaking quickly and quietly, she told him what she knew about Brij.

'Oh, Maggie, I'm sorry.' He looked like he meant it.

'Yeah, well. I don't know what I can do for her right now. More public comment, from me, might be counterproductive. When the news about Brij drops, it will be all anyone will want to talk about, and trying to segue over to the topic of an Income will look ruthless.'

Kinnear mused. 'Things will move on, sooner than you'd believe. But for now, I think your instincts are right. You've set things to spinning. Now you need to step back and see where it all lands.'

'I think so, yeah. We've made our case, and if it's meant to be, some of our friends in OzProg will pick up the ball. They're the ones who need to bring it on for a vote.' Deliberately, Maggie tried not to think about how others might turn Brij's situation to their own advantage. This was another reason that things should be left to others in OzProg: as desperately as she wanted an Income, Maggie didn't think she could bring herself to leverage her mentor's condition for tactical gain. 'Actually, that's why I called. You mentioned that if I ever wanted to get away from Canberra' – she used the colonial name as a way of alluding to the capital's insular political bubble, rather than the place itself – 'you knew some people.'

'I did say that.' He paused, as if weighing something up. Perhaps the timing of Maggie's request was awkward, or

Kinnear had misgivings about burdening his contacts with someone at the centre of a political storm. 'Give me a moment.' His avatar froze.

Half a minute passed, and his mouth moved again. 'Can you get to Bankstown Airport this afternoon?'

'Back to Sydney?' Maggie asked, and Kinnear offered a shrug.

'Hangar one one two. Ask for Captain Jelly. They've got a delivery for some friends in the Surrender, and I'm sure it won't be any trouble to ferry you up at the same time.'

'This isn't anything illegal, is it?' Maggie felt stupid for asking, but she couldn't afford more controversy. It unnerved her to think that in a few hours she could be travelling out of her country for the first time in her life.

'Absolutely not. It's ... outside of official channels. Some private donors ship medical supplies. While officially the government doesn't participate, it serves our interest to avoid any kind of crisis north of the border. Over the years I've accumulated the right kind of contacts, so I help facilitate. Have done for years. The Minister knows all about it, as did their predecessor.'

'Oh.'

'You can say you're volunteering, or fact-finding.' When Maggie didn't respond, he said, 'Buck up. You're making the right decision. I think this will be very good for you.'

MAGGIE SWUNG PAST HER APARTMENT TO PACK A bag. She'd been shuttling back and forth between cities for months, living out of a large suitcase, but for this trip she would need to travel light. She packed underwear, socks and versatile clothing that would see her through a few days. Two portable chargers for her shroud. She didn't know much about what it would be like on the other side of the border, other than occasional items on news feeds. Queenslanders might have felt differently, but people from the southern states tended not to think too much about the situation in the Cape. There were plenty of other problems closer to home.

For an aggravating half-hour, Maggie tried to formulate a message that she could send to Allie. An IRL visit to the hospital would not be welcomed, Maggie sensed; she would only be in the way. After battling with her AI ghostwriter, and deleting the last of several tortured drafts, she settled for a mashup of the usual platitudes.

Should she have fought Cass harder for control? But it had been an ambush, and anyway, she wasn't interested in overseeing Brij's entire program. Office admin would be nothing but a distraction – as long as Cass stayed true to her word. The only thing that Maggie could do for Brij was to get the Income put up for a vote, so that once Brij recovered, they could watch the numbers tally and break in their favour.

There was no time, no time to take a breath, she felt like she was pinballing from one crisis into another. If anything important happened, her shroud would let her know. But in her body, Maggie ached for escape.

CTRL+Z

TEZ GAREWAL, FORMER ELITE B-FLY HUNTER (CUR-rent ranking in freefall) is still running. He can't say what he's running from, or toward, but there is constant frantic move-ment in the high-intensity training centre of his mind.

Item one: he can't stop lucid-dreaming about Hanabi. In the early hours, as he edges close to the fuzzy boundary of sleep, she appears to him, and he doesn't have the will or inclination to make her leave. When his eyelids close, he is in some non-descript locale, skinned in his Decartes avatar, and she resolves in front of him. She slowly raises her mask, just like she did the last time he met her. As then, it's like catching a glimpse of some sexy god. Her features are somehow delicate and strong, imperfect in a way that a facegen app would struggle to achieve without heavy tweaking. Emerald eyes, keen but ever-so-slightly asymmetrical, and long hair so dark it eats the light, swept back and tied in some sort of loose, faux-effortless arrangement that probably reflects an on-trend style that Tez has never heard of. The bridge of her nose is thin, widening out into a broad, flat apex. She has an amber complexion that doesn't quite mask sporadic acne scars just above her jawline. She and Tez must be close in age. In his vision, she gives him time to study her, an act of forbearance, before she reasserts herself.

[On the ground, dude.]

Aware at all times that he is dreaming her, and not the other way around, he nonetheless complies. She stands over him, mask resting firmly on the crown of her head, her floor-length scarlet robe obscuring the shape of everything below her shoulders.

[Watch me. Don't look away.]

And he can't, and wouldn't, as she undoes a clasp at her throat and the robe billows to the floor, revealing a body taut with youth and insolence. She stands proudly facing him, feet comfortably apart, ready for his attention. Again she pauses, but this is not hesitation on her part; it must be for his benefit, to give him time to take her in. Tez, a man happily lost in his own fantasy, gazes without shame. He can't quite decide if she would have retained or removed her pubic hair, leaving her labia either clearly visible, or not, and in his excitement he doesn't much care. She moves forward, kneeling on either side of his hips, and leans over him so that he is looking up into her eyes.

With his right hand he reaches out, but she intercepts, gripping him by the wrist. He relents, and this makes her smile.

[Neither of us is really here.]

[I know.]

And he does know it, even swept up as he is, and the scene swerves, and he is reclined on the casting chair in his actual bedroom. And impossibly she is still with him, still on him, even though his shroud has disengaged, and he feels her, feels himself pressing against her. She has pulled her mask back down over her face, but otherwise remains unclothed. She starts to move.

'We need to be quiet,' he says out loud, and she continues, ignoring him.

Evening after morning after evening, the same sequence plays out. It's not like he's conjuring it up. It's more like an autoplay vid that, having stumbled upon randomly, he can't bring himself to turn off. He hasn't accessed conventional porn in weeks.

After these visitations, Tez feels both gratified and disquieted. Hanabi – whoever she/they (she?) really are – could be an actual terrorist, responsible for death, injury and erasure. He hates that she still has claim over him, even if only in his own mind. Some days he is tempted to try and track her down again. He is desperate to know her truly, and why she played him. To know if her meatspace body aligns with her avatar, and his vivid fantasising. But he refrains, and for once it's not because he's scared. She has started something in him, he is beginning to realise. But the rest of this process is for him to execute. For good or ill, she has done her work, and if all algorithms run true, they won't meet again.

And so notwithstanding – or maybe therefore – item two: he's corresponding with some of the activists he met in Goulburn. At first, it was a half-hearted attempt to glean whether they knew about the DHS plot in advance. Has he been hanging with murderers, or at least their sympathisers? If so, does that necessarily make their worldview invalid?

But from all he can tell, the Goulburn crew were as surprised and disgusted as anyone about how the protest ended up. There's no one camped at DHS now – it's a crime scene IRL and in shroudspace, so not a great place for anyone to loiter – and there's no consensus from within the movement about next steps.

If his new friends down south come to learn that Tez has a sister prosecuting the case for an Income, they'll think he's a spy. But that's an almost perfect inversion of the truth. Tez has absorbed too much, has been persuaded about the righteousness of their cause. Even with everything that's happened, he wants to help them. Has begun to help them, in his way, even though it feels like familial disloyalty. By following the trail Hanabi laid out for him, he might have inadvertently sabotaged Maggie's career; might have put her in danger. Those possibilities are real and, for the time being, unconfirmable. They make him feel clenched inside, but they don't change what he has come to believe, or what he aspires to become.

Item three: he's looking for a place of his own, a little semi-private dorm cell somewhere down Theodore way, where it's cheap. A radical (if that's what he is now), however timid, can't live with his mum. Before he can make the move, he'll have to save up some basket, but through an old uni contact, he's got a lead on a freelance gig running a team of customer service bots. Night-times, he's also lined up work pouring drinks at a local bar, having fabricated a CV and a certificate from a hospo course. How hard can it be to mix a few cocktails? He'll practice on Liv and Raman before his first shift.

This menial work has the potential to crush his soul. But only, he figures, if he leaves his soul lying around to be crushed. Tez has other plans.

It was the Goulbourn crew that gave him an answer. None of them have two doges to rub together, but they do have work, an economy. They work for each other, for the community, and their economy exists to facilitate those exchanges. And once he had the realisation, Tez couldn't believe it had taken years to arrive: *no one can stop him working besides himself.* The world at large can refuse to pay him. Can deem his contribution to be valueless. But, privileged in all the ways that he is, Tez has absolute discretion to work, or not, and to share the results of his labour, or not.

Thus, item *n+1*: he is building a locale. A publicly accessible environment showcasing a design that, as he describes it on his brand-new blog, *fosters interaction between meat- and aug-perspectives in a mutually enriching, accessible and integrated realm.* Even now, many IRL spaces are not built to gracefully accommodate virtual guests casting in, or they inhibit comms between meatspace and virtual occupants. Tez's plan calls for semi-sheltered pods with good sightlines, perfect for casting into, as well as RFID-studded thoroughfares reserved for meatspace folks, so that they can move without feeling like they need to dodge avatars or turn down their shrouds. Augmented themes complement real, moveable furniture, positioned to break up the open plan without causing congestion. An identical, purely shroudspace mirror of the room allows neurodivergent or socially anxious folk like Tez to practice being there in the safety of the virtual, so that if they visit later in meatspace, they know precisely what to expect.

Tez has modelled occupancy at peak times and during events. With cork floors and a patterned cloud ceiling, the acoustics work. Negativity triggers are minimised, and a canopy of climbing plants just above head-height adds greenery without obscuring the light from the new clerestory windows. There is flex so that catering, meetings, common spaces and breakouts can all be achieved. As a communal area it *works*, and it makes him content, a new and welcome feeling.

He's publishing plans, bills of materials, cost estimates; everything that builders, of varying qualifications and levels of experience, can use to embody the design. He's made it free for the taking, for anyone who wants it, but the example dimensions map the godawful lobby of that high-rise he got squished into down at the Academy site in Goulburn. He's talking with some of the complex managers there about knocking out walls, remodelling. Early days, but Tez thinks they get it.

If he was doing this as another oblique attempt to land a paying gig, then it would be demeaning, just another way of devaluing his own labour by working for exposure. But he's almost certain this is not what's happening. He means this as a gift.

Tez Garewal, former elite slacker, is a compendium:
volatile / lustful / talented /
arrogant / fretful /
busy.

His work will be valued; is being made manifest, if not in the way he would have expected. There is no time for malaise.

CHAPTER 18

With travel restrictions easing and a powerful new suite of broad-spectrum prophylactics hitting the market, in-person travel is easier and safer than it's been in decades. 'Curated e-tours are great and certainly have their place', explains Chris David Michaelson, head of Tourism Australia. 'And clearly they'll continue to dominate the market. But if it's been a few years, or maybe even longer, since you've been on the road for real, I beg you to give it another chance. Live a little. Smell, and touch, and taste. Without a little risk, there's no reward.'

— Intro, '17 Safe Australian Road Journeys'

FROM THE LANDSIDE END, THE CORRUGATED IRON hangar appeared so shabby as to suggest dereliction. It was only when she knocked for a third time, hard against the nondescript off-white door that was the only entrance, that an older man with a sizeable paunch shoved it aside and squinted at her, waiting for an explanation.

'Captain Jelly?' Maggie ventured.

He laughed and shook his head. 'She's out the back. Come through.'

The hangar was crowded tight with old jets and smaller monoprop planes, nested at angles to fit within the confines of the structure. Off to the left, a small, carpeted, cube-like workspace huddled, like the front office for an auto mechanic. The place smelled of metal, oil, and something almost cloying, which Maggie guessed was aviation fuel.

Sat on a fold-out chair behind a card table, an elegant blonde woman, skin immaculate but with the slightly brittle look of someone older who'd stuck religiously to a treatment regimen, was worrying at a piece of paper with a biro. She didn't look up until the man who'd let Maggie in cleared his throat. 'This is, uh …'

'Maggie Garewal. Tim Kinnear suggested I see you.'

'Angelique Kleiss.' She offered her fingertips. 'Timmy said you were on your way. We can always use another pair of hands on a trip like this.'

'She does prefer to go by Captain Jelly,' said the man, who still hadn't introduced himself. Angelique fixed him with a stare, but he continued unperturbed. 'Check out the dedication to the craft, working out a fuel load on paper like she's Nancy Bird Walton.'

Angelique looked Maggie up and down. 'What do you weigh? There's not that much to you – usually my hitchhikers are large and oafish, like Frankie here. I might need to run these numbers again.'

'Thanks for agreeing to take me. I hope I haven't put you to too much trouble.'

'Not at all! We'll make you work for passage. Frank, show Maggie where to put our cargo.'

He led her to the small office, which was littered with red canvas duffel bags. 'All of this stuff,' he said, grabbing a bag off the floor. 'And everything in there.' He pointed at a small refrigerator.

Maggie grabbed a bag and followed him back out and past two planes. He stopped at a relatively compact, gunmetal-grey jet, and opened a panel in the fuselage. 'Just dump it all in there.' He started to walk away, and added, 'Some of it's fragile.'

The jet's single engine perched on the roof of the aircraft like an aerodynamic hump. The body of the craft was bulbous at the front end, tapering off to a slim tail with V-shaped control surfaces. Maggie loaded the aft compartment until it was full, then started piling bags in the rear row of passenger seats inside the cabin. Angelique had jumped in the pilot's seat up front, and was jabbing at a keyboard in the centre console. A map appeared on the display, and lines sprang up, charting a path up the coast. Noticing Maggie taking it all in, Angelique said, 'My pride and joy. Practically an antique, one of the first personal jets, from the mid-twenties. Probably older than you are, Maggie. You wouldn't believe how much it costs to run. I mean, it was always expensive, but now with the synthfuel converter, the offsets … it's astronomical. She's a temperamental old bird, too, but nothing's more fun to fly.'

It was another hour before they were ready to take off. Frank and Angelique hauled open the huge airside hangar doors, and started tugging planes onto the apron so that they could get Angelique's jet out. For the most part, Maggie stood and watched, feeling useless. She checked again that her own large backpack had made it inside the cabin and, curious, she unzipped one of the red supply bags. Inside were bandages, bottles of steriliser, blister packets full of small white pills. She felt the plane jolt, and quickly zipped the bag back up, and poked her head out of the cabin door. Frank had attached the mechanical tug to the nosewheel of the aircraft. 'Get out,' he said, not unkindly. 'Hard enough without dead weight.'

Once the jet was outside, they had to re-park the other aircraft they'd moved. Standing on the apron with Angelique, they watched as Frank waved at them perfunctorily, walked back to the hangar, and began to slide the doors home.

Inside the cabin, the three rear seats were crowded with red bags, and Angelique motioned for Maggie to take the copilot's chair.

'Is this okay?'

'Sure. Just don't touch anything.' The seat was comfortable but cramped, and Maggie's feet brushed lightly against two pedals on the floor. She drew her legs back quickly, sitting curled up and silent, watching a couple of other aircraft depart and land while Angelique ran through a long sequence of pre-flight checks. When she was done, she threw Maggie a URL. 'So you can listen to air traffic control. Turn on your noise cancelling while we take off.'

When Maggie synced her audio, she could hear chatter between the tower and aircraft in the vicinity. It was hard to decode the meaning of the quick bursts of dialogue, and then Angelique added her own voice to the mix. 'Good morning Bankstown Ground, Vision Delta Romeo Lima to Cairns with two onboard, we are holding in the southern runup bay, request taxi and airways.'

'Delta Romeo Lima, not a problem, continue taxiing via alpha and alpha eight, hold short runway two nine right, remain on this frequency.'

'Hold two-niner right at alpha eight, staying with you, Delta Romeo Lima.'

'Delta Romeo Lima, number two in a controlled airspace, following the twin that's lined up runway centre.'

'Delta Romeo Lima, no problem.'

The sensation of the jet rolling forward was problematic. Although they were advancing in a measured way, Maggie was surprised to find herself gripping the armrests. The feeling was different to being in a car, less controlled, more like one was being shunted from behind by a giant hand, and the windscreen afforded her a view of the centre lines of the runup bay slipping under the nose of the small craft. Maggie had only been airborne a couple of times in her life, in newer, much larger electric jets. Maggie knew that she should let Angelique concentrate, even as they held waiting for permission to take off, but her nerves craved a distraction, and she asked, 'Why do these supplies need to be flown? Why not send them by road, or rail?'

Angelique didn't seem to mind talking. 'A lot of this is fragile, perishable and expensive. The other surgeons at my practice have all donated, and I wouldn't trust this cargo with anyone else. Anyway, the roads get bad north of Townsville. You'll see.'

Bankstown Ground jumped in with their clearance, and after that, things happened quickly. Maggie watched as Angelique hit a few more buttons on the console, then edged the throttle so that they rolled onto the main runway. When they'd straightened, Maggie heard the whine of the jet as it spun up, past the aural dampening provided by her shroud. The craft punched forward, gathering speed as Angelique worked to hold the wheels on either side of the centre line, until Maggie felt the craft pitch back and the air take them.

Angelique was busy with chatter from air traffic control, getting clearances for flight levels and a route out of controlled airspace around Sydney. There was something romantic, if disconcerting, about such a complicated system being overseen by humans. Perhaps irrationally, air transport was one of the rare fields in which the important decisions were not entrusted to machines. Managing traffic was, at its heart, an almost trivially solvable problem in a mathematical sense, but Maggie could understand most people's reticence to board a flight routed entirely by an AI.

She strained upright in her seat to look past the nose, over to the right side of the plane and the centre of the city. Her shroud labelled all the major buildings and landmarks for her: the white sails of Opera House poking above the seawall, the Harbor Bridge, Casino Point. In minutes it was all behind them, and they were over forest, coastline far away on the pilot's side.

Maggie studied Angelique. She was a model of composure, her eyes frequently moving from horizon to the centre display and back, but her movements were unhurried and precise. Maggie was curious, but before she could work out how to frame a question, the older woman must have noticed her glancing. 'I got into the wrong line of work,' she explained. 'I practice at the more elective end of my specialty, and that keeps me in av fuel. But it comes with a karmic deficit.'

Now that they were airborne and hurtling above the land, the realness of what she was doing, their destination, hit Maggie in a new way. The Surrender was dangerous – that was one of the reasons the Roy Government had put the entire peninsula in the too-hard basket, to the relief of most of the nation. Surrendering the land, excising it from Australia's and Queensland's borders, had meant that no one needed to take responsibility for the ever-larger numbers of climate refugees washing ashore. It meant no more ugly suppression of the independence movements that kept flaring up, led by Traditional Owners. No more reconstruction efforts bleeding the taxpayer dry every other cyclone season. And for the military – the military of Australia's strongest ally – it was a dark zone, the perfect training ground and test-bed for hostile tropical conditions. Although travel was not formally restricted, it wasn't a place that right-thinking Australians tended to go.

'I saw you on my feed,' said Angelique, cutting into Maggie's thoughts. The pilot had settled back in her seat, content to let the plane keep them steady and pointed forward. 'I don't know whether an Income's a good idea or not, but it's made all the old windbags at my practice cranky.'

Maggie laughed. 'Delighted to hear it. I don't know what'll happen. Maybe nothing.' For the last few hours, Maggie had been able to think about other things, but now her mind turned back to her mission, and she felt her stomach tighten in the old familiar way. 'Most of the time it feels very abstract, not like … I mean, Jesus. You're literally piloting a jet to deliver much-needed medical supplies.'

Perhaps Angelique heard bitterness in Maggie's voice. 'You've got to give it a shot, though, right? You're young, and this is filling you up. But ideas are ways to impose your thinking on others. Ideas are colonists! One day, you'll get them out of your system.'

It was stuffy in the cabin and the afternoon sun slanted into the cockpit from the aircraft's ten o'clock. Maggie tried to fight the drowsiness that was stealing over her. Angelique seemed glad to have a companion for the flight, and to pass out now might come across as ungrateful. But it was to no avail: Maggie hadn't slept well in days, and after a comfortable silence had descended somewhere north of Roma, her eyes tucked themselves in and drew the curtains. Some indeterminate time later, she felt a hand on her arm.

'Hey, sorry to wake you, but we'll be touching down in Cairns in ten.'

Maggie felt disorientated. 'Cairns? We're not landing in the Surrender?'

'God no. The paperwork for a cross-border flight is horrendous, and the landing strip up there isn't much better. From Cairns, you drive.' Angelique squinted at her. 'How much did Timmy K tell you about us?'

'Not much. A while back he mentioned he had some friends up north. Said if I ever needed to get away, he could think of worse places to go.'

'Ah. Well, Pablo and Frew are the loveliest boys.'

'That's who we're meeting?'

'That's who we're meeting.' Angelique seemed quietly amused. 'For the last couple of years, they've been running one of the main aid programs out of Dug. They'll look after you north of the border.'

'Wait – you're not staying?'

'I've got surgery tomorrow. Don't tell me Tim didn't mention *that*? You'll have to make your own way home.'

Maggie nodded, but didn't trust herself to speak.

Angelique's attention was diverted as she made contact with Cairns air traffic control, and followed their assigned route for the descent. The ocean had come back at them as they neared their destination, and by the horizon, tiny white wisps of cloud surfed above like the ghosts of dead coral. Maggie wondered whether these kinds of flights were possible in the wet season. Perhaps the supplies they carried would form part of a stockpile to help ride out the summer months.

Their approach took them directly over Admiralty Island, over the river and the stunted low-rise buildings that occupied the city's centre, like blocky bonsai plants on top of a cliff. It must have been low tide, and beyond the crumbling embankments, mud flats and twisty mangroves swept out halfway to the horizon, dwarfing the scale of anything human-made.

The landing was less exhilarating than the take-off, and more purely terrifying, as Angelique made small rudder adjustments to compensate for a crosswind, feathering them down the runway at an ever-so-slightly oblique angle until the tyres bit and Maggie was sure the plane would flip over. But of course nothing like that happened.

'Thank you,' said Maggie. 'You're an excellent pilot.'

Angelique kept her eyes forward, letting her work speak for itself.

THE SKY WAS DARKENING BY THE TIME ANGELIQUE and Maggie had managed to stow the jet in a squat concrete hangar. Maggie was starving, but there was only water and instant coffee on hand in the tiny, filthy kitchen onsite. Near the landside exit loomed an ancient truck with an open tray at the rear, its body sitting high off the ground, bonnet sporting a massive bullbar that looked like it had seen action. Maggie could see a steering wheel in the cabin.

Next to the vehicle, dwarfed by it, a pair of young men waited in apparent contentment.

'What've you got for us this time, Jel?' one of them called out. He was wearing worn moleskin trousers and heavy brown boots, which must have been uncomfortable in the humidity.

'Hey, Frew, lovely to see you, too. This is Maggie. Kinnear sent her to help for a couple of days. You'll take care of her, right?'

Frew's companion, dressed in a check shirt and tight blue work shorts, narrowed his eyes in a look of mock scrutiny. 'Well, if she's got opposable thumbs, she can tweeze hookworms out of feet.'

'That's the spirit.'

Now that Maggie was closer to them, she noticed tell-tale scars flanking their noses. She knew there would be similar scars at the openings of their ear canals. They'd had their shrouds removed, in adulthood. They could easily have had the scars concealed; no doubt Angelique could have helped them. The fact that they had failed to do so made it a statement.

The four of them worked together to shift the medical cargo from the jet to the rear of the truck, which was already near-full with rice flour, cooking oil, canisters of distilled water, and netted piles of second-hand clothes.

'Wanna drive?' Pablo asked Maggie.

'I haven't in years … and I'm not sure this is a good time to practice.'

Pablo shrugged, and opened the right-hand side door. Frew claimed the squeezy middle seat in the cabin's single row.

Before she joined them, Maggie clasped Angelique by the shoulder. 'Thanks for the ride, especially at such short notice. I hope we run into each other again.'

Angelique waved her off, to indicate that it had been no trouble, and turned for the hangar.

Once they had the doors slammed shut, Frew and Pablo each tugged at safety belts that unwound from over their shoulders, clipping them at buckles near their waists. Watching this, Maggie felt around for her own belt, sliding the clasp home in an unfamiliar, awkward motion. Pablo pressed the start button, provoking a whine from the electric engine accompanied by an intermittent rhythmic shudder that Maggie felt in her legs. Out on the highway, they headed north.

Ten minutes out from the airport, Maggie spotted drones running a line out west, glinting in the dusk. She knew they'd be policing the border, shuttling from here to Carpentaria and back. Down below, there was more ground traffic than she'd expected for a mid-size town. Maggie supposed there was still plenty to do, for those prepared to live here. As the northernmost Australian city on the east coast, Cairns was an important logistical hub. Judging from the number of military vehicles they passed coming the other way, the Yanks had a large official presence in town, not to mention soldiers visiting on leave. The buildings that they passed were hardened, with few if any windows, their designers reluctant to send more than a storey or two skyward. Drainage channels marked the land, doing what they could to alleviate the worst of the torrential rains that visited the place in the wet.

They pulled off the road just as the sun sank, when Frew spotted a roadside shack selling banh mi. 'You hungry, Maggie? We'd better grab something.' Frew unclipped his seatbelt. 'The food is both less and more interesting on the other side. They're trying some crops up around Cooktown, engineered to be more resilient, but we've had a couple of bad seasons in a row, so it's back to tinned stuff for the most part – or you take your chances with the local catch.'

They munched their rolls sitting in the car, parked by the highway. The only lights came from the nearby stall and the headlights of other vehicles passing. As their only mutual acquaintance, they swapped stories about Kinnear. When he'd finished with his meal, Pablo pulled them back out of the car park and kept them pointed north.

'I did a stint in the econometrics division of Human Support,' Frew explained, 'before Pabs and I went feral. I only spoke with Kinnear a couple of times, but when I resigned to go northside, Kinnear looked me up, told me to keep in touch. Said he could help with logistics.' He laughed, and there was no bitterness in it. 'Dult collects people like they're NFTs.'

'I guess he's collected me, now, too.'

'Looks like it. But he's been good to us,' said Pablo. 'He's strange, but I think the strangeness comes from a big, scheming, generous, frustrated brain, if that makes any sense.'

'Did Kinnear introduce the two of you to each other?' asked Maggie, leaning past her seatbelt so that she could see the faces of both of her companions.

'Nah, we studied together. Commerce at UQ, which is one way of getting a tour of how deeply fucked things are.'

'You should see our student loans,' added Frew.

'I hooked up with Frewie at a pub crawl in second year, and we've never looked back. Of course, then I got caught up in student politics, all the running battles with the Young Right.'

Maggie couldn't join the dots. These men were erudite, educated, with the necessary connections. What had led them to a life so far from the core? When Maggie had graduated, she'd felt the weight of obligation – to succeed, to embody the faith that her family and her society had invested within her person – compelling her toward power, toward the establishment. That, she had understood so clearly at the time, was where one repaid the debt.

Ahead, traffic had banked up near a red-bricked roadside tavern, and they were forced to slow. On the footpath between the tavern and the road, a shaggy, bare-arsed man in thongs and a T-shirt was attempting to navigate a hopscotch course, while his mates howled encouragement or derision. Brief honks issued from some of the other vehicles nearby.

Frew drew back in his seat, wincing. 'Well, that's a look.'

'Is this ... a thing up here?' Maggie didn't try to hide her confusion.

In the driver's seat, Pablo shook his head. 'Absolutely not. But also, I guess, welcome to the Cape?'

It had been a long, strange day, and a pantsless man wasn't worth dwelling on. Maggie took a few moments to anticipate what the rest of the evening might hold, and what she could do to smooth the ride. 'Hey, speaking of looks … I noticed you've both gone naked. No shrouds, I mean.' Pablo nodded, but they both waited for Maggie to continue. 'I don't know how important that is to you, but full disclosure, mine is still installed.'

Frew smiled. 'Thanks for checking. That's cool, we're not militant about it or anything. But a lot of our clients have had, shall we say, lived experience with surveillance. So this' – he pointed to a scar above his eye – 'reassures them. You might want to stay offline while you're here. Not that that'll stop people watching through your eyes if they really want to.'

Maggie almost laughed, and then caught herself. 'You think that sort of thing really happens?'

'I know it does,' said Frew. 'But I doubt anyone'd bother for the likes of us. The government doesn't want a humanitarian crisis, so we're basically doing their dirty work for them. Perpetuating the status quo. That's why Kinnear is able to help us – we're a tool of the regime.'

'Don't get him started,' said Pablo. 'He'll be like this the whole way to Dug.'

Quietly, Maggie set about putting her shroud into deep hibernation, instructing it to only reactivate if she received a message from Cass, Allie or Tez, or any other update about Brij's condition.

They drove on for another five minutes before they hit Palm Cove, a crowded shanty-town with signs hawking immigration agents, army surplus stores, dental clinics and bulk food emporiums. On the far side was a zone cleared of trees, buildings and debris for about one hundred metres. No need for a fence. Approaching from this direction, the border amounted to nothing more than a sign informing travellers that they were about to leave the Commonwealth of Australia. No checks on the way out, but across a concrete divider, the incoming road-way fattened into a dozen lanes, with vehicles held up at boom gates and staffed entry booths. At this, the busiest crossing point in Australia, Customs and Immigration were working to make sure nothing unwanted made it over the threshold.

They passed on through, and the road worsened immediately. Pablo hunched his shoulders and leaned over the wheel.

CHAPTER 19

Flesh x flesh touching is gross.

> Get your DIY IVF kit today.

> – Billboard, Southern Cross Station, Narrm

'PINEAPPLES AND COCONUTS, COCONUTS AND pineapples. I'm over it, Pabs.'

Pablo smiled beatifically, and threw a wink at Maggie. 'Do you want a mango?'

Frew glowered. 'I want a divorce and a bacon and egg roll.'

When Maggie woke in her bunk, her first thought had been to check her feed – but that was the impulse of a long-ingrained habit, and she resolved to ignore it. It had only been a day, less than twenty-four hours since she'd observed Cass looking much too comfortable as she perched behind Brij's desk. The point of this journey was distance.

The bunkroom was a cramped underground space that slept eighteen, with an adjoining toilet and shower and no other concessions to privacy. Pablo and Frew had their own room on the ground floor, and the bunkroom served as a crisis shelter for anyone who needed a night or two away from their current situation. With the wind noise from the surface all but muted, the only sounds were from other sleepers – the ruffling of sheets, the sag of a tired mattress as someone turned over. Snores, soft and louder. By the time Maggie had arrived the previous night, and had helped to unload the truck, everyone else staying in the dorm had already turned in. In the semi-dark, she had set about wiping down her mattress with cloth and disinfectant. With so many people sharing the space, she worried about pathogens, then worried that her concern revealed an unconscious racial bias. But no: she had been just as anxious back in the hall in Belconnen, sleeping three to a rack with students and job-seekers, before she'd landed her role with Brij. Still, the population here would naturally be less vaccinated, and had arrived from all over the hemisphere, carrying alien flora. She tried to let these thoughts exist and pass by, but they lingered, running laps.

Waking in the morning, she had found herself among strangers. She traded nods and timid waves with a few dorm-mates, who ranged from adolescents to the untreated elderly. By the way she dressed, even by the mint condition of her backpack, they would have been able to tell that Maggie was some sort of volunteer, or a tourist, and for the time being she was glad that she'd inherited her father's colouring. She could guess with low levels of confidence at ethnicities: locals with Djabuganjdi, Kuku-yalanji or Yidinjdji heritage; Islanders who'd left their drowned, doomed homes behind; refugees fleeing still-contested regions of the Malay Peninsula. Maggie wondered what had brought them into Pablo and Frew's orbit, and where they planned to go next.

Above ground, breakfast was served on long tables in a clearing next to the main building. The sky was streaked with high cloud, and the air felt oppressive, but no serious weather was expected that week. The compound was squat and contoured, hugging the earth and slathered in thick concrete to withstand the winds when they came. Frew introduced Maggie to some of the longer-term residents, and they swapped outlines of their lives, Maggie keeping things vague and mentioning that a friend had suggested she come up and volunteer. A handful of young men had recently arrived here in Dug, looking for work, and were staying at the compound until they were able to find somewhere more permanent; others hinted obliquely at family troubles, or a destitution so entire that Maggie had no reference point for it. There were plenty of unemployed people in Australia proper. But between government and community, hardly anyone went hungry in the way that an older woman described to Maggie, of being caught unprepared by the last storm, of losing everything she owned, and thereafter picking through refuse piles. As she listened, Maggie tried not to glance at the bowl of fruit placed on the table between them.

In time, Pablo wandered by. 'I'm heading north today, visiting one of the farming settlements. Want to tag along?'

'Sure,' Maggie replied, trying to match his casual tone. She followed Pablo back inside the windowless building, down the corridor until it opened into a rudimentary clinic and dispensary. Frew stood behind the counter, and he slid a cardboard box toward Pablo. 'Be safe,' he said.

'You're not coming?' Maggie asked.

'I'm not fond of Pablo's little road trips.' The tired way he said it suggested to Maggie that this was well-trodden ground. 'And someone needs to stay here.' He glanced behind him, at the medical supplies stacked haphazardly on wire shelving along the wall. 'We've never had a problem, but better safe than sorry.'

Maggie helped Pablo repack the truck, and they edged out onto the road. Pablo and Frew's compound was at the bottom end of Davidson Street, the main thoroughfare out of the old town, and here at least the structures looked permanent, reinforced. Most other buildings had a tapered shape like concrete anthills, hinting at excavation below. Here and there, ramshackle sheds had been erected to provide more expansive, albeit precarious, forms of shelter, and on stalls out the front of some of these buildings, traders were displaying their wares: fresh fruit and vegetables, tinned goods, clothing, building supplies. Roll-out solar panels, the kind the UN handed out after disasters, were battened to the tops of tin roofs, and strings of portable batteries dangled like rope ladders down the sides of walls.

Pablo pointed out a squat, squarish concrete building that had been painted a cheery terracotta. 'That's the post office.' Even though it was early, Maggie could see that a queue had formed, snaking away down a side street.

'People send, what, physical mail up here?'

'Not exactly. It's run by a Kuku-yalanji woman, Lana. There are so many groups here now. She's taken on the job of keeping the register. Names, where everyone's staying.'

They were following Port Douglas Road now, and as they left the town centre, the structures became more chaotically situated, and flimsy. It had been dark when they'd arrived the night before, but now Maggie could see just how large the settlement was. Treeless, interspersed with areas of marshland, it sprawled as far as Maggie could see. And people everywhere:

emerging from houses, lining the sides of the roads, pedalling slowly on bicycles. 'What's the population here?' Maggie asked.

'Just for Dug? Best estimate is four hundred thousand, but it fluctuates depending on the season, and how bad things are further north.'

'And this Lana, she keeps an address list?'

'She gets help from the different communities, but she holds the master roll. It can't be easy. People move around a lot, and that's in between times. When a decent storm hits, all bets are off.'

'What do you mean?'

'There are thirteen designated shelters up here, built deep in the years before the Surrender. When a storm comes in, people take what they can carry with them. All of this ...' he pointed out the driver's side window at the shacks lining the roadside, and shook his head. 'Afterwards, there's a rule of thumb: if you've got a foundation and at least one wall still standing, you're entitled to reclaim your site. Otherwise, it's a land grab. Problematic, because people leave shelter too early, to salvage what they can and claim high ground even while sheet metal is still whizzing around overhead. Still, it's the only system that most people can agree on.

He shrugged. 'Actually, it stops a lot of fighting. If there's a dispute over a structure, the parties go see Lana and she consults her lists. The communities see the value in having an umpire, and they back her.'

'And the mail?'

'Well, a lot of people up here are naked from birth, or they've been through trouble and had their shrouds removed.

So, yeah, you want to get a message to someone, you go see Lana, and she'll get one of her people to deliver it for a small fee.'

'It must be a lot of work to keep those records up to date.'

'You've got no idea. One night she showed me her books. A stack of ledgers up to here.' Taking one hand from the wheel, he raised it almost to the roof of the cabin.

'Wait, she uses real books? Like, pen and paper?'

'No one round here wants their location in bits, waiting to be scarfed.'

They turned on to a broader road that must once have been a highway. Now, Pablo took it slowly, navigating around massive pot-holes. 'One of the main problems we've got is sanitation. Cyclones make permanent plumbing tricky, so first thing during a re-build is to dig communal latrines. We usually get some engineer cadets up from Brisbane, and they try to model water flows to keep waste from ending up where it shouldn't. No one wants to see another typhoid outbreak like in 37.'

Now that they were a little further inland, there was more green to occlude the rich red mud that the storms had exposed closer to the coast. Juvenile trees reached tentatively upward between the broken bodies of those that had tried before. Maggie and Pablo lapsed into silence. It was stifling in the truck, and Pablo kept swiping his palm across his forehead to clear his too-long fringe out of his eyes. Maggie appreciated his company. He was generous with answers, with the uncomplicated manner of someone acting in accordance with their convictions. Last night he'd joked about being a tool of the state, but as Maggie saw it, there was a short, clean line that started with him and Frew, and ended in good outcomes.

They passed almost no traffic coming south. Pablo explained that they were on their way to a small farming community north of Wonga, on the banks of the Daintree River. A small community of Tongans and other drowned Islanders were running crop trials. Wild rice, sorghum, mungbeans, sunhemp, sesame – they were trying little plots of just about everything, and waiting on the next bad storm to see what would bounce back quickly, and what would be a dead loss.

There were people back in Dug watching with interest, but Pablo explained that it was a hard life in the interior of the Cape. Usually there was not enough water, and then sometimes there was far too much, and at those times the roads were cut. Pablo and Frew could help by making sure the workers were vaccinated. 'Jel keeps us stocked with antivirals, so we can at least cover the usual strains. But whenever something exotic reaches the Cape …' Pablo shrugged. 'Wildfire.'

Guiltily, Maggie thought of her annual appointments, where she received a jab to defeat all manner of covids and flus. In a few years, she would need to decide whether to start taking anti-aging treatments. Sitting in this truck, the thought struck her as obscene. She thought about Dada-ji: what he must have seen growing up, and the decisions he'd made.

The foliage was now above head-height, impinging on the sides of the highway, making the road feel like a corridor through a primordial world. Occasionally, in the shade of the trees, Maggie could make out people, most of them femme-presenting, milling by the roadside. The clothing they wore – micro-skirts, short shorts and skimpy tops – looked unsuited to the conditions. As Pablo's truck approached, they would look up, and then away.

'Are they—'

'Yeah. The Yanks operate out of Cooktown, or what's left of it, and this is the main road up. There's not a lot to do for coin up this way – you can go out on one of the fishing boats, or you can give the soldiers something they want.'

By the time they reached the farm, it was almost midday. After finding the turn-off from the main road, they edged up a gravel track past an orderly patchwork of crops that Maggie couldn't name. As they approached a central cluster of sheds, Maggie could see workers break off what they were doing and move to assemble in the central courtyard. When he exited the truck, Pablo was pulled into a bear hug by a large man wearing a baseball cap bearing the logo of an electronics manufacturer that had failed in the early thirties.

'Willy,' Pablo said. 'You're still here.'

The larger man chuckled. 'Still here. Mungbean harvest soon, then we'll be feeding ourselves, and doing huge farts, and you'll never get rid of us.'

They set up at a rickety outdoor table, a queue forming quickly in front of them. Pablo explained that Maggie's job was to pick vials and prepare syringes, which Pablo would then administer, before Maggie applied a plaster.

There wasn't much to it, but Pablo insisted on trading banter with each patient, causing the line to move slowly. No one seemed to mind. Once the dults were all done, it was the turn of the children whose parents laboured on the farm. They were a shy gaggle, about twenty of them all told, and with coaxing from their elders, they took their injections without much complaint. Now Pablo took more care, and it was only a couple of the younger ones, lingering at the back of the queue, who cried when it was their turn.

'Sing them something,' suggested Pablo.

Maggie squatted down next to two snuffling kids and hummed the melody of the first thing that came into her head: an old pop song about monkeys in a tree, shouting and waving to each other from their different branches, that had been inescapable a couple of years earlier. Halfway through, too late to stop, she remembered that it was probably a coded meditation about the pleasures and social complexities of VEMM, or virtually-enhanced mutual masturbation. Pablo raised an eyebrow, amused at the choice.

She didn't think these kids had shrouds, but they looked healthy enough. Maggie wondered how they were educated if they didn't have feed access. Perhaps there were terminals in the main buildings with satellite links, that would operate like the old workstations and tablets her parents described from their childhoods.

Pablo waved at her. 'Willy wants to talk business for a second. You right here?'

Maggie nodded, and sat down in a circle with the kids. She asked them for a song, and they happily obliged, and Maggie realised that she was a guest. The kids were striving to entertain her, talking over the top of each other as they told stories about their lives here, adding embellishments and gesticulating, with all the energy of loving creatures who had a place to sleep, and calories to burn.

IT WAS MID-AFTERNOON BY THE TIME THEY GOT back on the road, after a lavish vegan feast there had been no hope of refusing.

'The kids took a shine to you,' Pablo said as they rolled back on to the highway for the return journey.

'I didn't have much say in it,' Maggie replied. 'I think they just liked having someone new to talk to. They remind me of the kids I look after back home.' She explained that she volunteered at a childcare co-op, which made her remember Kei, and all of the problems she'd left at the border.

Half an hour after that, they were forced to slow. Maggie had been lost in her own thoughts and it took her a moment to register vehicles parked on the verge, the military green of them blending almost perfectly into the shaded foliage that flanked the road. Pablo said nothing, but they both took in the scene as they edged past. A group of eight or nine soldiers surrounded three men on their knees. The captives were lean and dark-skinned, clad in ill-fitting, muddy clothes. They were oriented to face away from the road, hands cable-tied behind their backs.

'I might have to stop. Okay?' Pablo asked Maggie.

Not sure what he was really asking, she nodded.

'All right. Hang on, sorry.' He guided their truck down over the steep lip of the asphalt, just beyond the other vehicles, and wasted no time killing the engine and jumping out. More slowly, Maggie exited on the other side, and made after Pablo, who walked briskly toward the soldiers, arms by his side, palms presented and held away from his body.

The scene was like a photograph, a frozen moment in time.

The detained men must have been aware of their arrival – the straightness of their bearings indicated that they were alert, and sensed that something had changed – but not one of them turned their heads to look. Most of the soldiers kept eyes on their captives, but two of those closest peeled away, and moved to intercept Pablo. 'Get back in your vehicle and move out,' one of them barked, a stocky man dressed in fatigues like the rest of his comrades. His mid-west American accent sounded jarring in this place. His hands moved to cradle the weapon slung over his chest, a compact assault rifle. He didn't raise it, but the threat was obvious, and intentional. A few feet away, his colleague adopted a similar stance.

Pablo didn't budge. 'Looks like you're having a disagreement with these men. Perhaps I could help translate.'

The soldier wasn't buying it. Raising his voice, he shouted, 'We are members of the United States Infantry Corps assigned to Operation AusShield. We have designated this area as a temporary exclusion zone for the purpose of training activities. You are required to remove yourselves. *Now*!' He dismissed them with a flick of his head.

Pablo's shoulders dropped. From a few paces behind him, Maggie watched as he motioned to her with his left hand, waving her back. She wanted to return to their truck, but she couldn't move – she was worried that if she did, the soldiers would somehow take that as a provocation.

With a tremor that was audible, Pablo said, 'I'm an Australian citizen, as is my friend back there. And this is the Surrendered Territory formerly known as North Queensland. We're not in the exclusion zone set aside for AusShield. I have more of a right to be here then you do.' He took a half step forward. 'I'll ask again: is there anything I can help with?'

The soldier locked eyes with Pablo, and then turned to Maggie. He appraised her, now, for the first time, and after a moment of indecision, he looked behind. One of the other soldiers gave a shrug. Without speaking, they broke away from their positions and walked calmly to their trucks, saying nothing to their former prisoners or to Maggie or Pablo.

Once the rumble of their vehicles had receded, the men on the side of the road regained their feet, and turned around slowly. They looked like they were in shock, their expressions slack. They, too, said nothing while Pablo fetched a pair of cutters from his truck. When their hands were freed, they rubbed their wrists. Finally, one of them bowed his head solemnly toward Pablo, and again to Maggie, and then in unison, they fled into the dense growth, their forms lost to view almost immediately and the noise of them gone not long after.

'Come on,' said Pablo. He held his shaking hands out in front of him.

It was only after they'd been travelling for a while, and they were nearing the outskirts of Dug, that Pablo spoke again. 'Don't tell Fru-fru what happened back there. It'd just worry them.'

'What *was* that?'

'An execution, I think. Or it would have been. Plenty of bodies turn up in the jungle near that road, shot and dumped. We all know who's doing the shooting.'

Maggie couldn't believe what she was hearing. 'Why would they ... murder those men?'

'I reckon they were traffickers. Drugs, people. They'd be in the business of selling to soldiers. Maybe it was an argument about product, or payment. It wouldn't matter to the Yanks, there's plenty more where those three came from.'

'Can we report it?'

'Who to? There was no crime. Some federal laws apply to the Surrender, but the Americans have immunity as part of the outsourcing deal. Killing stateless migrants is the least of any-one's concern.'

'Then, when we stopped ...'

'I felt like we'd be okay. If they detained us, there'd be ques-tions about what those grunts were doing there in the first place, and there'd need to be interviews and records about what we'd seen. Too messy. And if US soldiers were found to have shot at Australian citizens, well ... that really *would* cause headaches.'

'Still—'

Pablo nodded. 'It was dangerous, and I didn't give you much choice. I'm sorry, Maggie, but I couldn't drive past, you understand?'

Maggie nodded and looked out the window. She supposed she mostly did understand.

THAT EVENING, MAGGIE EXCUSED HERSELF AND strolled down to what was left of Four Mile Beach. After what had transpired, she gave no thought to safety as she left Pablo and Frew's compound and walked along Davidson Street toward the water, mingling with crowds heading home from a day working on the main street, or moving toward the gatherings and entertainments that this place offered in the evenings, which Maggie could only guess at. The noises she heard were cheerful, for the most part: people talking, children playing. The distant low thrum of a bass line to some song.

She'd been told that the old beach had been a wonder, but all that was left now was a twenty-metre strip of sand, which had to be approached via a raised boardwalk over a mildly foetid mangrove swamp.

Down by the water, the locals had cleared the sand of the detritus that tended to accrue on the mud flats up and down the coast: scraps of plastic, foliage and felled palm trees, bottles, fiberglass, and the carcasses of fish and birds. Bobbing in the water, she could see the outline of a net that Frew had assured her would keep out jellyfish. Whatever their situation, this was community at work: volunteers maintained this space, as a public good. Children and adults reclined on the beach, watching the sunset. Many more paddled in the water, most in swimming costumes but several others naked, no one taking issue.

Maggie was still dressed in the clothes she'd worn that day, and they felt heavy with the damp of the air and her sweat. The idea of water appealed, but her thoughts turned to the bodies it contained, and she contemplated the chances of infection.

But that was no way to live. Once the sun had sunk below the waves, she peeled off her shirt and shorts. She left her crop top and briefs where they were, and wandered down to stick a toe past the lapping shoreline. A PET bottle bobbed morosely, partly disintegrated, washed here from a long-ago time and an unknown source. Feeling the warmth around her calves, she waded forward until she was immersed. It was like swimming in stale tea, and she paddled for ten minutes, feeling cheated.

SHE FOUND HER PLACE IN THE DORM AND TURNED IN early. She didn't resent Pablo for his choices out on the road, but after what had gone down, she couldn't stomach the thought of speaking to anyone.

The following day was less eventful. She put in a solid ten-hour shift as Frew's assistant in the dispensary, helping him perform a stocktake, and updating records so that when regular patients presented, Pablo and Frew would have a basic history. It was all done on little index cards kept filed in a locked drawer.

'Maggie was a godsend,' Frew gushed to Pablo, as the three of them shared rum and pineapple juice in the ground-floor office that evening. 'She doesn't talk back. She doesn't malinger. She just goes about her work.'

Pablo shrugged his shoulders. 'You should give her a job, then. Fire me, and I'll start an open-air cinema.'

'Oh, I would,' said Frew. 'But I think Maggie's destined for better things.'

'I don't know about that,' Maggie replied.

'We hope you are,' said Pablo. 'Or else why are we plying you with booze and lobbying the hell out of you?'

'Lobbying?'

Frew avoided her eyes, stirring his drink with a tongue depressor repurposed as a swizzle stick. 'In our own smooth way. What did you think was happening? Why do you think Kinnear sent you up to us?'

'I needed to get away for a few days. He was doing me a favour …'

Frew and Pablo both laughed. 'That's Kinnear for you,' Frew said. 'Somehow we all come out feeling like we owe him something. Machiavellian as hell.'

Frew moved to top up Maggie's glass, but Maggie put her hand over the rim. 'Hold up for a second. If you're lobbying, then what are you trying to achieve? I mean, aside from the fact that I'm basically a nobody, what is it you want?'

Frew made to speak, but Pablo waved him into silence, and said, 'You've been here for a couple of days now. Seen more than you probably expected to.' This was accompanied by a knowing glance, and Maggie couldn't stop her eyes flicking over to Frew. 'What do you think this place needs?'

'Resources, clearly. Food, medicine, farming equipment. Power generation. Refrigeration. Engineering equipment to help recovery after storms roll through …'

'So far, so obvious.'

'But … the main problem seems to be a lack of coordination. There's the beginnings of it, with the First Nations groups up north. In Dug, there's a rudimentary civil society – that's you guys – and even a judiciary of sorts run out of the post office. The different groups are at least talking, and from the little I've seen, there's not much conflict. Perhaps this is what you'd expect me to say, given who I am, but I think what Dug needs is a government. *Self*-government. Without that, the Surrender and its people can't move much further.'

As Maggie puzzled it out in front of them, Frew and Pablo had started to smile quietly. Now Frew said, 'I got a good vibe from the moment I met you, Maggie. I can see why Kinnear's collected you, just like he's collected us, and Captain Jel. Think about what people could do here, if they were allowed to get organised. They could get visas, travel. Get bank accounts, get connected, at least as much as they wanted to. They could participate.'

'What do you mean, "if they were allowed to"?'

'Well, there's the problem. Statehood for the Surrender is quietly opposed by Australia. They don't want another viable nation on this continent. And as for the US, they appreciate having a place free from the rule of law. What if the people of the Cape formed a country and decided that the Yanks were no longer welcome? No. Much better to keep the status quo: no humanitarian disasters, but no coordination, either.'

Maggie chewed at her bottom lip, taking it in. She had never been confronted with the realpolitik of the Surrender before now, and that couldn't have been an accident. There must have been a consensus among the major parties to leave well enough alone, with no mileage to be won by trying to fix the Cape. 'That is immensely shitty.'

'Maggie, you *are* the government,' Pablo said. 'Just a tiny part of it, sure. But you'll go back down south, and you'll work with other, more powerful parts. And if you're lucky, one day you'll be heard. They'll listen to you in a way that no one will ever listen to us.'

'After all, we're just a couple of deranged, shroudless radicals,' Frew added serenely. 'Now, can I top you up?'

LATE THAT NIGHT, OR PERHAPS EARLY IN THE MORN-
ing, there was screaming. It was the inconsolable throaty pitch
of a child in pain, and Maggie came fully awake in seconds, feet
hitting the sticky polymer floor as she reached into her backpack for a pair of shorts. In the bunkroom, others were stirring,
but no one else appeared to share her sense of urgency. This was
someone else's crisis.

In the hall, Maggie saw Frew crouched over a small form.
It was hard to tell in the half-light, but it looked like a child
of seven or eight, and it was unmistakably the source of the
noise. There were dark smears along the far wall, and a woman
stood close, speaking in low, urgent tones to Frew in a language Maggie couldn't place. But Frew nodded, and hoisted
the child in his arms, blood dribbling from the child's leg
has he turned. Seeing Maggie, he said, 'Take the mother to
the lobby. Try and explain that this is a deep cut. I'm going to
sedate the kid, and clean and stitch the wound.' He moved off
toward the clinic.

When her child had disappeared from view, the woman
stretched out an arm and leaned against the side of the corridor,
watching the floor and stepping carefully forward as if to follow
the trail of droplets left behind. As gently as she could, Maggie
positioned herself in front of the surgery door, holding up her
palms in an appeal. She pointed to the other end of the corridor,
beckoning as she moved away.

Once Maggie had the woman seated, she did her best to
explain. There was no acknowledgement, and not knowing
what else to do, Maggie left to retrieve a cup of water. When it
was placed in her hands, the woman edged forward in her seat

and sipped mechanically, her gaze never straying from the doorway that led to the clinic.

Maggie didn't know how she was supposed to give comfort. She didn't know what had caused the injury – but what good would knowing do? Frew was at work. He had the hard job, but at least he was achieving something. Maggie was here, too anxious to speak in case she said something wrong.

The woman's hands were streaked with drying blood, and seeing this, Maggie felt revolted. Fighting this response, because that seemed like what a good person ought to do, she knelt forward and reached out her arm, squeezed the mother's hand, and found her eyes to check that it was okay. And when she saw, Maggie came to sit close, and took the woman in her arms, and they remained like that for the long minutes until Frew returned with news.

It was like the Truvies had said: her reasons were all wrong. When Maggie offered consolation, she felt driven by a sense of propriety, calculating her actions so that no one could say she'd been heartless. She could only surmise that there was an absence within her; a supermassive hole around which all thought circled. One day it would surely be exposed.

CHAPTER 20

The present invention is a method for creating a virtual representation of a physical space using data gathered from headsets worn by occupants of the space. The method involves collecting visual and audio data from each headset and processing it to create virtual representations of the space and its occupants. The virtual space updates in real-time to reflect changes in the physical space and the occupants' movements. Additionally, non-occupants can project a virtual representation, or avatar, of themselves into the virtual space to interact with the virtual representations of the physical occupants.

In addition to projecting virtual representations of non-occupants into the virtual space, the present invention also allows for physical occupants to see and hear the virtual visitors through their headsets. The headsets project augmented-reality representations of the visitors into the physical space, allowing for a more immersive and interactive experience. This feature provides a sense of presence and connection for both physical and virtual occupants, enabling them to communicate and interact in a more natural and intuitive way.

The ability for physical occupants to interact with virtual visitors in real-time can provide new opportunities for remote collaboration, teleconferencing, and virtual socialisation, offering a novel and innovative approach to bridging the gap between physical and virtual spaces.

– Kemeny et al, abstract, patent application
no. 20310080503, USPTO

Once the investment committee disconnected, I looked around this tiny universe that we had made possible. Why did the veneer on the walls look so cheap, the pattern subtle but repeating relentlessly, millions upon millions of iterations without variation or error? In that moment, I recognised myself as a charlatan.

– Mei Lan Kemeny, Unfolding the Shroud, 2039

LONG INTO THE FOLLOWING MORNING, MAGGIE dozed in her bunk and listened with eyes closed to the sounds of others shuffling about. There was something in the noise that put her in mind of a large family, and she remembered childhood sleepovers with her cousins.

When she finally surfaced, she tapped her temple to activate her shroud, realising that it had been dormant for almost three days, which might well have been the longest such absence since she'd had it installed as a pre-teen. Nothing about Brij had made it through the filter she'd established. Still lying beneath the sheet, watching the boot sequence, she felt a kind of nostalgic anticipation, like she was about to play a sport at which she'd once been adept.

At first, she found it hard to care about the messages that flashed for her attention. Mostly, these were minor pieces of administrivia: meeting requests, and polls about the next shroud theme. Judging by the quality of this traffic, Cass had instructed the office not to bother Maggie with anything of substance. She wondered what was being withheld, at the same time relieved that there were no crises demanding her immediate attention.

Her shroud had been archiving reacts and opinion-pieces about her appearance on *Oskar*, and she flicked through these to get the general tenor. Plenty of support, mingled with ad-hominem attacks about her position working with Brij, her relative youth, her ethnicity, and her ideological leanings. All of which was to be expected. It was only when she scanned the headlines that she realised there had been a shift. The fourth story on *Compactus*, a widely-consumed news aggregator, read: *Alpen Warms to Income Plan*. If the sources quoted in the article could be believed, the PM was now firmly supporting the initiative in the face of resistance from some within OzProg and many without. Face running hot, Maggie read that draft legislation was almost complete, and that a pleb could be held as early as next week.

What had *happened* in three days? This was being rushed through while Brij was incapacitated, while rumours and speculation about her illness still swirled. Couldn't Treasury have held off for another week? There was something Maggie wasn't seeing, some motive force she had failed to discern. But it didn't matter. Despite everything – Brij, Cass, Kei – finally, finally, this was a chance, and she knew it would be wrong to hide.

At breakfast, she told Pablo and Frew that she'd be leaving. Both expressed their disappointment – 'We could've used you for a few more days.' 'Are you sure you can't stay?' – but she suspected that one way or another, they were across the same news.

'Go get 'em, tiger,' Frew enthused, pumping his fist. 'Just remember us when you're running the country.'

Maggie smiled. 'How could I forget? No promises, but I'll do what I can.'

Pablo volunteered to drive Maggie back past the border. As she carried her backpack out to the truck, Maggie's bunk-mates shouted goodbyes, waving and grinning like she was an old friend about to leave for a holiday. Soon, Maggie would be back in the south playing politics again, and these people would still be looking for a place to live.

Pablo and Maggie drove in a companionable silence until they reached the arrivals queue at the border. When it was their turn for clearance, and Pablo exited the truck and stepped through the biometric scanner, there seemed to be no issue, but when Maggie did the same, the immigration officer frowned and made a weird grunt. 'Errr ...'

'Is there a problem?' Pablo asked.

'I'll just need you to drive over to that bay. Shouldn't be more than a minute.'

Pablo and Maggie did as directed. One minute turned into ten. 'What do you think it is?' asked Maggie.

'I don't know. I've been selected for enhanced checks before. Apparently random, though everyone knows that's bullshit. But this feels like something else.'

A different officer approached the truck. Almost negligently, he announced, 'Sorry for the wait. You can get on your way now.'

When Pablo left her at the train station, they embraced, and Maggie realised it was the second time she'd wrapped her arms around someone else in the space of a few hours.

'Stay clean. Be safe,' she said.

'You too.'

MAGGIE HADN'T REALISED HOW SLOW THE SLOW train to Brisbane would be. Limited to a top speed of two hundred kilometres an hour, the journey would take most of the day. She watched, bouncing in her seat, as the train sliced through cane fields. Above, the clouds bore distended, water-laden bellies. Inside the carriage the air was cool, but still heavy with moisture.

An hour into the journey, Kinnear messaged her. *[You need to get back. Things are kicking off.]*

[I'm en route to Brisbane], she replied. *[Should be in a sleeper car by ten tonight. Back to civilisation tomorrow morning.]*

[Head to Sydney, directly to Treasury. You'll be needed.]

[What's happening?]

[Don't know exactly. Could speculate, but won't.]

Maggie spent the rest of the train journey hoovering up whatever she could glean from public sources. She reached out to Insalata. He responded tersely to say that he'd welcome Maggie's input on the draft bill.

With time to kill, she found herself scrolling the general news. The Leadbeater's Possum Revival Project had stalled, with all crowdsourced funds to be returned. Apparently, growing an implanted cross-species embryo was not as straightforward as had been assumed, and none of the brushtail surrogates had managed to carry a Leadbeater baby to term. For now, a large-scale rewilding project was impossible. 'We're not giving up,' one of the lead scientists on the project was quoted as saying. 'Human actions doomed these wonderful creatures, and it's our responsibility to bring them back. One day, it will happen.'

Arriving in Brisbane, she spent a few hours at a capsule hotel near the Loganholme Land Car Depot, listening to others come and go, trying and failing to sleep, before dragging herself into a shower at 3 am. She dressed for the office, in the only blouse and suit pants she'd had the presence of mind to stuff, folded, into her backpack when she'd left for Cairns. In the jaundiced neon light of the public shower block, she turned this way and that, checking to make sure that she'd steamed out all the rumples in her clothes, knowing that the five-hour drive ahead would render the effort moot.

There was no queue for a land car. There was hardly anyone around at this hour, except for a few bored attendants. She spoke to no one; her shroud took care of the details even as she crouched and rolled into the low-slung recliner in the cabin of her assigned vehicle. The hour and the unfamiliar location made everything surreal. Was this happening? It seemed like this was happening.

On this leg of the journey, time passed swiftly. In a fragmented haze, Maggie tried to plan how hard to press Insalata when she arrived at the office. She gamed out conversations in her head, but it was impossible: she didn't know how the bill was shaping up, whose support may have arrived or evaporated in the days she'd been away. Alpen was backing it directly now, and she didn't know why.

AT HORNSBY, SHE SWITCHED TO A TOWN CAR THAT would take her into the city centre. A broad underground concourse separated the land and town platforms, walls and grimy floor both tiled in white and green. A distance of about a hundred metres, and she'd made it almost halfway when the hum started.

At first it was quiet. Unmistakably, it was coming from inside her own head, like tinnitus. Too annoying to tolerate. 'Sever,' she said. 'Sever!' But nothing happened.

Checking her stride, she pulled up her task manager and muted all apps, but the noise persisted. Maggie huffed her frustration. By now it was eight-thirty, and it would take her another forty-five minutes to get to Market Street. With her fingers, she formed the pattern that would initiate a reset of her shroud. Until it booted again, she wouldn't be able to hail a car.

The task manager window remained before her eyes. She repeated the reset pattern, and when that didn't work, she tried to scroll through the list of running processes. Her overlay was unresponsive; frozen in a way that she'd only experienced a few times in her life. Tremor in her voice, she sounded out, 'Lumen, Antic, Disco, Revel, Kudos.' The personal override code she'd practiced as a child, and never invoked, should have produced a hard stop until she could get to a service point – but there was no effect. The humming was getting louder now, and now the lights of the concourse were flaring brighter. No, not the lights;

it was in her eyes. Everything was giving way to a harsh, bright blanket of white. When she screwed her eyelids shut, she could still see the lingering glare of it, and when she opened them again, the blinding field persisted. She blinked and felt herself swaying sickly. The hum was painfully loud now, making it difficult to think. She was gasping quick and shallow. Her cheeks felt wet, but it was hard to be sure.

'Sever,' she pleaded.

Someone or something brushed past her arm. When she'd still been able to see, the concourse had been busy with commuters heading to town. She tightened her grip on her backpack. She could still feel its strap in her hand, and the realisation steadied her a little as she dropped into a crouch. With a shaking hand, she brushed her fingers up the side of her face, searching for the edge of her left eyebrow. She tapped four times, firmly: another failsafe she'd known about academically but never had reason to use. The effect should have been instantaneous. It was supposed to prevent malfunctioning units from putting their users in danger. But there was no change.

The humming had taken on a distorted quality now. It might have been Maggie's eardrums capitulating to the sheer volume. She tried to think past the noise and blinding light. Maggie was in a public space. She could shout for help, even if she couldn't hear her own voice. For all she knew, she was already speaking her thoughts aloud, or sobbing. She could call for police—

Before she could do anything more, the hum moderated, and a voice boomed out, reverberating through her flesh like the Word of God.

'MAGGIE GAREWAL. WE HAVE CONTROL OF YOUR SHROUD. DON'T MOVE. DON'T CALL FOR HELP.'

Distorted. Modulated so that Maggie couldn't even tell if it was a human or a bot.

'What. What is happening.' She was almost sure she was speaking out loud.

'AN INCOME BILL HAS BEEN WRITTEN. YOU WILL GO TO TREASURY. YOU WILL PUBLICLY SUPPORT IT, AND YOU WILL BE CREDITED AS AN ARCHITECT. WHEN YOU COOPERATE, THERE WILL BE MANY OPPORTUNITIES FOR YOU IN THE NEW GOVERNMENT.'

It was impossible to fathom. Support the Income bill? But it was *her* bill.

She tried to steady herself. Tried to talk quietly, calmly, so that anyone nearby wouldn't hear. But without being able to discern her own voice above the raging hum, she couldn't know how loudly she was speaking. 'You must need me. You must be worried that I won't support it.'

'YOU WILL.'

'Maybe I will.' Her fingers brushed over the slick floor tiles, tracing the lines of the grout. 'I don't know where it's at. But it will be my decision.'

'YOU WILL SUPPORT THE BILL. OR YOUR BROTHER WILL BE ARRESTED FOR HIS PART IN THE DHS BOMBING.'

'He had nothing—'

'THE EVIDENCE WE PRODUCE WILL BE CONVINCING.'

Maggie stiffened. So there it was. The naked threat.

'AND THE INCOME LEGISLATION WILL STILL PASS. THIS IS NOT A DIFFICULT DECISION. WE WILL BE WATCHING.

DO THE RIGHT THING FOR YOURSELF, YOUR FAMILY, YOUR
COUNTRY—'

—and immediately, the light and sound of the hack
desisted, and the world returned. She was on all fours, saliva
dribbling from her open mouth. Sobbing, she raised her head.
The concourse was still busy, but a pocket had formed around
her, as commuters averted their gazes and bent their trajectories
so that they would not have to engage with this person crawling
on the floor.

Unsteadily, Maggie found her feet and walked to the nearest
bathroom. She locked herself inside a cubicle, threw up, wiped
her mouth. She allowed herself several minutes, concentrating
on her breathing.

When she was done, she found her towel and toiletries kit
in her backpack. She was going to work, and she needed to look
presentable.

BUT IN THE CAR OVER, SHE COULDN'T SLOW HER
breathing, and she twisted in her seat. Her mind, which had
been bludgeoned by the assault, now careened from thought to
jangled thought. They were going to try and implicate Tez in the
violence at DHS. Was it possible that they – whoever *they* were –
who *were* they? – had perpetrated the attack? They might well
be responsible for Brij's condition. Who had the capability to
do those things? Not to mention the hacking of a shroud, which
was supposed to be inviolable?

And – she realised with a sudden sick lurch – if they'd been
spying on her, through her eyes and ears, then those leaks to

the news wraps – it needn't have been Kei. When she'd accused him, his anger and hurt had felt genuine. He'd had no sensible reason to betray her like that. They'd framed him; taken him from her, too.

They'd told her to proceed to Treasury, and that made her want to go anywhere else. But she'd been headed there before the hack, and she needed information. She couldn't make any decisions, any plans, until she understood what had occurred in her absence. Alpen was supporting the bill – what was in the bloody thing?

The voice had not sounded Australian; it had a trans-Atlantic flavour. Did that mean anything? An AI?

She couldn't be still. Couldn't hide. She needed information.

Her car rolled down the busy thoroughfares toward the centre. Now, she kept waiting for a diversion that would carry her somewhere unplanned. Or a slowing, to halt in front of an unmarked van. Or a violent crash. If a shroud could be hacked, then vehicles would be trivial.

But they wanted her at Treasury.

Through the front doors. Credentials worked, because the elevator opened for her, took her to where it knew she was going. She watched the others in the lift. Were they all oblivious? Like she had been, an hour ago?

On the seventeenth floor, she stalked toward the cubes where the Income working group had set up shop. Insalata was there, maybe waiting for her, and he moved to greet her. *How had he known*— no. That was not the important question.

'Well?' she asked him.

'Uh.' He looked supremely uncomfortable. 'Before I catch

you up, Maggie, you should check in with Felix. He's waiting in conference room two.'

'Are you serious?'

Insalata gazed past her, already in motion. 'This way.' Confusion bled into fury as she was escorted down the corridor, for a meeting with the work experience kid.

Felix was seated, legs splayed, arms draped over the sides of his chair. He smiled lazily when he saw her. 'Mags, welcome back. We've missed you the past few days.'

Insalata nodded curtly to no one in particular, and shut the door behind himself as he exited. Maggie claimed a seat at the distant end of the table, as far from Felix as possible.

Before she could get a word in, he continued his patter. 'I saw you on *Oskar*. You blew up! You're a proper celeb now. One of my bonk-buds wants me to get your autograph, but I said that'd be tacky.'

Her hands were shaking. She put them in her lap. 'Just tell me what's happening.'

Felix laughed nervously. 'No worries. I … heard you might be having a rough start to the day. If that's true, then I'm sorry. I really am. But I've got great news!' He leaned forward so that he was looking at her face-on. 'Polling after your appearance shows that the public is now strongly backing an Income. That's brought OzProg firmly into line behind us. We've drafted a bill, and there's no shortage of support in the Reps. It was *you*, Maggie. Your sales job made this possible. Made it almost obligatory, and a couple of people had to do some quick and dirty judo to get on the right side of this.'

'And the bill?'

'Drafted. Salad Boy's been very accommodating. He's worked his team hard to get this done so quickly.'

'Will it pass a pleb?'

'Yup. Chase has confirmed his support. Mackay, too.'

'Mackay?' Something lurched inside her. Three days ago, Mackay had railed against an Income on a nationally syndicated vid. 'How did you get him?'

'Well, we had to make some compromises to get buy-in from a range of stakeholders …'

'Just tell me.'

'The before-tax payment for the Income will be 10,800 Aussie per month.'

'That's … below the poverty line. Wait, did you say *before tax*?'

'And there won't be supplements for dependents.'

Maggie seethed, her lips tight.

'And … the bill will discontinue the national minimum wage.'

There was no grappling with it. Maggie heard a ragged sigh escape her throat. When she could speak, she said, 'There are too many people, not enough jobs. That was what an Income was supposed to fix. But this … with the labour over-supply, this will push wages down until they sit just above the Income rate. It'll push millions into destitution.'

'But people will finally have a choice, Mags. To work, or contribute in some other way. It's what you wanted.'

'This is sick, and you know it.'

'It's what the majority supports. And maybe one day, we can raise the rate to something more comfortable.'

'People won't want this, not once they understand.' Sudden

realisation felt like cold sweat running down her back. 'But you're scamming them. I ... helped scam them; made them believe we were doing this progressive thing ...' The revulsion she felt – which absolutely encompassed Felix, and his uncle, and Mackay, but which was primarily directed at her own credulous part in this disaster – was a seething, physical force. She tasted bile at the back of her mouth.

Felix pursed his lips and furrowed his brow in an unconvincing simulation of concern. 'Try not to overthink. We're both going to do well out of this, and all we have to do is swim with the current. In the right circles, you'll be acknowledged as the architect of this historic change. And there's talk of making me a Senator next election. It's kind of a bullshit job, I know – no real power – but Chase says it'll look good on the cv.'

It was already too much, but Maggie needed it all. Flailing, trying to see the shape of this conspiracy, she asked, 'What about the Americans? They all but threatened to abandon us ...'

'Mackay talked them round. He pitched it as a natural experiment in Matevian economics. And besides, this kind of Income will serve as a counter to the European version.'

'Mackay ... on *Oskar*, he told all of his proxies, the whole country, that an Income was basically the same as full communism. How's he going to walk that back?'

'Mackay's proxies don't follow him for his ideological consistency. He'll brag that he's won some important concessions. Which is true: Mackay saw the potential earlier than anyone. He was all over your white paper, and when OzProg won the election, he got in touch with Chase, told him there was a way to make this happen ...'

'So from the start, Mackay wanted to hijack this? All his criticisms were just for show ... and your uncle just let him?'

'Chase is pragmatic. The government will bog down soon – they won't get anything done. And Alpen wants a quick win, doesn't matter what. This is how real change happens, Maggie: driven from the centre, with popular support, built on compromise and a blend of inputs. You should be proud of your part in it.'

'And you. Your part in it ...'

'Chase sent me to Brij so that we could keep an eye on you; make sure you'd sell the thing properly, win over the left. He needn't have worried.'

Maggie shook her head. 'This is deranged.' She stood up, steadying herself against the desk. She was still shaking. 'You've got more rat cunning than I gave you credit for.'

Felix nodded. 'I know this must be a lot to process. But please try to see this as a win, Mags. You're on the winning team!' His carefree expression slipped, and he spoke his next words slowly and quietly. 'It's important that you stay on the winning team. This'll happen with or without you, or me – it's beyond us now.'

'I ... need to think.' She edged toward the door, still eying him, as if he might leap up and accost her.

'Sure,' he replied, chipper again. 'Just don't take too long. We've got a videographer coming in this afternoon, to document this historic moment. And Chase has asked me to confirm that you're with us. Believe it or not, I've liked working with you, Mags. I want you to land on your feet.'

There was nothing more to say. She strode quickly through

the open plan, needing the exit. Insalata approached, his face scrunching in mock empathy. 'Big couple of days?'

Maggie didn't even try to disguise her contempt.

IT HAD GROWN UNCOMFORTABLY HOT AND STUFFY outside, now that the sun was rising above the building line. Maggie was moving through the city with no plan, no intent; but her body must have had a notion. She performed a deep power-down of her shroud. She didn't doubt that she could still be tracked, but it might make it harder for them to see through her eyes, hear through the subdermal microphones in her face. She found herself working quickly northward up York Street, as if some subroutine had taken over. Rage was dominant. Confusion, and fear, and hurt at the betrayal: yes, all of that, but rage was working the levers as she made her way into one of the low-rent malls that functioned as a climate-controlled tunnel through the bowels of the city, filled with junk shops and shisha bars and shoe polish kiosks. She barrelled into a likely-looking vintage tech emporium, selling pre-shroud antiques, and made a selection.

When she went to pay, she hesitated, thinking about Tez. She wasn't the only one in danger. He was oblivious, and vulnerable. Brij was, too. But she had to put aside her regard for them, or risk paralysis. Had to keep going, give herself an option while she still had time. How much time, it was impossible to know. She felt like if she didn't articulate her plans, even to herself, then those surely watching through her eyes would hold off, too.

'Make it count,' she told herself out loud after she'd collected her goods and made her way streetside, veering downhill toward Darling Harbor. Under the Western Distributor, and past the tiny bars behind the aquarium, she butted up against the seawall, beneath the shelter of a footbridge. Here was as good as anywhere, if she was really going to do this.

She set up the tripod she'd purchased, and positioned the old-school camera with its independent link to shroudspace. Her own shroud found it quickly, and synced. Now there was no time for hesitation. She started a live, public channel, and sent an invite to everyone in her address book: Kinnear, Cass, her family, Kei. Friends and work contacts she hadn't 'faced with in years – the wider the net, the lower the risk of consequences for those who on-shared.

A red light on the camera blinked. She moved to stand in the frame.

'My name is Maggie Garewal. I'm a policy advisor to Brij Sutton, the proxy harvester who was recently hospitalised under suspicious circumstances.'

She had to get her message across quickly. She didn't know how much time they'd allow her.

'If you see this, repost it. I'm being blackmailed to support a corrupt bill that would introduce a universal basic income. I've fought hard for an Income – you might have watched me on *Oskar* – but this version is a fraud, and I was tricked into selling it.

'I think Brij might have been poisoned, because she'd have called out this travesty of a bill for what it was. My house has been broken into, my shroud has been hacked— ah.'

She felt a tingling behind her brow.

'They're in my head right now. I mean, this Income bill – the ends are all wrong. It's a trap to keep wealth in the hands of the few, and rob us of our power to make change. It's worse than nothing. If your harvester plans to vote for it, switch harvesters. If you voted for OzProg, tell them not to support it. At the very least, *own* your vote in this pleb—'

She couldn't hear, couldn't see. The pain behind her eyes was excruciating. She looked up, glimpsed an outline of towers staring back. Her knees buckled. Like a sheet being drawn over a caged bird, the world was stolen away, and Maggie could not have said what followed, or how fast it came.

SPRING

EPILOGUE

A contemporaneous profile, interposed with reconstructed/ retrieved passive chat logs, inquiry transcripts and ephemera, all dating from c. September 2058, as subsequently collated, arranged, exhibited and archived at the Australian Museum of Direct Democracy (Early Harvester Era Collection):

Waiting in the lobby, I hear the soft buzz of a hedge trimmer. Every few minutes a rooster crows, incongruously, from the community garden on the other side of the fence, the sound carrying through the tinted glass windows of Maggie Garewal's new office in the badlands. For settler-colonists, Canberra has always been a no-place; Tuggeranong is doubly so.

[– 'FRESH HARVEST', I. Musa, The Tri-Monthly (4) 2058]

[MAGGIE GAREWAL:] What have we got this morning?

[TIM KINNEAR:] Your first interview's here. Four petitioners waiting in the lobby, and another thirteen in the queue for a call. You've got the rats and mice club at eleven-thirty.

[GAREWAL:] Can you … do it all for me?

[KINNEAR:] As if you'd ever allow that.

[GAREWAL:] Well, show the journo in. Let's get this show on the road.

Garewal's Chief of Staff, former senior public servant Tim Kinnear, ushers me into his boss's office without knocking. Kinnear insists that this role is his version of semi-retirement. He does not draw a salary, adamant that it's a temporary posting. The contacts Kinnear has accumulated over the past four decades – notwithstanding his dismissal from Human Support at the start of the inquiry – have been useful to Garewal during this period of establishment. She later tells me that she dreads the day when Kinnear leaves her with a well-meaning and unsatisfactory replacement.

[MAGGIE GAREWAL:] Hi there.

[IMANI MUSA:] Harvester Garewal. May I call you Maggie? Thanks for giving us some time. Do you mind if I take audio, just for my notes?

[GAREWAL:] … No problem.

[IMANI MUSA:] Thanks. I wanted to start with a few questions about how you're recovering from your ordeal.

[GAREWAL:] Why does everyone insist on calling it that? Besides, I thought we'd worked through this with your editor.

This is meant to be about how the agenda is shaping up for the new session of parliament.

[MUSA:] Ah. The piece will be about that, mainly. But we wanted to round it out, show the human behind the proxies. People are still curious, you know?

For Garewal, the first month after the hack was a maelstrom. There was a police investigation, a parliamentary inquiry, and visits from more than one domestic security agency. Maggie has tried to answer all questions meticulously, reasoning that there is no longer any point in hiding what she's been through, including her unwitting presence at the DHS bombing. She insists that the Reeves must know more, but uncle and nephew have both issued full denials.

[SEN. RANDALL FÜNF, (APP):] And you attended the Treasury office on Market Street, Sydney, on the morning of 4 June?

[FELIX REEVE:] Yes.

[FÜNF:] And you met with Maggie Garewal, both of you in-person.

[REEVE:] Sure did.

[FÜNF:] And do you remember what you talked about?

[REEVE:] Really just how the bill was shaping up. I was trying to loop her in – she'd been away for a couple of days.

[FÜNF:] Did you say that you'd heard she might have had a rough start to the day, or words to that effect?

[REEVE:] I have no specific recollection of saying anything like that.

[FÜNF:] And if we were to check your shroud log for that morning?

[REEVE:] Like you'd already know, my shroud was glitching. My log got deleted.

[FÜNF:] I see. So when you met with Mx Garewal, you knew nothing about the hacking of her shroud, or any ultimatum that she support the Income bill.

[REEVE:] Absolutely not. And I've been advised to say that – uh, let me find this – yep. Any assertion to the contrary, if made beyond the confines of parliamentary privilege, would be defamatory and actionable.

In shroudspace, theories proliferate. Harvester Mackay and his supporters contend that Maggie was never attacked, and the whole thing is a hoax. Mainstream OzProg loyalists, with an interest in defending the status quo, grudgingly concede that a hack of some kind happened, but insist on describing it as an isolated incident, perpetrated by 'sophisticated, but apparently non-state actors'. On the far left and the far right, punters are certain that the US deep state, probably in the form of the CIA, is to blame; or perhaps it was the Chinese. Then again, maybe it was a plot by a cartel of megacorps, fearful of a basic income that had a chance of achieving its stated aims.

> [PABLO FLORES:] Think about it like this: seventy per cent of what happens in shroudspace is stressful, boring, distracting. You're reclaiming all of that time.

> [XAVIER FREW:] And when you want to speak to someone, just pick up the dumbphone.

> [MAGGIE GAREWAL:] Thanks, you two. You're right, I know.

> [FREW:] An IRL life slaps, in ways you can't see yet. But you'll get there.

> [FLORES:] In the meantime, think happy thoughts. And call us, girl!

In every important sense, Garewal considers herself lucky. After collapsing by the sea wall, a jogger on their way past spotted her and took the unusual step of calling an ambulance, rather than simply leaving the then-policy advisor to her fate. And when paramedics arrived, one of them had been aware of her broadcast, as it ripped virally through Australian shroudspace. This first responder had the presence of mind to do an EM scan, and register the activity from Garewal's shroud, and convince their colleagues to do an emergency extraction then and there. If any of those things had not happened, Garewal could have been permanently impaired. As it is, her doctors assure her that a new shroud graft will almost certainly take. But, of course, it isn't that simple.

[DR. CARMEN ETTA (CLINPSYCH MAPS FCCLP):] It may be that you never learn the truth.

[MAGGIE GAREWAL] I don't do well with ... not knowing. The break-in, the DHS bombing. Brij's poisoning – toxicology showed high levels of some pesticide meant for fire ants. There are too many questions.

[ETTA:] Do you find yourself thinking often about these events, and whether they are connected?

[GAREWAL] You have no idea.

Harvester Sutton's retirement was forced, but she could have chosen to anoint a successor. In the resulting vacuum, Cassidy Saye, another of Sutton's former policy advisors, was quickest to reach out to grantors and offer an alternative. Saye now speaks for around half a million, almost all of whom she has inherited from her former boss. Meanwhile, following the attack, Garewal found herself receiving unasked-for proxy grants. To be sure, most dults who viewed her panicked broadcast in real-time, as she urged them to vote against a plan that she herself had backed for many months, concluded that she was unhinged.

But a few listened closely, and dug deeper. And the trickle of grants turned into a torrent as the inquiry wound on, once further details of the hack on her shroud became public. In the end, Saye and Garewal have both ended up with large chunks of Sutton's former base, and now Garewal speaks for a few hundred thousand votes; just over the threshold to receive public funding, which pays for this cut-rate office in Tuggeranong, her Chief of Staff's outreach budget, and a couple of interns.

[BRIDGET SUTTON:] I still feel like I've been shat out of a cannon.

[MAGGIE GAREWAL:] … Shot?

[SUTTON:] No.

[GAREWAL:] Oh. Sorry to hear that.

[SUTTON:] Try and play nice with Cass, okay? You're still on the same team.

[GAREWAL:] I will. Most of the time it's not too hard.

[SUTTON:] Good.

[GAREWAL:] …

[SUTTON:] Okay Maggie, I don't want to be late for my second nap of the day. Talk soon.

[GAREWAL:] ...

[ALISABETH SUTTON:] Thanks for calling again.

[GAREWAL:] She's doing better.

[ALISABETH SUTTON:] She is. Her speech has improved, as I'm sure you noticed. But she still finds it hard to concentrate. The mountain air has to be doing some good.

Maggie luxuriates in the knowledge of having a whole seventeen minutes to herself before her next meeting, with a ragtag collection of minor harvesters. The goal is to present a united front on an upcoming omnibus spending bill, maximising their influence by negotiating as a bloc. In this kind of company, Maggie often finds herself playing the dult in the room, lowering expectations and reminding everyone of the need for some semblance of fiscal responsibility. This amuses and irritates her in equal turns, but she can't pretend she isn't suited to it. Her brief but intense career as an advisor has prepared her well.

Controller in hand, Maggie turns on the screen fastened to the wall of her office and enters the meeting code by manipulating a grid of touch-buttons. The ceiling-mounted camera angled in her direction makes her uncomfortable, but it is easy to physically unplug between uses. Given recent experience, she does not permit voice-activated tech in here, always on and listening.

[DR. CARMEN ETTA (CLINPSYCH MAPS FCCLP):] What you are describing is grief.

[MAGGIE GAREWEAL:] That's gross, though, isn't it? I'm alive, and biologically whole.

[ETTA:] But…

[GAREWEAL:] But it feels like exile. I need Kinnear just to learn what people are saying in shroudspace. And shroudspace is where everything happens! It's where people talk, meet, shop, fuck, and live out the majority of what I once would have called a life.

'I get to decide what I do next,' Garewal tells me. Here in her office, she puts on a brave face, but she admits that this doesn't stop the night terrors, or the hours spent quietly crying in the office of her new psychotherapist, as they carefully poke at Maggie's trauma. She tries to convince herself that the crisis has passed. Few entertain the idea that Garewal, or her brother, who has since moved away from Ngunnawal, had anything to do with the violence at DHS. Besides, she reasons, the very public nature of her broadcast, and the profile she's developed since then, might offer her brother, ex-Harvester Sutton, and Garewal herself some cover from further repercussions. If they were to follow through on the threats they've made, Garewal's attackers would be confirming the notion that shrouds are vulnerable to surveillance and attack.

[MAGGIE GAREWAL:] How's Tez doing?

[PABLO FLORES:] Great.

[XAVIER FREW:] Really great.

[FLORES:] We love that guy.

[FREW:] We've stolen your big bro, and made him our little bro, and you can't have him back.

[GAREWAL:] Is he still working on the post office?

[FREW:] The locals are vibing over the plans. A grid of skylights that can be sheathed when the wind picks up – genius.

[FLORES:] People have started to bug him for house designs.

[FREW:] There's plenty for him here, Maggie. He hasn't missed a beat since his hard disconnect. In fact, he's talking about a complete extraction.

[GAREWAL:] No way. Tez has spent two decades jacked in! What have you done to him?

[FREW:] Mwa ha ha ha.

As she's done so often in the last three months, Maggie splays her fingers, poised to input a command, before registering her loss. She rubs the skin on the bridge of her nose. Without cosmetic treatment, the white scars mark her, but for the time being, she wears them as a badge of honour. Shroudless, she must ignore the agricultural sounds from next door without the aid of technology. It's a good thing that there is plenty of work to be done.

[DR. CARMEN ETTA (CLINPSYCH MAPS FCCLP):] What helps?

[MAGGIE GAREWAL:] Unnecessary carbs.

[ETTA:] ...

[GAREWAL:] The messages of support I've had, from friends and strangers. My brother is doing well. And, it feels like I've been given a kind of extra life. Anything I achieve from this point on is a bonus, in some ways.

With the Income initiative passed, OzProg has been quick to claim victory. But plenty of people, not just Garewal's donors, overrode their own proxies to cast a personal vote against. Now that it has entered into force, and employers are firing people and offering the same jobs back at reduced pay, a collective anger is building. Already there is some old-school talk, about coordinated action, and withholding of labour until living wages are offered. Prime Minister Alpen and OzProg have begun to distance themselves, talking about 'tweaks', and 'version 2.0'. Garewal has a voice in the resulting discussion, and she seems half-convinced that a good Income scheme might still be salvageable. OzProg-era politics is proving to be so fractured that with the right messaging, any idea has half a chance.

[KEI ARAKACHI:] Hey.

[MAGGIE GAREWAL:] Hey. Thanks for jumping on.

[ARAKACHI:] I checked with the area manager, and I'm sorry but it's a no-go. Apparently if we let an unshrouded person volunteer, it voids our insurance. Something about needing to be able to summon help in an emergency.

[GAREWAL:] Oh. That's kind of bullshit.

[ARAKACHI:] Yeah. You get to keep your credits, though.

[GAREWAL:] Thanks for trying.

[ARAKACHI:] No worries.

[GAREWAL:] And, Kei. I know I'm repeating myself, but I'm really sorry.

[ARAKACHI:] I followed the inquiry. That must have been hell for you.

[GAREWAL:] It was not the best.

[ARAKACHI:] Oh, hey, I've got to run. Micah's trying to tip over a shelf . . .

[GAREWAL:] !!! Good luck. Stay clean.

[ARAKACHI:] You too.

For all that has been taken from her, plenty remains. After this interview wraps, Garewal will listen to the opinions, anxieties and interests represented on the teaming call. She will find a way to swallow her frustration and work in concert with her fellow harvesters, including former colleague Cassidy Saye. When that's done, she will admit the people waiting in her IRL lobby, one by one, and hear their prayers and complaints, for no other reason than because they have come to her. Nursing manifold wounds of her own, she will spend the rest of the day making the small corrections that are within her reach. And on this night she will return to her childhood home, because if nothing else, she remains dutiful. Garewal will eat dinner with her parents, Raman and Liz, and with her grandfather, who has recently returned from a tour of the drowned islands.

[IMANI MUSA:] Thank you, Maggie. I realise we've gone over time, but I have one more question. It's for background, you could say.

[MUSA:] You're a minor celeb now. There would be plenty of ways to monetise your experience, that don't involve sitting … here.

[MAGGIE GAREWAL:] True.

[MUSA:] So why this particular boulder? This hill?

[GAREWAL:] …
    It's like this.

In every moment that passes, so much could be achieved. It accumulates ... this is the work that has found me. I'm doing the best I can, and it will never be enough.

GLOSSARY

AUGMENT — To overlay meatspace with virtual reality elements.

AVATAR — The virtual projection of an individual into augmented reality. An avatar may, but need not, emulate the meatspace appearance of the individual.

BARBECUE, THE — Pro-meat protest group, and/or the locale maintained by that group in shroudspace. (Alt: Big Barbecue)

BASKET — A collection or spread of different currencies, which may include government-issued, corporate-issued and crypto monies.

BOMB, THE — The prospect that thawing of arctic permafrost might lead to runaway climate catastrophe. (Alt: Polar Bomb)

BOT — An artificial emissary, usually human-like in appearance, programmed to deliver messages in shroudspace.

CAST IN — To appear virtually in a location or locale. (Alt: spawn)

DEPARTMENT FOR HUMAN SUPPORT — Commonwealth department responsible for delivery of welfare programs and anti-poverty measures. (Alt: DHS)

DOXX	To reveal personal information about an individual, usually with the intention of causing harm or embarrassment.
DULT	(*slang*) Commonly-used gender-neutral term for an adult human.
FEED	A curated and customisable information flow of news, gossip, opinion and/or trivia, delivered via shroud.
FIVE-YEAR	A celebratory gathering, customarily held on the date five years prior to a planned voluntary end-of-life event.
FLÛTTR	Squad-based virtual game involving the hunting of butterflies.
GRANTOR	An individual who has granted a proxy to another.
HIT SHUFFLE	(*slang*) To practise polyamory while in a primary romantic relationship.
INCOME	Proposal for government to make regular payments to every dult, regardless of personal circumstances, in order to maintain a specified standard of living. (Alt: basic income, universal/unconditional basic income, UBI)
LOBBY	Private locale created by and for an individual. Lobbies can be, and often are, heavily customised by their owners.
LOCALE	User-created virtual space that may or may not have a meatspace analogue. Locales can be public or private.
MEATSPACE	Physical, original-flavour reality.

NARRM	Capital of Victoria; former name 'Melbourne'.
NGUNNAWAL-NGAMBRI	Capital of Australia; former name 'Canberra'. (Alt: Ngunnawal, Ngambri, Nganbra)
OVERLAY	Visual/auditory augmented layer superimposed over meatspace to create augmented reality.
OZPROG	(*slang*) The Australian Progressive Party, formed via merger of the Australian Greens and the Australian Labor Party in the early 2040s.
PING	A very short message delivered via shroudspace.
PLATE REFORM	Proposal to ration naturally-grown meat purchases, with the aim of reducing consumption and/or increasing equality in distribution.
PLEB	(*slang*) A population-wide vote on proposed legislation. Bills that pass a pleb and at least one other chamber of parliament are, by convention, enacted. (Alt: plebiscite, 'scite)
PRIV	(*slang*) Derogatory term referring to someone who benefits from unearned privilege.
PROJECTION	Emplacement of a virtual object into real space, to create a hybrid or augmented reality.
PROXY	Legal authority to cast a plebiscite vote on behalf of another.
PROXY HARVESTER	A person who invites others to grant proxies to them. Due to their control over the outcome of plebs, successful proxy harvesters wield considerable political power.

SHROUD — Set of devices implanted in a human face to enable ready engagement with shroudspace. (Alt: augmentation, implant)

SHROUDSPACE — The universe of augmented and virtual realities.

STAY CLEAN — Commonly-used parting phrase, expressing a wish for good health.

SURRENDER, THE — Region of the mainland Australian continent, encompassing Cape York north of the Cairns-Karumba Line, excised from the Commonwealth of Australia's territorial borders in 2041 by the Roy Government.

SYNTHMEAT — Synthetic protein, typically lab-grown and intended to emulate the flavour and texture of meat.

TREATMENT — Cocktail of personalised anti-aging, anti-senility and cosmetic therapies facilitating lifespans exceeding one hundred years.

TRUVIES — (*slang*) The True Values Party, a socially conservative, faith-based political party, formed as a breakaway from the Liberal Party in 2033.

TRYST — Social gathering, often but not always involving group sex.

ACKNOWLEDGEMENTS

Trying to chart the near-future is a foolish undertaking. In the seven years it took to write this story, I revised major plot points again and again, as world events – wars, political drama, pandemics and scientific breakthroughs – overtook my more outlandish predictions. Worse still, the introduction of a Basic Income was my main character's central motivation – but I'm not an economist. Any generalist understanding I can claim is derived from reading econ-bloggers like John Quiggin, Joshua Gans, Paul Krugman and Noah Smith; and from economics texts pitched at general readers, along with scholarly articles about the hypothetical and observed effects of introducing a UBI. The childcare co-op that Maggie works at was inspired by the real Capitol Hill Babysitting Cooperative in Washington DC, which Krugman used as an allegory for the paradox of thrift. All errors and misconceptions, whether they pertain to economics or, say, the practical implementation of an augmented reality network, are mine.

A novel is a sequence of tiny lies that, with any luck, add up to some kind of larger truth. For that trick to work, the lies need to be expressed with at least a basic degree of lucidity. I am indebted to many early readers of this story, beginning with Patrick Allington, who mentored me while I sketched out early chapters and tried to work out who Maggie was. Later, in chunks, I inflicted a whole draft manuscript on Wayne Marshall, Jake Dean, Alex Cothren and The Weaz. Their honest and supportive feedback, and the pleasure of reading their work in exchange, has kept me going. I am especially grateful to Alex for the use of 'Here Are My Demands' as a title, which is lifted from 'The Eater', a captivating, filthy Cothren short story.

Michael Bollen, Maddy Sexton, and the team at Wakefield Press, past and present, have been wonderful to work with across two books. Their support for arts and artists in Australia, and particularly South Australia, is epic. Maddy brought perceptivity, positivity and the right amount of gentle nudging in her role as editor of this story, and I'm appreciative of everything she's done to improve the version I originally submitted.

Thanks to Duncan Blachford for another knockout cover and gorgeous typesetting. Working in dialogue with talented artists like Duncan is one of the best parts of bringing a book together.

Thank you to my agent, Martin Shaw, whose keen eye, friendship, and insistence that I write a novel – not another short story collection; a *novel* – were essential supportive elements.

A shout-out to Amanda and the rest of my many talented and creative cousins, on both sides of my family, who have led the way.

Thank you to Sarah, without whom ... none of this.

An early version of one of Tez's scenes, which was an experiment in writing from his perspective, was published as the short story 'Flûttr' in *Futures,* an anthology of speculative fiction available through Glimmer Press.

This project was supported by an Independent Makers and Presenters Project Grant from the Government of South Australia.

This book is for Finley who, as an infant, impeded the writing for understandable reasons; and who remains a source of joy and inspiration. The future had better look out for you.

www.ingramcontent.com/pod-product-compliance
Lightning Source LLC
Chambersburg PA
CBHW060541030726
47498CB00004B/1272